DREAM MAKER

LAS VEGAS VIPERS BOOK TWO

STACEY LYNN

Dream Maker

Las Vegas Vipers Series

Book Two

Stacey Lynn

Content Editing: My Brother's Editor

Proofreading: Virginia Tesi Carey

Cover Design: Shanoff Designs

Dream Maker is a work of fiction. Names, characters, places, trademarks, and incidents are used fictitiously or are the product of the author's imagination.

❀ Created with Vellum

PROLOGUE
JOEY

Dude. Get your ass here. Everyone's heading to Malley's.

I shook my head at Alix Halvrick's text. He was one of my best friends on the team, but as single as they came. When he said *everyone*, he meant every single guy looking to score. I hadn't been that kind of guy in years, really never, considering I was drafted to the Las Vegas Vipers when I was twenty and started playing as soon as I graduated from college.

I wasn't surprised the guys were headed out to celebrate. We were headed into late November, the trade deadline was over a month away, and we were killing our division, currently up by three games. The team was incredible, all of our lines working together like we practiced twenty-four-seven, even in our sleep. I was on top of my game, scoring a hat trick earlier in our road game to Arizona.

I was also exhausted, my ribs aching from one too many slams into the boards by their defenseman who should have been a football linebacker.

I'm out. Next time, I texted back and shut my garage door before entering my home.

Lenora had a matinee earlier where she worked as a burlesque dancer for Las Vegas's premier show on the Strip. I wanted a drink, my wife, and a few hours of catching up on our lives while I'd been on the road for the last week. Some sex. And a long night of sleep.

Although that sex part could have been in any order.

God, I missed my wife. We both led crazy lives, but when we were home together, she was the calm to my constant rush.

Tucking my phone away, I entered our house, a gorgeous six-thousand square foot home, all modern and bright, but with finishing touches Lenora had made over the years. She'd turned the behemoth structure from a house to a home. Careful not to leave anything out where she'd trip over it, which drove her crazy, I dropped my bag into the mudroom and kicked off my shoes.

The house was quiet, but that wasn't unusual. Lenora lived a lifestyle that involved so much loud music and constant flashing lights she said it overwhelmed her senses and she craved the quiet when she was out of her performing mode.

Which meant since she wasn't on the main floor, in the kitchen, or reading a book in the family room, she was probably upstairs. Maybe napping.

Hopefully soaking in our bathtub.

Her car was in the garage, so she was home. A bath would explain why she hadn't answered any of my texts after we landed letting her know we won. She might have been married to a pro hockey player, but when it came to the game, she gave no fucks about it. Barely watched it, occasionally came to my games, but never really enjoyed them. I didn't fully blame her. Some women could be judgmental bitches when they heard what she did for a living, but I'd always been damn proud of her and impressed.

She was incredible on stage, even if I didn't love the fact she did it with barely anything left to the imagination. Guys got hard-ons to my wife's moves and tits and her abs she worked hard to maintain, but only I saw the person she was outside the performer.

And she was fucking awesome. Captured my attention the moment I saw her grabbing a coffee. I was a young, cocky little shit who'd recently moved to Vegas. I took my shot, got shot down, and continued to get right back up. For weeks I stalked her at the coffee shop, made her laugh. Once I realized she ordered the same thing every day, a skinny caramel latte with no whip, I'd have it waiting for her when she'd walk in.

The third time I had her order ready, I'd already been sitting at a table, two cups of coffee in front of me. As soon as she entered, she didn't even look toward the line. Her gorgeous blue eyes scanned the small shop, landed on me, and she came straight to me.

She sat down, grabbed her coffee and said, "One date, you crazy man. I'll give you one date."

I was done for. Now, every time I was on the road, all I wanted when I got home was to fall into my wife's arms, talk about our lives, and then spend the rest of the night making love.

Soft music filtered down the hallway from our bedroom. A light jazz. Her favorite.

I picked up my steps, thinking of finding her in the tub, bubbles surrounding her full breasts that would already be peaked and hardened. I'd tear off my shirt, and she'd begin grabbing her tits, playing with them so I could watch her get herself turned on while I finished stripping.

Oh yeah. Fuck Malley's and spending time with the guys. I saw them enough. All I needed was my wife.

I worked at the belt of my dress pants, yanking it through the loops and undid the button. The sooner I could join her, the sooner I'd have everything I needed.

With my belt in one hand, I pulled off my shirt and reached for the door handle and opened it slowly, softly, so I could surprise her.

Instead, it was me that was fucking surprised.

My jaw might have slammed into the floor and I blinked several times, trying to make sense of what I saw in front of me.

Because my wife wasn't in the bathtub.

And her hands weren't on her own tits. They were on another woman's, who was sitting on my wife's face, her back to me.

"What in the fuck?"

"Oh shit!" Lenora screamed and the woman who was on top of her jumped to the side, grabbed the sheet from our bed and tangled it around herself.

"Are you..." I blinked, trying to clear my vision. "Are you fucking kidding me?"

Pain like I'd never known before slashed right through my chest. I might as well have been shot at point-blank range with my dad's hunting rifle.

"Joey. I didn't know you were coming home yet."

Was she fucking high? "To my own home? What in the fuck is going on?"

I mean, it was obvious. I'd just walked in on my wife, not only fucking around on me but fucking around with another woman. Pissed. Hurt. None of those words described what I was feeling. A roar rushed through my ears and I locked my knees so I didn't collapse. Was this *seriously* happening?

"Fuck, Lenora." If the person she was cheating on me with was a man, I'd probably deck his ass. Instead, a quick glance told me it was Rhianna. Fucking Rhianna. They were friends. Had been for years.

And Lenora hadn't held secrets from me. At least I hadn't thought so. Not until now. "How long?"

Lenora blinked at me, eyes shimmering with tears. She'd told me early on she was bi. I'd worried about it for months. It'd taken a lot to be confident in what we had, Lenora assuring me she just loved everyone, regardless of gender. She wouldn't leave me just because she got sick of dick and wanted variety. It wasn't like that.

Which meant I never, in my wildest dreams, even when I knew she thought Rhianna was attractive, could have imagined walking in on this—with Rhianna still currently scurrying around *my* bedroom, grabbing clothes and apologizing.

Yeah.

Me too.

"How long?" I asked again. Lenora stayed on the bed, a pillow in her lap. and for the first time since I met her, I had no desire to glance at her breasts.

"A couple of months."

A couple of months.

Four small words.

And my marriage imploded.

I spun on my heels, threw my shirt back on, and grabbed my phone from my pocket.

I'll be there in fifteen minutes, I texted Alix. Because fuck this. If I stayed, I'd yell. I'd punch a wall or hell, I... I had no idea what to do with what I just saw. Heard.

Halfway down the stairs, I shouted back up to them, "I'm heading out. Get your shit out of this house and be gone before I get back or we have problems."

She listened.

I returned home the next morning after crashing on Alix's couch, calling an Uber to take me back to the bar to get my car.

By ten the next morning, my house looked like she'd never lived there.

I cracked open a bottle of whiskey and got trashed.

Again.

1

JOEY

Champagne fell from the air like rain, the shouts of my teammates as loud as a roaring thunderstorm. The floors shook from our jumping. The screams of men and women so damn jubilant I almost forgot. For a moment, I almost forgot I was there alone.

Arms were thrown over my shoulder. Alix, my best friend, yanked me to him and shoved a bottle of champagne in front of my face.

"Drink up, motherfucker! We're champions!"

And I'd helped take the team there. A hat trick in game five of the playoffs where we won the series four to one. At home. The arena was still trembling either from fans refusing to leave or the ground shaking from the hoards making their way down the ramps to exit.

I grabbed the champagne, tugged down on the Stanley Cup Champion hat I'd already had tossed at me, and chugged.

Around the locker room, it was a haze of bubbly being shaken, confetti sticking to everyone's uniforms, and wives. Girlfriends. Family members. My parents were there, my brothers and their wives and their kids. Lizzie was holding on to Garrett's waist and Katie, her best friend and my brother Jude's wife, was clinging to her arms, laughing so hard she was using Lizzie to hold herself up. In Jude's arms was his baby daughter and my newest niece, Marissa, looking adorable and ridiculous with noise-canceling headphones over her ears that were twice the size of her tiny, seven-month-old head.

And there I was.

Chugging champagne, seething with jealousy at the guys who had their women with them.

It'd been seven months since I kicked Lenora out of our house. Five months since our divorce was finalized. Three months since she started posting pictures of her and Rhianna on her social media pages.

Three hours since she sent me a text, texts that started coming once we reached the playoffs.

Good luck tonight. I know you'll do great. I'd love to talk when you can. Followed by a kissing emoji that'd made me want to smash my cell phone into my locker and then slash it to pieces beneath my skates.

Every time her name popped up on my screen my gut rolled. They weren't personal. No questions asked. No hellos. A simple good luck text like we were still friends and they kept coming even though I hadn't responded to any of them.

Partly because I couldn't figure out why she'd start texting me now. Asking me to call her? For what fucking purpose?

Lenora never gave a shit about hockey. One of the things I loved most about her. Once I got over my own insecurities with her, there was no doubt she was with me for *me*, not the game or the excitement or the money. At first, she'd tried to understand the rules. She'd listen while I talked about the game or my team. She came to the occasional game, but outside my family who liked her, she never fell into the whole hockey wives and girlfriends' traditions of watching games together. She'd had her own life, one she loved.

I'd always thought her independence and confidence was sexy as hell—until that life of hers ended up naked and riding my wife's face in my own fucking bed. One I burned as soon as I was sober enough to do so without setting my backyard on fire. I'd slept on my couch for two weeks before my new bed was delivered.

Possibly—not my greatest moment in life but whatever.

Alix went to take the bottle out of my hand and I grabbed it back. "It's mine now."

He threw his head back and laughed. "Damn straight." He just shook his head and grabbed a bottle from Max, one of our defenseman, next to him.

As soon as he did, Max hip-checked him, shoving Alix into me so hard I almost stumbled on my skates.

"We're getting fucked up tonight, boys!" Max shouted.

"Hell yeah!" Alix screamed right back, waving the champagne bottle in the air and drenching us further. He turned to me. "You in?"

How I wanted to. Badly. "Can't." I shook my head and pointed the tip of my champagne bottle toward my mom and dad.

John Taylor Sr. was surrounded by our coaching staff and veteran players. Everyone flocked to him. As a man who was now in the NHL Hall of Fame, I didn't blame anyone for their interest in him. Hell, he was still one of the best men I'd ever known. "My parents insisted we all had dinner tonight first, win or lose. Johnny and Jason and their families head back home tomorrow." Had we lost, we would have hit the road and headed back to Boston for game six. Johnny had planned to watch us there, since they lived in New York, but Jason and Tessa couldn't handle all the traveling, not since we just learned she was pregnant. The Taylors procreated like bunnies. My parents had been thrilled. I'd left the room, burning with jealousy.

"Fuck. That sucks. Meet up later? Kane just got word Lavo's shut down the terrace for us tonight and opened up the VIP section. We're busing it there."

"I'll be there," I assured him.

The last place I was going was home tonight. Not to an empty house since my parents and family had suites in a downtown hotel. I'd told them all they could stay with me but Dad didn't want to interfere with my traveling and need to focus. Silly, since the entire team was required to stay in a hotel the night before games on lockdown for the same reason.

I might have been twenty-six years old, but I'd long since learned that arguing with my parents was useless.

Coach Vik shouted out and the room went silent as he praised us on our wins, congratulated us on an amazing season and told us to stay strong in the off-season. Then, like Coach tended to do, he shouted for us to stop acting like Neanderthals, get dressed and get the hell out.

An hour later, I was pulling up to the restaurant where my parents had reserved a private room, to find it packed.

Garrett and Lizzie were already there, along with his mom and sister who'd been staying with them for a few months. At the sight of Gabby, my chest did that strange tightening thing it'd started doing lately whenever I saw her. A few months back, she and I had spent an hour in a waiting room together where she'd lost her shit thinking of Lizzie losing the babies she was still currently carrying. I'd brought Garrett to the hospital the moment we arrived back from an away game after he'd received alarming texts when our plane landed. While he went to be with Lizzie, it'd been me Gabby had turned to.

"I can't... what if she's in trouble. And God, I barely know you. You don't need this."

"Hey." Without thought, rhyme, or reason, I draped my arm over her shoulders and pulled her to my chest. "It's okay. You're allowed to be worried and if I didn't want to be here, I wouldn't be."

She cried softly, knee bouncing as it continually brushed against mine, and I focused on the medicinal smell of the hospital instead of the minty scent of her shampoo.

God, she was gorgeous, and if you put Gabby and Garrett next to each other, no one would ever suspect they were siblings. His lighter hair and blue eyes were the exact opposite to Gabby's chocolate brown hair, thick, piled on top of her head right now but there was so much of it, I couldn't help but wonder how long and thick it'd be when it was down.

Holy shit. Where'd that come from? Not only had I never seen her that way before, but she was also my teammate's little sister —my friend's little sister.

"Thanks," she said, and pushed off me, as she did, my fingers didn't loosen on her shoulder and I didn't let her go.

Not in time for her to almost brush her lips over my jaw as she tried to sit up.

And shit. Her eyes were golden, so bright and beautiful with flecks of coal that sparked from her irises and out.

"Joey," she whispered, and I swore her hand hit my knee. Trailed to my thigh.

Shit. What was I doing? But I couldn't pull away. For the first time in months, my heart was hot, my chest heaving, and where her hand was at my thigh, applying pressure, the heat from her touch was shooting higher, straight to my dick.

It was then I realized her hand wasn't on my leg holding me to her but trying to push me away. I released her like I'd been burned and cleared my throat.

What in the hell was happening to me? "You good?"

"I'm okay." Her dark brows, thick and perfectly shaped, furrowed. "Are you?"

"Yeah." I wiped my hands down my thighs. "Of course I am."

But I wasn't. I was anything but.

I lusted after my teammate's little sister. It might have only been for a few seconds, but those seconds were everything.

For the first time in months, I actually envisioned myself with someone other than Lenora.

Talk about shitty timing and the worst person to suddenly find myself attracted to.

I shook off the memory, the sensation that made my chest grow warm every time I saw her now.

The rest of the team had begun filtering into the waiting room then, allowing me to put space between us. Lots of space. Space I'd kept up since then.

Until now, because surrounding the table were my brothers, their wives, a handful of kids and babies in the mix, our parents... and the only empty seat at the table?

Right next to Gabrielle Dubiak. My teammate's sister. My friend's little sister.

And the woman who admittedly, since that night in the hospital, had been someone who'd been both unwelcome and welcome in my nightly dreams.

I'd also been right, with her hair down and curled, it was long. Thick. Luscious.

Hair I wanted in my fist and on my pillow.

Fuck.

2

GABBY

H air spiked at the back of my neck and tingles created an unwanted, full body shiver as they danced down my spine. I didn't have to turn to know who'd I find entering the private room.

Joey was here.

Joey who'd held my hand and looked at me like he wanted to kiss me months ago.

Joey, my brother's teammate, and great friend and all-around sexy as hell but also incredible guy. The guy I couldn't stop thinking about since that night he'd held me. Comforted me. Looked at me like he'd wanted to slip his hands into my hair and press his mouth to mine.

The guy who'd been able to make me think *Kurt who?* whenever Garrett or Lizzie asked about my ex-boyfriend and if I was still hiding out in Vegas so I didn't have to deal with him.

Joey Taylor, the king of the ice who'd scored a hat trick in their final game tonight to help his team win the Stanley Cup.

Joey, who was saying hello to everyone but me because

he'd barely looked at me since that hour we spent alone in the hospital months ago. Who was now pulling out the chair next to me, settling his hand at the back of mine and leaning in.

"Hey Gabby," he said, and his lips moved so perfectly, slightly hidden behind his dark, thick scruff. His matching black hair was long, in desperate need of a cut. And *God* how I'd love to get my hands in his hair—in a way that had nothing to do with my chosen cosmetology profession.

Joey Taylor might have been the youngest Taylor brother, the youngest guy in this room, but he was hands down, the star of all my recent fantasies, so much so my mouth went dry at the sight of him, the fresh scent of his cologne he must have applied after his shower, the glimmer in his piercing dark eyes and the way his lips moved as he asked me something.

"Huh?" I asked, like a complete fool.

Oh God. How long had I been staring at him?

He blinked, gorgeous dark lashes fanned his lids and then those full, pink lips of his with the perfect bow at the center top, kicked up at the corner.

Amusement lit up his eyes. "I said hello. And how are you?"

"Oh. Good." I reached for my water. The icy condensation on my glass chilled my palms and fingertips. Did nothing to squash the heat pulsing in other places. Places that pulsed with need whenever I thought of him. I took a sip then chugged half the glass and as I licked my lips, cursed myself.

"I'm good," I repeated, because he'd stolen my brain cells. "Congratulations. You should be proud of yourself."

He leaned back, away from me, but I could still smell

him. Still feel the warmth from where his hand brushed against my shoulders. "Had a great team working with me."

"You can't be that modest. You played awesome."

His hand reached up, ran beneath his bottom lip, tugging it to a corner like he was thinking, but then he was jostled from the other side and his hand fell.

"Thanks," he murmured before turning to the interruption, his brother Jason, messing his hair at the top of his head.

"Damn good game, kid."

He smirked and shook his head, clasped his brother's hand in his, and yanked Jason down to slap him on the shoulder. "Not a kid."

"Aw. Come on. You'll always be our kid brother."

His features twisted into an arrogant smirk. "What can I say? Mom and Dad had to keep trying until they reached perfection." He shrugged his shoulders and tossed his hands up in a *what can you do* gesture that had Jason throwing his head back and laughing.

"Sure thing. You keep telling yourself that, runt."

I forced myself to turn back to the table, to where Lizzie sat across from me, barely able to squeeze herself close to the table due to her rapidly growing belly. She and my brother got married only a few days ago, right before this final series started.

I couldn't be happier for them.

I also couldn't stop the tiny green-eyed monster who lived deep inside my gut when I caught the way they were smiling at each other. Googly-eyed barely described the way they looked at each other as Garrett rested his hand atop her belly, carrying their twin boys.

"You okay?" he asked.

"I'm good. Promise."

He kissed her cheek. "We won't stay long. I think it's time we start planning that honeymoon."

Her cheeks turned pink, and her smile widened. This was what I wanted. Thought I had with Kurt. Stupid me for thinking I'd find it with him, though. I'd fabulously ignored all the red flags he'd waved like a matador in my direction.

I reached for my water, drinking the rest of it when the servers assigned to our room returned with trays filled with drinks we'd already ordered, and appetizers Garrett and John Taylor Sr. requested ahead of time.

Soon, the table was filled with food, alcohol flowing. Laughter bounced off the walls, and through most of it, I was an outsider.

Until my mom reached out and set her hand on my forearm.

"So, honey. What are your plans now?"

My mom was wise. She was smart beyond smart. A single mom since my dad died when I was five, she was a detective with our local police department back in Washington. I loved her with my whole heart, but when we were around each other, we were oil and water. I couldn't remember a time when we'd truly gotten along, or when she hadn't condemned one of my current life choices. She had a very linear way of believing how life should be lived.

Like making plans. Sticking to them. Never deviating. The very idea of such structure was enough for me to break out in hives.

I took a sip of my red wine and slid my arm from beneath her soft touch, settling it into my lap. "I haven't thought about it much."

She was famous for looks that spoke a million words with her eyes and mouth alone. Currently her look was full of disapproval, bordering on losing her shit with frustration.

Thankfully we were in a room filled with people she'd in no way make a scene in front of.

"You don't actually think you can keep living off your brother and staying with Lizzie now that they're *married,* do you?"

Of course I didn't. "Knowing what I can't do doesn't mean I've decided what I want to do."

She rolled her eyes, her lips thinning as she brought her gin giblet to her lips.

What my mom didn't know was that I had plans. Lots of them.

Okay, so maybe they weren't *plans* necessarily. But thoughts. Dreams. Ideas. They were plans in a hazy, *I should go do this,* kind of way. I had mountains of those. Just none I'd ever actually done before.

But now?

I could do them, right?

I could do anything. I had no job. No man. Few friends back in Seattle mostly because I'd met Kurt shortly after I started my new job at the salon and while my coworkers were great, I spent most of my free time with Kurt and his friends. Fortunately for me, and because my big brother was the most awesome man I'd ever met, he'd insisted on paying for my apartment so I could save my income until I had a decent enough clientele to live off of comfortably.

Sure I'd argued about it. I'd outright refused. Then, I figured what the hell. If my brother wanted to give me a few grand out of his millions to ensure I was taken care of, what was the harm? After all, that meant I could save my income for all those dreams of mine.

Now, what was stopping me?

"Gabrielle," my mother sighed. "We've talked about this."

Technically, she'd talked about it until she was blue in the face. I settled in for the lecture I'd heard a half dozen times in the last week alone since she'd been in town and cupped my wineglass in both hands.

"I don't know how you think you can continue to keep living like this. Letting Garrett fund your lifestyle when he has his own family to provide for now, jumping from one job to another. You're twenty-three, almost twenty-four years old. Don't you think it's time to start finding some stability? I mean, for God's sake, look at your brother—"

"Hey, Gabby, can you pass me the salt?"

I jumped at Joey's voice, the way his shoulder nudged mine.

My mom, just getting started in her *why can't you be more like your brother* rant that began filtering in one ear and out the other before I was eighteen, still had her mouth slightly ajar.

"Sure, Joey." I reached for the salt he could have easily grabbed himself and when I handed it to him, I swore his hand held mine longer than necessary.

"Thanks." His head dipped in my direction. Dark eyes met mine that sent a swirl of something warm straight to my stomach. "You okay?"

"Fine."

His eyes scanned my face, tiny little lines dug in at the outer edges of them. He'd heard. Awesome.

"Sure?"

"Sure I'm sure."

"What are you doing after this?" He set down the salt-shaker, not bothering to use it. Awesome, he really had asked for it just to interrupt my mom's rant. How much he'd heard, how humiliated I was, were questions I wasn't willing to ask.

"Sleeping." *Finding a new place to go*, because really, my mom was right. The season was over, Garrett and Lizzie were married. I couldn't use the excuse to stay in town because he was on the road so much. I could go back to my Seattle apartment, but then what? I hadn't wanted to live in Seattle since high school, but I kept staying. In part because I didn't want to leave my mom there alone. Mostly because I had no idea where else I wanted to live.

"I'm meeting the guys at the Venetian where they've shut down the outdoor terrace at one of their clubs for the team. Want to come?" He glanced at my mom, my brother, and then his brothers and family. "I think they'll all be headed back to their hotels early."

I hadn't planned on doing anything, but Joey was right. Lizzie would be home and asleep and the last thing I needed now was to be suffocating in their home with my mom on a roll of *let's get Gabby's shit together for her since she can't do it on her own spiel.*

"That sounds like fun," I lied. "Thanks."

"Should be a blast."

Somehow, he didn't exactly sound like it would be fun for him, either, but what the hell.

He'd saved me when I needed it. I'd make sure we both had an epic blast.

3

GABBY

My eyes were so dry I practically had to peel them open with my fingers. As they unstuck, a groan fell from my sandpaper scraped throat. Holy crap. Had I swallowed sand last night? Chugged saltwater by the gallons? Every bone in my body ached as I rolled over, groaning again, and then squinted.

Where in the hell was I? The bedroom walls were a dark, rich gray. White woodwork surrounding them. The dresser along the wall held a variety of mishmash items. Cash. Coins. Bottles that looked to be cologne or perfume. My body screamed in agony as I tried to sit up, grabbing the white, and comfy as hell duvet cover covering the silkiest sheets I'd ever touched, dragging it all up and over my chest.

"Holy shit," I whispered, scanning my surroundings and freezing as I saw the bundle of covers next to me. The shape of a body beneath them with only a shock of dark hair visible.

My pulse raced and I quickly dipped a look beneath the covers. I had on a shirt. But not *my* shirt. My legs were bare. Underwear on. As panic bubbled and my heart sped, at least there was the familiar, physical proof that *nothing* had happened down there the night before. But as I tried to figure out how in the hell I got to this strange room, memories of last night were a large, black and blank slate.

"Oh fuck," I whispered.

Joey and I had left the restaurant and headed toward the Venetian. On the way, we'd grabbed drinks outside, in those long bottleneck things that were draped around necks with a lanyard. I laughed so hard at one point I bumped into him and told him I had to pee. We had to find a bathroom, and as we stumbled through a casino I couldn't remember, there were muted lights and the ringing of slot machines.

And then... nothing.

But I'd been with Joey the entire time. Right?

I swung my head in the direction of the body next to me. Dark hair. All I could see. A quick glance again at his hair, settled me further.

Joey.

It was him sleeping next to me.

At least I didn't hook up with a random in Vegas. God, but still, how embarrassing.

Somehow, we must have gotten back to his house. He was a good guy. My brother's friend. He wouldn't have taken advantage of me.

Nothing happened. Of course nothing happened. We probably got drunk, came home and crashed—at least, I was assuming we were at his home.

As I tried to convince myself, I swung my feet over the edge of the bed. Huge mistake. The bedroom spun and the bed tilted and wavered.

"Oh shit," I groaned and palmed my forehead until the room settled. As I did, a scrape of something hard and cold scratched across my forehead.

I pulled my hand back, frowning, and... oh hell *no*.

Oh hell no. I jumped out of bed so quick and spun around, faced Joey, still sleeping, his back to me. His muted snores ratcheted up my panic level so much I almost collapsed back onto the bed, but despite the room going topsy-turvy and my stomach threatening to upheave, I couldn't stop gawking at my hand.

The sharp object? A ring. And on the top of that ring? A diamond. And *bling* put the size of the rock on my finger to shame.

"Holy shit," I gasped, right as my stomach flopped again.

I turned, raced toward one of the closed doors, and covered my mouth. Thank God I guessed correctly. I ended up in the bathroom and sprinted toward the small door at the end.

Please dear sweet heaven in all things holy, let it be the toilet.

I fell to my knees right as neon colors from last night's last remembered drink ended up splattering all over the toilet.

I puked until there was nothing left in between, staring at the ring on my finger. My ring finger.

Left hand.

There was no way.

This had to be a joke. Right.

Had to be. There had to be some explanation. Maybe we'd been joking around. Maybe he won this for me in an arcade. Maybe he struck it huge playing poker or something and bought this for me as a prize for patiently standing next to him.

Not that I remembered *any* of those things. But I sure as hell didn't remember him sliding a rock the size of Mount Rainier on my finger either.

"Fuck," I moaned and once I was certain I'd emptied my stomach of last night's contents, I scrambled off the floor and headed toward his bathroom that was almost the size of my living room apartment back in Seattle. All white. Stark. Marble counters, a shower with seven jets from multiple directions, and a bathtub that could possibly fit four. For a moment, I thought of climbing into it. Filling the tub and passing back out in the enormous thing. I swayed on my feet and made my way to the sinks where I splashed water on my face, used the hand soap—gross—to wash my face and remove mascara and makeup, and then found his toothpaste on the counter where I did a quick cleaning with my finger.

What in the hell was going on?

There was no way we got married. Not in Vegas.

A laugh bubbled from my throat as quickly as the thought hit my mind. No freaking way.

There had to be another explanation. Along with one of how I ended up in his room. In what I assumed was his shirt.

Because absolutely, one hundred percent, there was no way I got married to my brother's teammate. Not Joey. Not the guy who'd never once looked at me with anything but mutual respect despite the flutter my heart gave every time he was near me. Except, there was that one time...

No. Stop it. I kicked thoughts of the night he'd gazed at me in the hospital, me sick with worry, Joey quick to comfort. He'd pulled me to his hard chest like he was built for being the protector and as soon as my heart had fluttered, I'd stopped it.

No, that wasn't true. As soon as I noticed how sharp his jawline was, how close I was to it. As soon as I inhaled the mild scent of his cologne, that hint of campfire and spicy man dressed in plaid carrying an ax. That's what made me pull back from him, push him away.

He'd been too damn tempting and I had to have been imagining all of it.

But this?

Oh dear God. "My mom is going to kill me."

A scattered, nervous, and almost hysterical laugh bubbled in my throat. So much for not living off my brother anymore like she'd accused me of. Nope. Classic Gabby. I jumped right into a freaking marriage with another rich man to cover my bills.

Oh God. Tears burst into my eyes. My mom would *kill* me for this. Shoot disappointed daggers so deep into my eye sockets I'd die on the spot. I sniffed, splashed more water on my face, and forced down that image.

We didn't get married. Sure, I wasn't a planner and I was more dreamer than foot settled firmly on cement, but to do something *this* extravagant?

I wouldn't.

"Right?" I asked the reflection in the mirror. My skin was pale, a slight green hue to it. My brown eyes were dull, but that wasn't shocking. My body felt like I'd drained it of ninety-eight percent of the fluid it typically contained.

As I scanned myself in the mirror, looking for any signs of anything that could make this make sense, my reflection had no answer.

Not helpful.

But surely Joey could figure this out. He'd remember.

Right?

Right.

I turned and opened the door slowly. It was silent, and I took a second to inhale a deep breath. This had to be a misunderstanding. Of course it was.

Instead of Joey sleeping, his back turned to me with that quiet—and adorable, in retrospect—snoring sound, he was sitting up in his bed. Back to the pillows, scrubbing his hands down his face.

And on his left hand?

A fucking matte black band on his finger.

"Oh fuck," I said, and his gaze snapped in my direction.

His hands fell to the duvet and eyes widened as he took me in right before his head thunked against the headboard and his eyes closed. "Thank God it's you."

Not comforting. If he didn't know who he was in bed with, did that mean he didn't remember anything either?

"Um." I stepped into his room. "I think something happened."

"I know. We must have drunk every fucking bottle of alcohol in Nevada last night if the way I feel is any indication."

Despite myself, a quiet laugh slipped from my throat. He was joking. This was good. At least, not horrible.

But did he not know? Had he not seen the ring?

"Um. This might be the dumbest thing I've ever asked in my life, but did we get married last night?" As I asked, my knees wobbled. His eyes had still been closed, but at the mention of getting married, they flew open and his jaw fell.

"What?"

I gestured to his hand. Held up mine. "We have rings."

As he glanced at his own hand, his lips pressed together. Slowly, taking several long minutes, his gaze lifted. Tortured, pained dark eyes swept over my face before settling on my left hand, still in the air, ring and diamond so big it'd be visible from a mile away. "What the fuck?"

"That's exactly what I thought."

"No." He shook his head, swung it side to side and

groaned as he flung himself out of his bed. He was wearing shorts. Athletic ones that hung low on his hips and nothing else. I couldn't help it. He was *ripped*. Everywhere. That V-muscle of his on display and his chest heaving.

Fuck. Don't check him out!

He's your husband, the stupid part of my brain whispered.

He's not! my more rational side screamed. I whipped my gaze to the wall behind him, and tears burned my eyes.

"I don't remember anything," I said and my chin wobbled. Goddamn. I was not this girl. I didn't *cry*. I didn't cry when Kurt was banging his bimbo assistant when I showed up at his work twenty minutes early for a lunch date. "I can't... I remember the drinks. I know we walked toward the Venetian, but after that..."

"Fuck. I can't be married to you." He was right. Of course we couldn't be. Still, a pain whipped through me at his words. He started and must have seen my expression. "I didn't mean it like that."

I waved him off. "I get it."

"Lenora and I have only been divorced a few months."

"I said I get it." The words came out harsher than intended and I took a step back even though we were so far apart it wasn't like I had anything to be concerned about.

He hadn't touched me last night. That I was certain of.

"Shit." His hands dropped to his hips and his head fell forward, staring at the gleaming wood floor beneath our feet. "This isn't... I can't.... Fuck." He laughed and lifted his head. "I don't even know what to say. I don't remember. You don't remember. I mean, hell, maybe we just fucked around at a jewelry store or something?"

I shrugged. His guess was as good as mine. "That's what I was hoping for."

"Maybe that's all we did."

"Sure." Because how could I argue. He *could* be right, but even as I tried to agree, there was a niggling memory in my mind, like a finger tapping glass, trying to break free. And there was me on the other side, a white dress, a clump of pale pink flowers in one hand. And I was walking...

I shook that out of my head. Wrong. I didn't get married.

No way.

No how.

"I need food," I blurted, and Joey's pale, stunned, and regretful expression changed. Lips kicked at a corner. "I need to piss and shower. But I can show you where the kitchen is?"

At least he'd confirmed we were in his home, not some hotel, although I'd already gathered that. Couldn't be too sure these days. His bedroom was twice the size of my brother's. Decorated like it could be a hotel outside the clutter all over the dresser top, but who was I to judge?

I was a shit housekeeper.

"I think I can find it, but um, do you have a pair of pants or something I can wear?"

Outside the clutter on his dresser, there were no clothes on the floor. Especially nothing of mine. Most definitely not Garrett's jersey I wore last night with jeans. Where in the heck were my *clothes*?

A pink stain rushed to Joey's olive-colored cheeks, making me fidget where I stood. He really needed some clothes, too.

His nakedness could distract me when I was running on full throttle. I couldn't handle him while I was running on empty.

Crap on a cracker. How did I get into situations like this?

Joey moved to his dresser, shaking off whatever thought

he had when I asked for pants and set a few things on his dresser.

"I'll be down in a few minutes," he muttered, not looking at me.

Once he was gone, I dashed to the dresser, grabbed a pair of flannel pants, pulled them on and tied them around my waist, rolling them several times so I didn't trip over the length. Dressed, still nauseous, needing caffeine and for someone to walk me through last night, I made my way down his hall to a grand staircase, wide enough for the entire first line of his team to stand shoulder-to-shoulder on. The house was enormous, all of it looking professionally decorated with natural hues and small pops of color that made it feel more homey than bare and cold, but there were few personal touches.

Not that it mattered. I didn't care about Joey's house, his life... or I shouldn't have, but I found my steps slowing once I hit the main level. The tiled floor chilled my feet, but I still gazed around. There were two small sitting rooms, a closed door with glass panes that looked like it led into an office, Joey's most likely based on the sports jerseys framed on the walls and a few different baseball caps set on shelves. The only personal items in the whole house were in that room I figured, while I found the enormous living room, a vaulted ceiling that was at least two-stories high with wood beams. A ceiling fan hung in the middle, swirling slowly and silently. It did nothing for the airflow, or the nerves pressing down on me.

If we'd done something so ridiculously stupid as to get married, how did we fix it?

He was a good guy, but practically a stranger. I knew him through stories and secondhand information, enough to know he'd been with Lenora for years. And obviously he wasn't over that…

I can't be married to you.

He'd spit it so angrily.

I finally found the kitchen beyond the main living area, but it took another minute to find the coffee pot, tucked into a mini kitchen behind his behemoth of a professional kitchen that looked industrial and cold, through a walkway, around a corner, that took me to a smaller area where there was a stainless-steel pot on the counter along with a microwave.

Who in the hell had two kitchens right next to each other?

I shook my head.

Again, who cared?

Joey had to make millions. He was one of the fastest wingers in the league. His parents and family came from money. A dynasty of Taylors whose father had played pro hockey and all four sons followed in his footsteps.

Thankfully, the coffee pot looked simple enough and after a quick search of cupboards above it, I found mugs and more boxes of coffee pods than a grocery store contained. I grabbed one, not bothering to see if it was flavored, desperate for something normal. For caffeine. For something to erase the headache and if possible, the decisions of last night and as it brewed, I explored a little more. Around a different entrance to this mini kitchen, my eyes popped when I found another staircase. Narrowed, more normal, it led straight up to the second floor.

A door behind me showed the garage, four stalls, two empty.

The gurgling sounds of my coffee quieted and I moved that way, slid the coffee mug into my hands, and blew on it before my first sip. As soon as the heat hit my tongue, my eyes closed and a quiet moan escaped.

Coffee. Almost everything I needed to erase this hangover.

I headed back to the kitchen, hearing footsteps sound almost above my head and a few moments later Joey appeared through the mini kitchen and into the eating area where I was seated.

His hair was wet, dark locks swept to the side and he was scratching his beard while thumbing through his phone almost maniacally. I'd never seen fingers move that fast.

My phone.

Where in the hell was my purse?

I set my mug down and the noise must have startled him because his head whipped up. Dark, tortured eyes almost burned my skin with the intensity in his look.

And then he dropped the bomb.

"We are married. I want to stay that way."

4

JOEY

Coffee sputtered from her mouth and her hand that flew to her mouth did nothing to catch it as some of it splattered on my shirt.

Of all things I'd done in the last fifteen minutes since waking up in a hungover fog, Gabby spitting coffee on me was the most minor.

Still, her cheeks burned a hot pink and she apologized, scrambling to search for a towel or something to clean me off. And as she did, repeating *I'm so sorry* on a ridiculous loop, the sight of her in my clothes distracted me from the problem at hand.

We'd gotten married.

Worse, there were viral images of us leaving a chapel. Some TikTok creator had managed to catch us on video, Gabby's ass slung over my shoulder, a bouquet of flowers in one hand and a manila envelope in the other.

My phone had died at some point during the night but as soon as I turned it on, it went off like a rocket, beeping and buzzing all over the place until I finally unlocked it and started scrolling through the messages.

Every single text notification tightened my chest. This was *bad*. Really bad. Everyone was freaking out. My coach, my teammates. And then my heart dropped to the floor.

Two words, really, from the team's manager. *"Morality clause."*

I'd scrubbed my hand through my hair and cursed until those words blurred together. How in the hell could I stay married to a woman I barely knew? How could I divorce her? Two marriages... two *divorces* in less than a year? What kind of guy did that make me look like?

Not a good one, in anyone's eyes, especially my own.

"You what?" Gabby asked, and it hadn't occurred to me she'd dropped to her knees in front of me, swiping coffee splatter off my tile.

Like I gave a shit about coffee stains.

Gabby. On her knees. All that hair for me to fist and hold on to, those eyes wide with wonder and her cheeks still flushed.

She looked torn up from a long night, in my clothes, hair a frazzled mess...

Looking like sin on a platter, ready for me, waiting... ready.

Not good. Not good at all, asshole.

"You have to be joking." Her light brown eyes blinked, the color of caramel that made my thoughts short circuit and sizzle.

Enough. If only I could remember *something* about last night, but hell, the last thing I remembered was sucking down those long-neck drinks and practically falling into the Flamingo casino in search of a bathroom. Gabby was right. After that, everything was hazy.

We needed to figure this out. And I couldn't do that if my

dick got hard while she was on her knees, showing exactly how attracted I was to her.

I barked out a laugh and she froze. "I need a minute," I muttered and headed toward the butler's pantry. I was losing my mind. Had to be.

Was it possible to have a mid-life crisis heading into your late twenties? Maybe one of the hits I took into the boards last night scrambled my ability to make decent decisions.

I filled my coffee, grabbed another for her in case she needed a refill and once both were full, I found Gabby leaning against the island. Hands to her head, elbows on the counter. Her ass jutted out, filling out the backside of my pajama pants I'd tossed her way.

As I stepped into the kitchen, I slid her fresh cup onto the counter and brought mine to my mouth. "We need to talk."

She was already shaking her head, not bothering a glance at either of her coffee cups. "We... we seriously got *married*?"

"Yeah. My phone's freaking the hell out, so I turned it off again, but some pics were taken and have gone viral. Listen—"

"No. We can't. There's no way. I mean, the rings were a joke, right? Because we didn't..." She slapped her hands to the counter, straightened her arms. The green hue to her skin had faded, the flush now back, but there was something about the way her golden eyes sparked with a fire that froze me to my spot and made it difficult to suck in a breath.

God, she was beautiful.

"We did." I turned my phone back on. "Like I said, there're photos. And a video—"

"Video?"

"Yeah. Someone put it on TikTok. Tagged my team."

There was a flash of skin and then my phone disappeared from my hand and was in hers. Her body pressed to my side, her fingers frantically punching at my phone.

"Holy shit," she gasped, one hand to her mouth, covering it as the video came to life and there we were.

Me. Wearing the same black suit I'd had on when I met up with everyone for dinner. Only my profile was visible but it was clear it was me. And then there was Gabby, thrown over my shoulder. Her black hair bounced through the air as I readjusted my hold, one arm raised to flag down a cab and then my hand was at her ass, spanking it playfully while she kicked her feet in the air. Petals from the flowers in her hand fluttered to the porn card littered street and she waved the envelope in hand while shouting something we couldn't hear over the screen's music singing *This is the way we live..."*

"Shit. This is bad," she said, the words falling from her like someone was pulling on them. She swung my phone in my direction and I took it, almost afraid to get too close to her.

Gabby apparently had a fire inside of her and that fuse was set.

She could blow at any moment and I figured it could go either way. Either find this the most hilarious adventure she'd ever been on or tear the house apart in her anger.

"Listen, Gabs. We need to talk about this."

"Does Garrett know?"

"I have about a hundred texts but I didn't see his name, and he hasn't called, so I don't know."

"Shit." She shoved her hands through her hair, flinching as she scraped through tangles and then slammed her hands back to the counter. "We have to fix this."

"We will." And we would... "But I can't yet."

Her head lifted, slow, and that fuse lit earlier sparked hotter. "Excuse me?"

God, she was pretty. Even growing pissed at me, slightly hungover, those full lips of hers pressed into a frown, my dick noticed all of it. Liked all of it. My chest heated as she glared at me with that questioning look.

"I have a morality clause in my contract. And honestly, I don't think it'd be an issue any other time, but we just won the Stanley Cup *last night*. We have the parade in a few days. *Anything* that could bring attention to the team right now in any kind of negative light could mean I face suspension, hefty fines. I could lose my endorsements..." The text from the team's manager wasn't clear or specific. The threat alone was enough to have me panicking. "Please. Can we just... give this some time? A few weeks? Let the dust settle and then we can handle this, but if we rush off to lawyers and a courthouse today or while the celebrations are going on, this could be bad. For me *and* my team."

I clung to the small hope she wouldn't want the team embarrassed since her brother was on it.

I closed my eyes and dropped my head. One night and it was ridiculous how something like this could screw everything up for me.

"If we wait," I continued. "It wouldn't be seen as a drunken mistake, or something foolish and embarrassing, for either of us. It could just be... it didn't work out. I have endorsements, and I help sponsor a youth baseball league. If people get the wrong idea about this, or the right one, I guess, but think it's wrong, I could lose a lot of that. And the league's support with those kids. Please?"

I lifted my head, afraid of what I'd see there. Terrified she'd storm out. From what I could see, no one knew who

I'd married yet. We could spin this. So I fell in love with my teammate's sister in a few weeks. Our families had history together. Either way, a press release saying we were so overcome with joy we couldn't wait any longer would settle ruffled feathers much more so than a public record of annulment after drunken stupidity.

Hell, maybe I needed to call my brother, Jason. He and Tessa had eloped to Vegas a few years ago for that very reason. And wasn't it similar? Tessa had a brother who played for the Ice Kings, Jason's team. The teammate's little sister.

How fucking ironic.

Granted, they planned their elopement. They didn't wake up with hazy memories, headaches, and rings on their fingers they couldn't remember even purchasing. However, the receipt I saw earlier on my nightstand proved I'd done exactly that for the massive diamond Gabby was currently tapping on the countertop.

"What do you expect me to do with this? You're essentially blackmailing me into staying married to you, Joey. We barely know each other. Garrett's going to lose his shit. And for what?"

"To not embarrass me or your brother's team. I'm not trying to blackmail you." I pushed off the counter, moving closer to her. She was right. Besides having fun with her last night—the parts I could remember—and liking the way she looked in my clothes, we barely knew each other. The more I thought about this, the better it was. Hell, like I wanted to be twenty-six and twice divorced.

Maybe we could actually work this out. Relationships started with less, right? I *was* attracted to her. I liked talking to her. She was smart. Sassy. Hell... yeah... maybe we could actually do this. But it wasn't like I could let her know the reason I wanted to stay married was also because I didn't want to look like a complete loser, unable to stay married.

Lowering my voice, I worked hard not to let the hope thrumming through my blood scare her off. "I'm asking for help, Gabby. That's all. And maybe I can help you, too?"

She scoffed, rubbing the back of her neck like she couldn't handle the stress anymore. "How?"

Thank God I was quick on my feet. We could *do* this. "Last night, with your mom. When she asked you what you planned..." As I spoke, the memory of her mom made her lips thin. I could barely believe the way I'd heard Rachel talking to her daughter. I'd always liked the woman, but man... I'd never heard her be so nearly hard on Garrett, and as soon as she started that line I knew would end with *why can't you be more like your brother*, I'd found my hand clenched in a fist.

My brothers and I were competitive, and I knew before I ever strapped on skates I wanted to be just like my dad. All of my brothers did, but never, in any of our history had our parents pitted us against each other like that. And it'd pissed me off.

"My mom," she said and all the shine in her eyes vanished. "She's going to *kill* me. Oh God, she already thinks I'm an idiot, too stupid or too immature."

Her chin wobbled and like last night and that time in the hospital, I went to her without hesitation.

"Hey." I cupped her cheeks in my hands, her warmth sliding into my palms. "Don't cry. Not about this."

"You don't understand." She sniffed and tears sparked in her eyes. "She thinks I'm so irresponsible, living off Garrett and everything and being here and I can't even tell her why I left Seattle because she *loved* Kurt. I'm sure she'll find some way him cheating on me was my fault and it's so humiliating."

I had no idea what her rambling meant, but one mention of whoever Kurt was cheating on her and my hands on her cheeks tightened.

"Gabby," I said her name roughly, regaining her attention before she could spill more than she meant. "Listen. We can *do* this."

"Do what?"

It suddenly seemed so easy. All our problems could be fixed…

As long as we stayed married.

"You told your mom you had plans, right? And you knew you couldn't stay with Garrett and Lizzie."

"Yeah…" she drawled out. She wasn't following me.

"Me getting divorced again, or getting an annulment would be bad for me, and your mom would think you're foolish if we got married because we were drunk and stupid, right?"

"Yeah." Dark, perfectly done brows tugged in.

We were so close, it finally registered she had no makeup on. There was a faint cluster of freckles across the bridge of her nose, something I'd never seen. Her lashes were long and thick as she blinked slowly and then her tongue darted out, slid along her bottom lip.

She wasn't beautiful, she was exquisite, and that pink of her tongue had me forcing down a groan.

On their own volition, my thumbs brushed the apple of her cheeks. Color deepened as I wiped away a tear that had fallen and she swallowed thickly. Her skin, soft like silk, was tempting. Made me want to drag my lips over the path of my thumbs, slide my hands to her throat to feel the speed of her pulse.

"I think we stay married," I rasped out. My throat was growing thick, other parts of me more so as I held her, as she didn't make an effort to pull away. Instead, her lips parted in wonder. "Let's sell this to your mom. Lie a little if we have to."

"A little?" A corner of her lips ticked up and God, how I wanted to taste them.

I shouldn't have felt this way, but there was something so undeniably sexy about this woman in front of me, bringing her hands to my wrists and curling her soft, warm palms around my skin.

"What are you suggesting?"

"Let's tell your mom we planned this. We've been seeing each other since earlier this spring. Wanted to keep it quiet from Garrett during the playoffs."

"What?" She blinked. Those long, thick eyelashes of hers fluttered wildly and her hands gripped me more firmly.

But she wasn't pushing me away, and I'd count it as a win.

At her adorably confused look, I repeated it. "Let's tell your mom we've been seeing each other. Wanted to keep it quiet. We can do this, Gabby. And in a few weeks, once everything settles down, we can reevaluate. But for now, you can move in here, get out of Garrett's house. And whatever plans you'd started making, whatever you were going to tell your mom you wanted to do, I'll help you."

"Help me."

God, she was adorable when confused. Good thing for me because based on the fire in her eyes earlier I doubted I'd win many arguments with her. I could imagine her, all that fire—all that *passion*—directed at me and how I'd react.

Equally passionate.

I bit down on my lower lip to stave off another groan and

slid my hands down her cheeks until my hands were gripping hers between us. We were so close, and my arms brushed her breasts, eliciting a surprised gasp from her.

Hot damn. Her nipples were hard beneath her shirt and if I wasn't mistaken, her own breathing had picked up.

It wasn't great waking up married to a woman I was attracted to without much memory of the night. But... if my *wife* was attracted to me, wanted me as badly as I was learning I wanted her—was it the worst thing in the world?

"You're insane," she whispered, and untangled her hands from mine, taking a step back and scratching across her forehead. The green and gold painted fingers grabbed my attention, quickly followed by the blinding sparkle of that diamond I'd apparently slid onto her slim, delicate finger. "Absolutely insane. Have you lost your mind?"

"Possibly."

She huffed a laugh and turned, grabbed her coffee and took a sip. Cringing, she made a face. "Gross. It's cold and" —she glanced at me— "and you're laughing at me."

Sure enough, my smile was wide, although I wasn't laughing. Not yet. "You're adorable," I said. "Let me refill your coffee. You think about this. But I swear to you, we can both win something from this, even if it stays temporary."

"How temporary? I mean, there *were* things I thought about doing this summer, places I wanted to go, and at some point, I need to find a new job—"

As she spoke, I hurried to the coffee pot, easily able to hear it mostly because with every word she spoke, her voice level increased. Her panic was palpable, but I wasn't easily deterred.

We could do this. And having this woman on my arm wouldn't be such a bad thing.

I brought her back her coffee. She was still ranting about

some asshole named Kurt and construction, but I cut her off.

We had more serious things to work out. Like, any minute, our families would wake up, turn on the news or their phones and I had no doubt they'd descend on my home, demanding answers and explanations.

As I told her this, she turned as white as my countertops.

"Oh shit." She gaped at me. I rolled my lips together to fight a laugh.

Yeah, I liked her. She was sexy even when freaked out of her mind.

"Yeah. So... I hate to rush you on this, but you're going to have to make a decision, and soon."

"Right," she mumbled. "Because I've done such a great job at thinking lately. You know that Garrett is going to kill you, right? Smash your face in with his goalie stick or something."

I chuckled, shook my head. "He won't."

He'd be pissed. Might throw a punch. But like me, Garrett loved his hockey sticks too much to risk breaking them over my head. Thank God.

"I need the bathroom," she blurted. "I'm sorry, but I just... I need a minute and I need to pee and this is all so much."

I fought the urge to yank her to me, to calm her down. At some point, I couldn't push this. She had to decide what she wanted. And if she chose to get an annulment, a quick divorce, I'd respect it, even if I hated it for my own ego's sake.

"It's down that hall, first door to the left." I gestured in the direction, the hallway past the living room. "Take all the time you need. We'll be okay with whatever you decide."

Even if I hated it.

5

———

GABBY

I found the bathroom where Joey told me it was and as soon as I stopped inside, my jaw almost hit the floor.

On the counter was a plastic bag, Garrett's jersey I'd worn last night poking out of the top. My purse was next to it, knocked over and half-emptied.

My phone. I snatched it up, found it dead and clung to it like a lifeline even if it didn't have any battery life in it.

At least I found my things.

I kicked a white bundle of fabric on the floor and blood drained from my face, making me shiver. Closing the bathroom door, I squatted down, ran my fingers over the soft, silky fabric. My fingers shook as I grabbed it and stood with it in my hands.

My wedding dress. It had to be and for a moment, my eyes burned. I'd gotten married. I'd worn a wedding dress, carried a beautiful bouquet of pale pink roses like I'd always imagined I'd have in my wedding, and I'd slipped into this beautiful dress and gotten married. Walked down the aisle. Most likely vowed to be faithful, for better or worse, sickness and health.

And I didn't remember a single moment except random flashes of Joey and me leaving the chapel.

Hell, I didn't even know *where* we'd gotten married.

Not the wedding I'd dreamed of, and yet I'd been aware enough to ask for a few of the things I'd always wanted.

Standing, I held the dress in front of me, chin wobbling with emotion. I was young when my dad died in a training exercise for the military. So young, some days it was difficult to remember him and I probably would have forgotten what he looked like completely if Mom hadn't kept our house full of photographs of him everywhere she could fit them, or constantly told me how much I looked like him. Sometimes, she'd say it with tears in her eyes and then leave the room. Didn't exactly make me feel great to know that some days just looking at me made her hurt. Her love for him was so large, so huge, and still, somehow so fulfilling, that eighteen years later she still told stories about him, still loved him.

That was the kind of love I'd always imagined I'd have when I walked down the aisle.

Tears slipped down my cheeks as I brushed a hand over the lace front of the dress. Even not on a hanger, rumpled from a night on the floor, it was beautiful. Elegant. It was a dress I would have scoured bridal shops for, taking days or weeks to find the perfect one and somehow I'd managed to find it in hours or moments. None of it made sense. How Joey had managed to buy me a gorgeous ring. How I'd been able to find a dress I would have chosen if I were marrying my soul mate. How we'd gotten the license and how it'd all come together in glimpses of everything I'd dreamed of as a little girl while I played with Barbies and Polly Pockets.

I was *married*, and despite my mother believing I was incapable of making good decisions, marriage was one I took with the utmost seriousness.

So what in the hell happened between Joey and me last night where we'd decided this would be a good idea? Despite being drunk, it had to have been something *huge*. Something powerful.

"What a freaking mess," I muttered to my reflection. My skin was pale, eyes red. I needed a shower and a fresh change of clothes and I definitely needed to get my shit together to deal with the drunken decisions we made.

Garrett was going to *kill* Joey. My mom would most likely disown me.

And Joey? What in the hell would his parents say? What would his brothers and their wives think of me? Sure, I'd met them before. Jude, Joey's next oldest brother, and Garrett had been friends for so long—since college—I knew him well. But a drunken Vegas wedding neither of us remembered wouldn't make a good impression on either of our families.

Oh dear. Maybe I was losing my mind. Could I do what Joey suggested and not fall in love with him? Hell, I was already attracted to the man, but what wasn't attractive about the guy with his trim hips, athletic body. A drool-worthy, panty-melting body with a wicked as sin smile. Every time Joey smiled at me, it felt like he was thinking dirty thoughts behind that twist of his lips and the gleam in his eyes.

Foolish. It had to be. I was just Garrett's sister, someone he barely knew.

There was no way I could stay married to him—too much time alone and I might find myself catching feelings.

A laugh bubbled from me, and I clamped a hand over my mouth to muffle it.

How absurd. Who didn't want to love their husband?

"Women who get drunk and hitched in Vegas, you idiot."

Right. That was how we started. I needed to remember that. Carefully folding the dress, I draped it over the bathroom counter, over my clothes when another thought hit me.

I'd woken up in Joey's bed, upstairs, down the hall in his mansion dressed in a T-shirt that wasn't mine and my underwear.

My clothes were all down here, in the bag, on the floor.

Holy *shit*. Had I run *naked* through his house? Had he seen me?

As the visual of that registered, another maniacal laugh burst free.

Screw Joey hearing me. I was absolutely losing my mind. How freaking *horrifying*.

Way to go, Gabby. Show your husband your side of ridiculous crazy the night you're hitched.

Oh God. What was I going to do?

I shoved my fingers to my temples, tried to massage away the pounding in my brain and sat down on the toilet. Elbows to my knees, I groaned. There was no good way to fix this. If we hurried off to a courthouse and got an annulment and Joey made the news for reasons other than their win last night, he could end up in trouble.

If I told Garrett what really happened, he could end up in prison. Hell, I could be a widow before I ever consummated my wedding vows.

I was twenty-three years old. I didn't want to be divorced, not even if the story would someday make me laugh. And Joey was just recently divorced. Did he want another marriage ending?

Shit.

As the thoughts raced, I closed my eyes, tried to tally up

the pros and cons of Joey's idea when another flash was brought to the forefront.

"Do you know what hurts the most?"

I threaded my arm through Joey's as we stood at the fence. In front of us, to the tune of "Luck Be a Lady," the Bellagio fountains danced and performed for the crowds.

"What?"

"I loved her," he said and his voice was so guttural my chest squeezed tight. "I would have done anything for her. Bent over backwards to make sure she was happy. Hell, had she come to me, told me what she was thinking... I might have... hell, if that's what was missing for her to be truly happy, I might have even given her that..."

His voice trailed off, jaw so tight, I wanted to run my finger along his jaw, but the pained look in his eyes held me back.

"Would you have? Really?"

He stared at the lights, the fountains bursting to the music and shook his head. "No. I loved her, but I wouldn't have been okay with sharing her either."

My hand flinched on his arm. The love he had for his wife was so obvious I could feel it radiating off of him.

"Do you love her? Still?"

He turned, looked down at me with his onyx eyes and licked his lips, swallowed so slowly I was mesmerized by the dip of his Adam's apple. "Not anymore. Not like that. I miss coming home to someone. Miss being with someone, but Lenora and I, we were always so different. When I look back objectively, there were core things, values we differed on that would have torn us apart eventually." He paused, rolled his lips together and I stared at him, that unwanted pulse at my core started to throb as I gazed at his lips.

His mouth was perfect. And that dimple in his cheek, right at the edge of his scruff when he quirked even the smallest smile threatened to undo me. Dimples should be outlawed. I'd curse God for creating that spot in a man's cheek that made a woman's knees wobble if I wasn't so afraid of him spiting me. At least he wasn't wearing his hat backward. That one-two punch might have knocked me off my feet. There'd be no way I could stand a chance resisting this man, even as he talked about his failed marriage.

He was the kind of man my dad would have loved. My chest tightened and I turned back to the fountains so he couldn't see the pain in my eyes, the loneliness in them. In all my life, I'd never been anyone's first choice, not like Joey was just describing, and sometimes... sometimes it hurt.

"You'll find someone, someday. You're too good of a man to not have everything you want in life." As I said it, my voice shook. I meant it with everything in me.

My reward was his smile. A genuine one that lit up his face and wiped away his pain. "Yeah? You think?"

"Of course I do."

He glanced back to the fountains, the look on his face changing to one of contemplation, and when he turned back to me, my knees went weak at the look on his face. Dark eyes that held so much, lips ticked up at the corners. "My parents have had an incredible marriage for forty years. I want what they have more than I've ever wanted anything, including hockey. If I ever get married again, I'll do my damnedest to make sure we can have that kind of life together."

A sob bubbled in my throat. I'd had a long string of boyfriends over the years. Some who just didn't work out, some that ended ugly. Some like Kurt that ended in humiliating and self-confidence-killing ways. But all I'd wanted as a girl, was to find the kind of guy who I could love like my mom still loved my dad, even though he died so many years ago. I wanted what Joey's parents had too, and I had no doubt the next time Joey fell

*in love, he'd do more than bend over backwards to give his wife
everything she wanted, he'd kill to make it happen.*

"*I think whoever falls in love and marries you next will be the
luckiest woman in the world.*"

And it was me.

He'd married me, and he wanted to stay that way.

Perhaps, in my inebriated state, I'd been right.

The girl who married Joey Taylor would end up being
the luckiest woman alive. So outside the ridiculousness of
this entire fiasco and the absurdity of us staying married
when we didn't remember doing it, what did I really have to
lose?

Outside my heart, anyway.

6

JOEY

I paced laps around my living room furniture shortly after Gabby disappeared into the bathroom. She'd asked for a minute, but she'd been in there long enough to remodel the damn thing. As the door opened, I spun from my view of my backyard and faced her.

Her skin held no more color than it had earlier, and in her hand was her phone. A silky white dress was draped over her arm. Along with the clothes of mine I'd given her, she wore an embarrassed little grin and her eyes crinkled at the edges.

She was dressed, though, in jeans and Garrett's jersey, the clothes she'd been wearing last night. Which meant...

"So, I found my stuff, which means I think last night I stripped down in the bathroom?" As she asked, her brows rose and a hint of pink appeared on her cheeks.

That was an image in itself. Add on her naked, streaking through my home and I brought my fist to my mouth to cover my laugh.

"It's not funny," she pouted. "Please tell me you don't remember it?"

"No recollection of it, I promise." But hell if I wasn't a little bit disappointed by that. I doubted we'd had sex last night. Both of us had woken up slightly clothed, but it wasn't until she draped the dress in her arm over the back of my love seat with such tender care, I actually remembered anything.

"What's your favorite cut?"

I twisted my head and grinned at Gabby. Her eyes were bright, slightly glazed from that last hurricane drink, but she was no less stunning. She laughed and shook her head, pointed to something other than the four-carat round diamond ring I'd had the store assistant remove from its glass case.

"I've never thought of it. But I know I don't want something that sticks up too high." Facing the assistant, she explained, "I cut hair. Do a lot of work with my hands and I don't want it scraping someone's scalp or getting tangled in their hair. Do you have something that will help with that?"

"Bien sûr, of course." The woman turned, headed to a different case and with a set of keys in her hand, unlocked another glass-enclosed cabinet.

"Are you sure about this?" I asked, but it wasn't the ring I meant. Gabby knocked me off my feet all night long. She played poker better than I did, she laughed more than any person I'd ever been around, and most of all, the entire night I'd been around her once I told her about Lenora at the fountains, I hadn't once thought about my ex-wife. Being around Gabby swept it all away. And if she had that effect on me in a night, what could she do with me if we had more time together?

"Of course, I'm sure," she said, and she gazed up at me so softly, so confidently, I hoped like hell she wasn't talking about the ring either.

"This is a three and a half-carat emerald cut," the woman said, returning and set down the most gorgeous mass of bling I'd

ever seen. Diamonds wrapped around the band and that emerald diamond barely rose from the band, just like Gabby had said.

"Oh my," she breathed next to me. Her shoulder hit mine and I draped my hand to her waist. She smelled good. Like lilacs and springtime and the hope of a new, luscious and beautiful beginning. "It's gorgeous."

"It's yours," I said. For whatever reason, I wanted this woman. Now. Tonight. Tomorrow, and hell, I'd keep her forever if the promise of her was half as beautiful as the night with her had been.

"What? Joey, it's..."

"Yours." I kissed her temple and inhaled another whiff of that sweet scent she wore. But I didn't even think it was the perfume, it was just Gabby. "We'll make sure we get it fitted properly tomorrow if it doesn't fit," and then turning back to the assistant I said, "Is there a wedding band that matches?" At her yes, I said, "We'll take that too. And now, what about my ring? Do I get one?"

Gabby tilted her head back, her pert nose crinkling as she laughed. "Of course, but you have to leave so it's a surprise."

"What? You just got to see yours!"

"Yeah, because you said you wanted help. I don't need help with yours. I already know what's perfect for you."

I glanced down at my left hand. The black band, wide and thick, was simple. Matte finish. It was cool to the touch as I brushed my thumb over it. A little loose. *We'll get them fitted.* Jesus. We'd really done this, and somehow pulled it off in a night. But she'd been right. The ring was perfect for me and at some point last night, I'd been sure she was too. That meant something, right?

"Joey?" I jerked at the sound of my name, at Gabby shuffling on her feet, brows tugged in. "You okay?"

"Last night." I cleared my throat. That had to have been

a memory but it was so vivid, it felt like it'd just happened. "When we looked at rings, you said you wanted one that wouldn't get tangled in your client's hair while you worked."

"Oh." She blinked rapidly, beautiful dark lashes fluttering and she reached for the couch like she needed an anchor, something to brace herself. "I told you at the fountains that if you got married again, the woman you chose would be the luckiest woman in the world."

A heat so fast, so furious, speared my chest it almost knocked me right off my feet. If only *I* could remember the way we looked at each other when those words were said.

She was remembering, too. She didn't look upset about it, either. Maybe we'd remember everything, maybe we wouldn't, but what I would never forget was the way she looked at me right then, saying those words she spoke, almost like she believed it was fully true.

I wanted her. And wasn't that hilarious? I wanted my wife, a woman I couldn't remember ever kissing more than the briefest brush at her temple or her cheek. But hell if I wasn't turned on while she brushed her hand over that dress as if it was her most treasured possession.

I rocked on my heels, shoved my hands to my hips and shrugged, smiling. "Then I guess it's your lucky day."

She laughed, slow and sensual and it was so beautiful I wanted to record her doing that same exact laugh so I could listen to it every time I needed a smile.

"I guess so," she agreed, still smiling. Still laughing, color finally returning to her cheeks and the rest of her before she bit her bottom lip. "So, I decided—"

A rapid, fierce pounding sound came from the front door and both of us whipped our heads in the direction. The doorbell went off, drowned out by the continual pounding on my glass door so harshly my chandeliers shook and the thousands of mini crystals hanging from it rattled.

"Joey and Gabby! Get your asses down here. NOW!"

"Oh shit," Gabby whispered, golden wide eyes meeting mine.

I nodded. "I think that means Garrett's heard our good news."

At least, I hoped it was good news because she hadn't told me what it was.

Her eyes widened, jaw went slack until at the very last second, she smiled. "Should we tell them, husband?"

That smile of hers wobbled but fuck that. If that was her way of saying she was ready to go along with this ridiculous plan, I was all in for it.

I held out my hand, held my breath until she placed hers gently in mine. Hers was cold, sweaty, and I swore from that moment on, my wife would never have to be nervous around me again.

"Let's do this."

~

GARRETT AND RACHEL barreled into my house, pushing Gabby and I back before I could welcome them.

"Shit," Gabby gasped, gripping my arm with her free hand as she stumbled back.

Lizzie, for her part, hands settled on her stomach, gave us a chagrined look before stepping in and giving us a quiet, *hey*.

"Explain." Garrett stood in my entryway, arms crossed over his chest. He breathed like a bull ready to charge and I was pretty certain steam could plume from his ears at any moment.

"Back down. Now." I gritted my teeth together. Next to me, Gabby was clinging to my arm like a woman afraid to take a step away from me out of fear of what her family would do. Or say. And fuck if that didn't feel good.

She was leaning on *me*. Not running to them.

"Are you fucking—"

"You don't get to come into *my* home and demand answers, G. So take a deep breath. Calm the fuck down. Get yourself a cup of coffee if you need it, but neither of us will discuss or explain anything until you chill the fuck out."

Gabby exhaled, a heavy, shuddering breath, and I glanced down at her.

They didn't need to know anything. We could spin this any way we wanted, all the ways we'd already discussed, but I didn't *want* to lie.

At least until her mom stepped forward, placing one hand on Garrett's bulging bicep. "How could you embarrass your brother like this?" she asked.

"Mom—"

Hell, even Garrett flinched at the question. "Not cool, Mom," he muttered. And glanced at Gabby. Eyes flickered to me.

"Shit." He scrubbed his hands down his face, through his beard before dropping them to his hips and stepping back. "Give me a minute, but then you're talking. Both of you."

He stormed out of my entryway, headed toward where I kept my coffee. He'd been in my house enough since he'd been traded to Las Vegas, so I left him to it and turned to Rachel.

"That goes for you, too. You don't get to come into my house and disrespect Gabby *or* me like you just did. None of this is about Garrett, and if you talk to your daughter like that again while I'm here, I'm going to be the one seeing you out."

I'd always respected Rachel. She'd always come across as a woman much like my own mother who was level-headed, proud of her boy for making it to the NHL. Until she spoke to Gabby the way she did at dinner last night, I never could have imagined that would have been the first thing she said.

"You don't get it, Joey," she said, sighing. "This is Gabby. This is what she does. Acts first, thinks last…"

"Enough." I squeezed Gabby's hand and pulled her close to me. "That's enough, Rachel, and I mean it. You want answers to your questions, you'll shut your mouth and listen or you'll be on the front porch and you won't be hearing a damn thing."

"Joey," Gabby whispered, pressing more tightly into my side. "It's okay."

"It's not okay." I tried to loosen my features, but knew I was scowling at her. "I got three brothers. Mom and Dad, they never pitted us against us like she's doing to you. She might love you, she might want the best for you, but constantly talking to you like you're fucking everything up and blaming you for all of it is shit and shouldn't happen, and I'm not going to stand here listening to it. Not anymore."

I slid my gaze to Rachel, wearing an expression similar to the one Garrett sported when he entered. "You get me?"

She glanced at Gabby. Back to me. With angry eyes and a pinched face, she huffed. "You'll see. You might not like what I'm saying, but that doesn't mean it's wrong either."

With that, she took off in the direction Garrett had headed, leaving Lizzie gawking at both of us.

"So… you're married." She grinned and then rolled her lips together like she was fighting a laugh. "That's exciting."

7

———

GABBY

In my wildest imaginations, I couldn't have predicted the whirlwind of this morning would have ended up with Joey Taylor, of all people, stepping in between my mother and me as she began to remind me how disappointed she was in my decisions.

As she opened her mouth, I'd braced for the worst, but she'd barely gotten anything out before Joey was there, defending me and protecting me. Never, not once in my life, had I ever had that. Sure, there was Garrett, who hated it when Mom pulled this crap, but like this morning, all he did was admonish her with a word.

He would hug me later, apologize on her behalf, remind me she loved me, she just didn't understand me. For a woman who solved puzzles and crime for a living, she was completely exasperated by that fact.

But even then, he'd never stepped up and said *Don't.*

For a moment, the briefest of them, I'd imagined a lifetime of being with Joey, believing I'd always have someone at my back in this way. It was fleeting, the bubble bursting almost as quickly as it formed, but now I wanted that back. I wanted to reach for it and hold it to me and believe this completely ludicrous plan of Joey's would work.

We'd feign a mad crush, a whirlwind romance we kept in secret, although who would believe that considering I'd barely left Garrett and Lizzie's on my own since I'd been in town? Maybe, for the first time in my life, I'd shut my mom up faster than Joey had done.

Leave it to Lizzie to know exactly how to lighten the mood.

I grinned, it shook and trembled, and I still clung to Joey like a suction cup, but I was smiling, shaking my head at her. "It appears that way," I said.

Her smile was bright enough to light up a room on a normal day. Today, it was cautious even as she stepped toward me with her arms outstretched.

I released Joey's hand, missed his warmth immediately and pulled her in for a hug.

"Your mom. She loves you but I doubt even Garrett will let that slide."

"We'll see," I muttered into the crook of her shoulder. She was growing every day and I had to fold myself over her stomach to hug her.

"You really got hitched?"

I stepped back, showed her the ring. "Yeah."

"Holy shit," she gasped. One hand covered her mouth and the other yanked my hand closer to her. "This is fucking huge!"

"That's what they all say," Joey teased.

"Shut up." She laughed, and I joined him, bumping my shoulder into his as he stepped up to me and settled his hand on my lower back.

"It's gorgeous," she said, still gaping at him, fingers shaking like she was afraid to touch it. I understood. I was terrified of the weight of the thing alone, much less playing with it. I couldn't even take it off. What if I lost it? This had to be more than the average person spent on a car.

Holy hell. I was *wearing* a Mercedes. A giggle worked its way up and I covered my mouth before it fell free. With my mom and Garrett in the other room, probably making coffee and talking in hushed tones about me so I didn't hear them, I allowed myself the moment of happiness as Lizzie smiled up at me, eyes shining but wary.

"You're happy? This is good?"

"It will be," Joey proclaimed, and it was just that. A promise. A vow, or at least a wish everything would work out.

I looked up at him, so much taller than me. The top of my head barely brushed the top of his shoulder but that was okay. It gave me a great view of that sexy indent at the base of his neck, his Adam's apple as he swallowed. He grinned down at me and I swayed on my feet.

The dimple. Holy crap. I'd forgotten about that dimple of his but there it was, on full display, digging into his cheek so perfectly I wanted to run my fingertip over it and then press my lips to his full ones.

"Yeah." Lizzie cleared her throat and stepped back, dropping my hand like the ring scalded her. "I'm just... going to give that look a moment of privacy."

I frowned at her, caught her smirk and the circle she made with her finger pointed in our direction before she waddled out of the room. Pretty sure her stomach disappeared three seconds before the rest of her did she was getting so big.

"So," Joey said, still holding me, still grinning down at me and making me stupid with that dimple. "I'm thinking we should call my family, get this over with all together."

Flashbacks of his dad calling refs donkeys and dick sucking zebras during calls he didn't agree with flashed into my brain and I flinched.

"Too much?" Joey chuckled.

"Um. Yes. But I don't think it could get much worse."

"Right." His smile flatlined and he grabbed his phone from his pocket. He grimaced, looking at his text strings before sliding his dark eyes to me. "Looks like they heard and are on their way anyway."

"Great," I muttered.

"Come on. Let's go get some more coffee, see what kind of food I have we can put out for everyone. By this afternoon, everything will be okay."

"You sound so sure."

"Listen to me, and listen good, okay?"

I could only nod at his expression, as his hand slid to my hip and he maneuvered himself from my side to my front where his other hand went to my cheek like it was the most natural thing in the world. Like we were familiar with each other and touched each other often, whenever the mood struck.

The warmth from his palm heated my skin, flushed my neck down to my chest. If only...

"Your mom might believe you act before you think, but mine know I don't. Mine know how serious I took my marriage to Lenora, how badly I wanted us to last forever."

At the mention of Lenora, my stomach sank, but he continued without pausing.

"I mean this, Gabby. Whatever else you believe today, know this. I wouldn't have gotten married at the drop of a hat because we were drunk and being silly. We might not ever fully remember what happened last night, but I know, deep in my gut and my conscience, *something* happened that made us think this was the perfect idea. We might figure out what that something is, we might not, but what I do know right now, is that we're married. And I take that seriously. No one will give you a hard time. I won't allow it. You're my *wife*, for whatever reasons that came about, and as long as you continue to be my wife, my job is to protect you. Emotionally. Physically. Financially, if you need it. Understand?"

I understood nothing. Not this speech. Not the intensity swirling in his dark eyes or the way his chest heaved with the force of his statement.

"Joey—"

It was all I got out before he tugged me forward and gently brushed his lips over my forehead. A barely there, gone before I truly registered it and yet sparks of pleasure worked their way down my spine, tangled in my stomach and drove deeper until my body felt alive for the first time since I could remember.

A kiss or a touch from Kurt never felt like this.

Never had my body responded so quickly.

I leaned in, rested against him, and then nodded. "Thank you."

"We'll figure the rest out as it comes."

And that sounded like a promise too.

"I JUST... I DON'T UNDERSTAND."

Sonya Taylor, the matriarch of the Taylor clan was standing next to her husband, wringing her hands together, making me feel approximately two feet tall. They must have already been on their way, a caravan of Taylor brothers and spouses and kids in tow, because they showed up a minute or two after Joey and I headed to the kitchen where Lizzie jumped in and helped us pull fruit out of Joey's fridge. Joey attempted to chip in, letting us know where to find everything, but Lizzie ushered him out of the kitchen with wide eyes and a whispered, *"You might need to go keep Garrett and Rachel company."*

I'd cringed, hating I didn't have the family who would at least wait and listen before jumping to conclusions of my extreme irresponsibility.

Not that the truth wasn't exactly what they thought. But damn.

For once, it'd be nice if I was at least given the benefit of the doubt.

Once he'd stepped away, shooting me a look I somehow was able to read asking me if I was okay and I nodded, I turned to Lizzie. "Please don't ask me questions."

Fortunately, she hadn't the time before the doorbell rang, the Taylors descended and all three of their wives helped us finish digging in the kitchen for essentials and what we attempted to pass off as a brunch—minus the champagne for mimosas, if he even had any. Based on their tightened expressions, surreptitious glances in my direction and Joey's, no one was in the mood for more celebrating.

It was once Joey called everyone into the living room, took my hand in his, tangling our fingers together like we'd been holding hands since our middle school days and declared, "As you've seen and as you've heard, Gabby and I were married last night."

The proof of it was with my wedding dress still draped over the couch and our marriage certificate he'd found upstairs and brought down at some point now sitting for all to see on the large coffee table.

"It's simple, Mom," Joey said. He slid a grin toward Sonya I imagined had a terrific track record of getting him out of all sorts of trouble. "Gabby and I started spending time together a few months ago, and last night, we decided we didn't want to wait to start the rest of our lives together."

He sold it so well. If we weren't around everyone who knew us best, loved us the most, and knew our tells, I had no doubt he would have been one hundred percent believed.

Except for Garrett.

"Yeah?" he asked, arms once again crossed over his chest, eyes narrowed. "When exactly have you been spending time together because last I knew, we were on the road or playing games and Gabby here was with me on the nights we weren't."

Next to him, Lizzie tucked in close, slipping her arm behind his back. She gave me the same questioning look, only half as menacing as Garrett was giving Joey.

"That's not true," I said. "There were lots of nights I left to give you and Lizzie time alone. Or nights when you two went out for dinner and baby shopping."

"So you were sneaking around? What for, unless you knew you were doing something you weren't supposed to."

"I'm not twelve, Garrett. Stop making me sound like a disobedient preteen."

"Then stop acting like it," he shot back and at my side, Joey's spine went taut.

"Don't," he snapped, leaning forward an inch, but with the way his anger spiked he might as well have been right in Garrett's face. "Don't you dare. We already had this talk. You don't get to stand here and be a dick to her. That's the last cheap shot you take before you leave."

Garrett's mouth thinned, but his anger was as much a living, breathing dragon as Joey's was next to me.

He leaned back and exhaled, running his hand up and

down my back. Whether he was trying to comfort me or soothe himself, I didn't know.

"Listen, I know you're all shocked. I know this isn't ideal and I know, Mom, that you're at least slightly disappointed you didn't get to get dressed up for another wedding."

At that, Sonya smiled, shook her head in an adoring way.

"But I already gave you that, and you didn't freak out like this when Jason and Tessa eloped to Vegas."

"That was planned," Jason pointed out, all blond-haired and burly and standing tall behind Tessa who was tucked into the couch.

Tessa turned pink and sank deeper into the couch.

"So? Doesn't mean it was a mistake and you didn't get the third degree."

"I asked him questions," Sonya said, but quickly frowned. "Although, in thinking about it, I only asked him one."

"Are you happy?" Jason said and grinned down at his wife. "And yes, I was. Still am. Best damn decision I ever made. Can you say the same?"

I fought against shuffling on my feet. Damn. The Taylors could be seriously intense, a surprise given how laid-back and jovial they usually were.

Without skipping a beat, Joey stood tall, arm around my shoulders like he was *proud* to be the man next to me and lied through his teeth. "Yes."

My mom, surprisingly silent through all this, watched the entire thing with an assessing gaze. Perhaps she had enough manners not to berate me in front of everyone. Perhaps, maybe for the first time, she was finally giving me the benefit of the doubt.

Hard to believe, but stranger things have happened.

"Okay then." Sonya came forward, smiling tentatively

but no less graceful than she usually did with her dark hair already styled perfectly this early and dressed to take on the world in a stylish summer wrap dress with fluttered cap sleeves. "Then I'm happy for you."

She pressed her hands to Joey's face, tugged him down to kiss his cheek and turned to me.

With the same gentle movements and touch, I practically melted into her as she stepped back, keeping her warm, soft palms against my skin. "Then welcome to the family, Gabby." She winked playfully. "Such as it is."

8

JOEY

I couldn't remember if I'd kissed my wife when we got married. I assumed we did the obligatory *you may kiss your bride* kiss. But was it a peck? Had there been passion? Based on the way I reacted to every touch this morning, I imagined I'd tilted her head back, slid my other hand across her cheek before the pull of her was too strong to withstand. I imagined I took her mouth in a kiss that would have been inappropriate for a church, but wholly appropriate for a Vegas Strip chapel wedding.

With my mom accepting her into the family so easily, the glimmer in Gabby's eyes, smiling so sweetly at her, I wanted that kiss.

Wanted to hold her in my arms, palm the back of her head with my hand and hold her tight to me, swaying to a song that would become our song. I wanted to hold our clasped hands together at my chest where the beat of my heart would be a rhythmic tune to the passion between us.

I wanted to slip my tongue into the sweet cavern of her mouth, memorize the feel and taste of her. Learn what she loved, what drove her into a frenzy and what would bring her to a slow, torturous boil. I wanted all of it with the beautiful woman next to me, despite lacking memories of how I grew to this place in such a short time.

Who gave a flying fuck. Gabby next to me, loving on my mom and then quickly thereafter being hugged by the rest of the Taylor women with congratulations and gasps of excitement over the ring, was all I needed to see to know I hadn't fully lied to my mom or Jason.

I was happy. Right then, I was the happiest I could remember being in a very long time—Stanley Cup win included.

And that was all my family had ever wanted for me, particularly over the last year when so much went to shit.

Tepid congratulations cooled further, until eventually, my mom suggested they all head out. Some of my family had flights and I imagined Katie and Jude wanted to get Marissa back to their home and on a regular schedule. Slowly, they began saying their goodbyes and soon, the house was empty save for Garrett, Lizzie, and Rachel. All of whom had been relatively quiet since I told Garrett to back off.

"Be good to her," he said, coming to me with his hand outstretched.

I arched my brow.

He could squish my hand and break every bone if he wanted to. I took it anyway, preparing for the overly hardened grip that never came. "I will."

"I still don't like this. But I've got your back. Always."

"Then have Gabby's."

Lizzie shoved Garrett out of the way, earning a playful scowl and she rolled her eyes in exchange. "He'll get over this. You know how protective you Dubiaks can be."

Gabby flushed, peered up at me. "It's possible I wasn't

the nicest when I learned Lizzie was here a few months ago."

"Not the nicest is putting it the nicest way possible. I thought she was going to climb through the computer screen and strangle me."

"Until you told me you were pregnant, I might have." Gabby settled her hands on Lizzie's stomach and the wariness she carried all day evaporated in a moment. "Make sure you take care of my nephews."

Lizzie chuckled. "Take care of my own boys, you mean? I think I can manage."

My heart swelled as Gabby ran her hands gently over Lizzie's belly. She looked incredible for having twins, and on a normal day I would have complimented her. But today, I was struck by the look on Gabby's face. Reverent and awed, she *loved* those babies already.

Unbidden, an image of her swollen the same with *my* baby inside of her flashed in my mind. She'd be beautiful. Probably cranky. A whole lot sassy but an enormous amount of sexy.

Would she want that? Babies?

It was one of the biggest things Lenora and I could never agree on. I wanted them. She wanted to wait. She couldn't exactly dance burlesque while expecting and she hadn't wanted to take time off work, worried she wouldn't return to the same size afterward.

I'd been okay with it considering my travel schedule. Our entire lives had been a revolving door of one of us coming or going. That wasn't the stability I wanted for my kids, so I understood to a point.

We'd had time.

But now?

I shook the thought away.

Gabby and I didn't even remember getting married. We didn't know if we were going to *stay* married. Thinking of babies was definitely putting the cart before the horse. Unfortunately, the image didn't clear as quickly as I wanted.

It lingered there, Gabby's hand wearing my ring resting her hand atop her own belly, smiling, gorgeous, and happy to be making a family with me.

I wanted that... the family with the kids climbing all over me as soon as I returned from an away game like my brothers and I had done to our dad when we were little.

"You'll be back?" Gabby asked Garrett. She'd already mentioned him bringing her things over so she could get settled here.

Scowl still firmly in place and deciding to act like I didn't exist, he nodded, bent to her cheek. "If you're sure."

"I'm sure." Her hand settled on his arm and squeezed. "You two need your privacy and don't argue with me. We all know it."

He sighed, shot a glare in my direction that could melt icebergs and took Lizzie's hand in his. "As soon as we get your things packed, I'll bring them back over."

"Thank you."

Her mom stepped up to her then, wrapped her in her arms. I didn't miss the way Gabby stiffened first before returning the hug nor the unhappy look still twisting Rachel's expression. "We love you. Always. No matter what."

"Thanks Mom."

She ended the hug and lifted a hand in my direction—huh. No hug for the new son-in-law. Not surprising based on her attitude. Couldn't really blame her either.

The three of them headed out, and right as Rachel got to the door, holding it open with one hand, she shot her final shot.

"And when this blows up, like I'm certain it will, we'll be here for you then, too."

The door slammed, making Gabby jump and she stared at the door like she hoped to set it on fire.

"Bitch," I muttered. Yeah, it was her mom, but that shit was unnecessary. What mom found some sort of sick enjoyment in making her daughter feel like a shitty loser?

"Don't," Gabby muttered too. "Don't say a thing."

She headed off toward the kitchen, leaving me in my entryway, the house near silent except for the sound of my fridge opening.

Not exactly the way I'd planned to spend the day after we won the Stanley Cup.

"YOU SURE KNOW how to set the world on fire."

Alix's chuckle was heartier than my responding one. "Yeah. That was the plan."

"Damn. How'd that happen?"

It hit me then, how many times we'd have to tell the story. How old it was already getting and barely half a day had gone by.

Less than an hour after the shitty departure from Gabby's family, Garrett returned with her suitcases. I'd stayed far enough back to give them privacy, close enough to step in in case he decided to pull a Rachel and leave with a shitty comment. Fortunately, he didn't.

I'd hauled her bags upstairs to the guest room over-looking the pool, two doors away from mine while Gabby had herself a glass of wine. Then she disappeared into the room, barely looking at me, sipping her wine and muttering how she was going to unpack. It was strange, knowing I was going to be living with another woman after being married for so long, and on the flip side, I liked it.

Maybe it was the fact I was the youngest of a family of six, but I'd spent so little time alone growing up, then roommates in college, the quietness ate at me.

A few minutes later, when I'd gone to pick up the phone to begin returning some of the thousand phone calls, my jaw had dropped and I'd forgotten the English language when Gabby reappeared.

Wrapped in a beach towel she must have found in my hall closet, her figure was completely hidden behind it, but the two straps at her shoulders told me she'd thrown on a swimsuit. With her glass of wine in one hand, her phone in another, her cheeks turned a hot pink when she nodded toward my backyard. "Do you mind if I get in the hot tub?"

"It's your house now, for the time being," I'd told her, somehow managing to shove my tongue back in my mouth and remembering I did know words. "You can do whatever you want. Any time. And I mean that."

She'd thanked me, padded outside on bare feet and before I could watch the towel fall from her, revealing all that smooth, olive skin, I'd put my back to her, only to get Alix's laughter ringing in my ear.

"Long story neither of us remember that much but don't go repeating that because that's not the story we'll be spinning later."

"No shit?" He choked on his laugh. "Lemme guess, you talked to Miles?"

My agent had been my first call.

"More like he talked at me, but pretty much. We have to sit down, spin this as some love at first sight bullshit basically. And now, all the wives are invited to the parade on Thursday. You're welcome by the way."

"Geez. Way to fuck over us single guys. Now we gotta stand there looking all happy and shit with that cup in our hands while you huddle up with your women. I'm so damn disappointed."

"Fuck off."

There was a reason he was my best friend. His faded Swiss accent and dry humor pretty much ensured everything and anything he said came across making him sound like an asshole.

"So, you going to fill me in on the true version or not?"

"Someday over beers, but mostly I wanted to return your call. Today's been a shit show and we've already had to face down our families. Frankly, I want to grab a bottle of whiskey and get plastered."

As the thought hit me, my eyes trailed to the hot tub. Where Gabby was. Practically naked. Drinking.

Seemed like she had a similar idea to me.

"Is this good? You know…"

"I don't even fucking know, man." I ran a hand through my hair and scraped it down my beard as I sighed. Out the back door, I could barely glimpse Gabby's hair piled on her head. The hot tub was mostly hidden from view from my spot in the kitchen, and while I could take three steps to see her, I stayed where I was.

She was tempting enough fully clothed or dressed in my pajamas. I wasn't sure what self-control I'd have if I caught a glimpse of her in a bikini. Enough thoughts were conjuring at the mere idea of her being a vision in scraps of fabric. The reality could prove too tempting.

"What do you mean you don't know? I mean, Dominick… hell, even Max I could see."

No shit. Max was the life of the party, recently broken up with a puck bunny no one but he liked and even then I doubted he found her all that enjoyable when they were both clothed. Hell, even our center Kane, also recently divorced, scored more tail than I had since mine.

Sighing, I dragged my gaze off the windows, the view of Gabby tipping the wineglass to her lips. "It might sound insane but there's something about her... I barely know her, and you're right. This isn't me. On the other hand, I thought Lenora was my one and only forever, so why would I have done this had I not felt *something* for her?"

"You are not usually a man who runs by the seat of his pants. That is for sure."

"It's fly." I laughed, unable to help it. Alix had been in the United States for over a decade but he still butchered random sayings. "Fly by the seat of your pants."

"That does not make any sense. You do not fly in pants."

"That's not the point," I said, still laughing. "But I hear you. I don't do spontaneous."

Outside the glimpse of ring shopping I had earlier, I hadn't been able to remember much more other than hazy flickers of her giggling, smiling, eyes glistening with happiness as she threw her head back and laughed. I wouldn't have married a woman solely because she laughed prettily. Marriage meant too much for me to base it on something so frivolous. There had to be *something* we hadn't put together yet.

"Listen, I'm sorry to cut this short. I'll explain it all someday soon, but for now, just keep this between us. Okay?"

"I have your back. Always, brother."

"Thanks, man."

As I hung up, I decided the rest of the voicemails from my team could wait.

We might have made a mistake, but I was exhausted

from repeating that all day. More exhausted from thinking about it. We might not know *why*, but surely there had to be a reason.

We needed time to figure out if whatever connection we felt last night was real, something long lasting. The only way to do that was to spend time together.

Which meant I was getting half-naked in the hot tub and joining Gabby.

Really, not the worst way to spend a day with my wife.

9

GABBY

How embarrassing. Absolutely humiliating. Not surprising, considering it was my mom and it didn't matter what I did, it was usually the wrong thing. *Go to college and get a degree.* I chose cosmetology school. *Find a stable guy. The guy who will set your heart on fire but keep your feet on the ground.* I dated those and lost everyone, not through most faults of my own but I figured Mom would think that once she found out what Kurt did to me. *Were you there for him enough?* As if his inability to keep it in his pants during the workday and wait until he got home was my fault.

But God.

The fact Joey sat there, practically brimming with rage until he took over was the worst part. No one wanted their parents to think they were a failure at everything they tried, but to have someone like Joey, whose family and parents were so wonderful, watching it?

At least they'd already been gone when she threw out her parting shot.

I took a gulp of wine and settled against the edge of the

hot tub. If only I could drown my sorrows in hot, steamy bubbles and this delicious Cabernet, it was possible everything could have been perfect.

It was the only place I could think of to escape after Joey had been so sweet to me. After he'd stood up for me. No one ever did that. Not even Garrett, not really. He might have been able to calm Mom down and get her off my case but he hadn't always been around, while I'd stayed close.

And even then he didn't stand up for me, he simply dissipated the tension.

Did I have some daddy issues? Pretty sure any therapist would say yes. Unequivocally. Tended to happen when a girl lost her dad before she turned five and then our mother spent our entire childhood making sure Garrett knew how important he was, how strong, how brave, how fast, how absolutely good he was at everything he set his mind to. I didn't blame her. Hockey demanded a lot of time. Garrett was ten when our dad died and he'd grown up overnight.

Me? I was always the little girl who still wished her dad could tuck her in at night, throw her high in the air. I had very few memories of him, but he sang. All the time. He made up songs about dinners and walks and folding clothes and what it was like to fly. My dad could take the mundane and turn it into an adventure with a melody.

Tears rose in my eyes and I splashed my face with hot water. I didn't need to lose it now.

And yet? Why the hell not? It wasn't even dinnertime yet and today had been the longest day in existence. Worse, there were no signs it would get better. I had a husband who I barely knew, who was probably still in love with his exwife, for fuck's sake. How in the hell I'd let him convince me to give this a shot was anyone's guess. More standard Gabby leaping before looking behavior probably.

No. I shook my head and closed my eyes, resting my head against the ledge. I refused to believe it. I'd always wanted what my mom had with my dad. A man in my life who inspired that kind of love and devotion years after they were gone. I wouldn't have taken getting married so frivolously despite my mom's beliefs.

Joey had to be right, at least right enough to consider his crazy plan. Something had to have happened. Something more than the safety I felt when he'd wrapped his arm around me earlier and protected me. Defended me. He'd do all that because that was the kind of guys all the Taylors were.

He'd done it for *me*, though. And my heart had fluttered, grown and stretched inside my chest with every touch from him.

I was attracted to my husband. At least there was that.

I snorted, took another drink and squinted at the bright sun. I'd barely eaten anything while everyone was there, my stomach too knotted to think about food. Probably, the smart idea would be to switch to water. Although if the last twenty-four hours proved anything, I wasn't great at making the smart, responsible choice.

Who cared if it hit me too hard and too fast in the heated water and the hot sun? Passing out and sleeping the rest of the day and night away would probably be the best decision I'd made in the last twenty-four hours.

The rush of bubbles, the buzz of the jets and the heat of the sun on my face, along with the wine I slowly indulged in eventually loosened my muscles and relaxed me, enough so I closed my eyes again, heaved a sigh and...

"Black and odd! Yes!" I threw my hands in the air, stacked chips toppling next to me and to my right, Joey leaned in, laughing at my outburst.

"*You're on a roll.*"

"*You must be my lucky charm.*" *I kissed his cheek, laughed at my lipstick print I left behind and went to wipe it away with my thumb.*

Joey grabbed my hand, brought my hand to his mouth and kissed the pad of my thumb. "*Don't. Leave it. Let everyone know you can't keep yourself away from me.*"

A fire lit in those dark eyes of his and sent a shiver through me in the most delicious way. Oh dear...

"*You electrify this whole room. Do you know that?*"

I was stunned. Speechless, gaping at him until the raucous alarms of someone hitting a jackpot at a nearby slot machine rattled the ground beneath my feet. Or perhaps the rattling was the way Joey kept looking at me. Touching me. Ever since I told him the next woman he married would be the luckiest girl in the world, something had shifted. He looked at me like he wanted me.

Perhaps it was the alcohol talking. Perhaps worse, it was the alcohol moving him to behave in such a way.

Regardless, I was having the time of my life with a man who looked at me like he couldn't wait to get me alone.

"*Joey...*"

His name was a plea. A prayer of hope.

He rolled his lips together, held the pad of my thumbs to his full lips with that stormy gaze of his glued to mine.

"*Place your bets!*"

I startled, glanced down at my mess of a pile of chips. Joey nipped at my thumb, shot a shockwave of desire straight to my sex and then took my hand in his, and began restacking the chips.

"*Place your bets, Gabby. You have more money to win.*"

Somehow, I figured I was already a winner.

I jerked to a start, splashed water into my face and over the edge of the tub. The bright sun blinded me right before a shadow stopped in front of it, blocking the brightness and my lips parted.

Joey was in front of me, a towel draped over his arms crossed in front of him, gray swim trunks hanging low on his waist.

"Hey," I said, pushing up to sitting. "How long have you been standing out here?"

His lips curved at the edges. He'd trimmed his beard, leaving only a scruff that I imagined would scrape perfectly against tender skin, skin that was currently heated and not from the water but from what I remembered.

"I didn't want to startle you. You looked lost in thought."

He was right. He dropped his towel and if I hadn't lost thought at the memory of last night, I certainly did at the sight of him. Broad shoulders, curved pecs with a light smattering of hair, the delineation of his abs that showed the strength of his body so perfectly, he could have been a model. Posed naked on the cover of a male health magazine with only his hockey helmet protecting his most valuables. The man was breathtaking. Jaw-droppingly sexy. My husband—who I couldn't remember so much as touching outside playful kisses and holding hands.

"I won five hundred playing roulette."

His head tilted, and a surprised but adorable smile took over his face. "Did you?"

"I did." His grin was infectious and I flashed him a matching one. "Are you going to join me?"

My knees trembled as I asked. He looked so good standing there, bronzed and strong, I could have stared at him for hours. It was probably better for both of us if he covered himself.

"You don't mind?"

"It's your house." I snorted, waved a hand in the air. "Oh,

but before you get in, would you mind grabbing more wine?"

He walked to the side of the tub, lifted the bottle I'd opened earlier and a spare glass. "Already thought of that."

"Wonderful. Come on in then."

He poured his glass, refilled mine and then climbed into the hot tub, slowly sinking down. I almost wept at the loss of all that carved perfection.

Tension turned as hot as the water and the sun beating down on us, and I found myself unable to look directly at him. Would he think my flushed cheeks was purely due to the hot tub?

Would he know where my thoughts had drifted?

Joey was a pretty smart guy, instinctual on the ice. Would that translate to life as well?

"Your smile is disarming."

"Disarming?"

"Yeah. You come across as a pretty straight-laced guy but that smile tells me there's a side to you few get to see."

"Does it?" His finger and thumb picked at a chunk of my hair, tucking it behind my ear and trailing that fingertip down the edge of my jaw. "What kind of side?"

Dark. He had a dark side. No, Joey wasn't dark. He was, "wild."

I'd said that to him. And those dark eyes of his practically burned my retinas it was so heated.

"You told me my backward hat made me a ten."

"What?"

My chest heaved beneath the water, pushing the swell of my breasts over the bubbles and I clung to my wineglass.

Oh sweet heavens. I'd said all of that to him.

I'd practically thrown myself at him.

"My hat." He chuckled, wineglass in front of his mouth

that I was pretty certain wore that same damn disarming smile I accused him of having. Hell if I was wrong though. That smile said he was wicked in ways I'd probably never considered.

I bit my lip to hold in my groan, perhaps a needy whimper, and blinked.

"That's right." I laughed. "You had that hat pulled low over your eyes and when I won, you spun it around."

"You told me I was a ten."

He wasn't a ten. Thirty-six on a scale of ten. Joey's physique alone blew other men out of the water. Add in his personality and charm and otherworldly morals and he was in a ballpark of his own.

And I'd said all that right before...

"I lied," I said, blurted rather.

"What?" His head jerked in surprise. "You mean I'm not a ten?"

Oh hell, I'd discuss the merits of where he ranked on the scale if it kept him from thinking of that conversation.

I rolled my eyes playfully. "Don't be self-deprecating. You know you're hot."

His hand went to his chest, barely visible over the bubbles as he sat across from me in the tub that could easily hold twelve. Even then, if I stretched my legs, I could probably brush his, run my foot up his calf. How high could I get before he stopped me?

Would he stop me?

"You wound me."

"Please," I spurted. "I'm sure your ego is large enough to withstand it. And yeah, with your hat on backward you're definitely a ten. But that's kryptonite to any girl. A backward hat automatically ups your appeal by several levels."

"So without it, I'm—"

This had to stop. If he was searching, hunting for how I truly felt about him, I couldn't do it.

I brought the wineglass to my lips and smirked. "A four."

His head fell back, mouth open, and the most jubilant laugh burst into the air.

Hot damn. My husband was hotter than the sun kind of hot.

If only he thought the same thing about me.

Joey's laughter was so enjoyable, I was still focusing on him, his mouth, and the sparkling humor in his dark eyes when it wiped clean. With a nakedness that stole my breath, something I doubted he'd ever let me see and something I hadn't been prepared to give him, he ran his tongue over his lips and said, "There may have been a time my ego could have withstood anything, but that's not so anymore."

"Joey—"

That nakedness slammed shut with a blink, lips quirking at the corners like he was just now finishing his laugh. "So go easy on me, would you?"

"I will." This was one promise to him I could keep.

Perhaps after all this mess was over, I'd have found a new friend, even if I was starting to realize why I'd wanted to marry him in the first place.

Joey Taylor was the kind of guy a girl could fall in love with in moments, and I was starting to fear I'd been stupid enough to do just that.

10

JOEY

I woke to the startling brightness of the sun shining through curtains I must not have closed the night before and the desperate need for hydration.

Two nights in a row of overindulgence after months of rarely drinking, alcohol bans at hotels during the playoffs, and I wasn't just hungover, I was pretty certain my body now only contained one percent of water.

"Shit," I groaned, and pushed out of bed. Fortunately, as I quickly rehashed through last night's events, it was clear nothing ridiculous happened I'd have to again answer for.

"Hell." I laughed, catching sight of my face in the mirror that looked as dehydrated and hungover as I suspected, and chuckled. "It wasn't like we could do anything worse."

No, instead, Gabby and I sat in the hot tub, flirted—at least I did—teased—she did it better—and talked about the day and how we'd spin the story based on Miles's suggestion. After we climbed out, I ordered pizza, another cheat meal I indulged in infrequently during the season. I gave myself one month of freedom from food and the constant daily stress of workouts after our season ended. Usually, anyway. With playoffs lasting so long I might have to cut that back to two or three weeks. Regardless, I pushed it all to the side last night. I gorged on carbs and greasy cheese, opened a second bottle of wine, and once Gabby began hiding her yawns behind laughter and the backs of her hands, suggested we head to bed.

In all, it was mundane, typical conversations—outside planning on how to effectively lie to millions of people.

None of it forgotten. Hell, I remembered all of it with such precise clarity even thinking about it had my dick hardening.

I *wanted* my wife. She smelled like heaven. She was witty, capable of making me laugh after I'd spent years struggling to do the same. Conversations, whether it was life or hockey or family—outside her mom—came so easily, with her quick wit and sarcasm and teasing looks she tried to hide behind her attraction to me. I could spend a lifetime speaking and laughing with her and never grow bored. The moment I expected her to go easy on me, like I'd requested, she had no problem challenging me. Small things, but meaningful ones too.

"Why did you buy such a large house?" she'd asked. I'd answered. I needed open air and room. I spent so much time on the road, crammed into hotels and airplanes and buses, I wanted to come home to something that was warm and inviting and something that wouldn't leave me crawling the walls before I hit the road again.

"What will you do after you retire, assuming you're not forced out due to injury?" Hopefully by then I had kids to coach like my dad. She'd given me a soft smile I'd wanted to capture in a photo so I could look at it always. Was it my devotion to the sport and love of the game or the mention of kids? I hadn't been brave enough to ask.

There was a peace that came with being with someone who not only enjoyed the game, but understood the sacrifice it took, the fear it could be swiped away with one wrong hit, one bad season. One injury, one slump.

It'd been years, if ever, I had that same understanding from Lenora. Sure, she didn't much care I played hockey which had been attractive, but there was something to be said for someone who truly *knew* the sacrifices, the pain, the dedication and not only understood it, but supported it.

Lenora and I never had that. The realization hit me like a stick to the gut as I got dressed to go work out. She'd come home and talk about her day. I'd ask her questions. I took her to the studio to learn new dances. Hell, I fixed her post-workout smoothies she loved and I encouraged her when she didn't feel like getting out of bed. But as soon as the conversation turned to my games, my hard work... somehow, those conversations turned back to her and hers.

Was it possible I'd missed for so long how little the two of us shared? Or was I looking at it through the lens of a man who was still bitter she cheated on me and left me? It wasn't even about who she cheated on me with, it was that she'd done it all.

"Damn." I curled my hands around the edge of our marble countertops and dropped my head. There was no point in this. What she and I had was done, and I wasn't going to ruin my mood, or the day I had ahead of me with Gabby lingering on thoughts and questions I wouldn't ever get answers to, but ones I wasn't even sure I needed anymore.

What was done was done.

With that, I shoved off the counter, brushed my teeth, spit, wiped my mouth with the gray towel before chucking it to the counter.

I'd had a gym installed in what should have been the pool house two summers ago so I quit having to go to the team's facilities every time I needed to work out. It'd basically become the backup gym for guys who didn't want to make their trek to the training center, too. At any time over the summer, there could be up to six guys working out together, giving each other shit, ending the workout by throwing each other into the pool and then spending the rest of the day drinking and chilling out. Would that change now? Now that I had Gabby? Lenora had never cared, but her busiest season for performing was the summer so she'd rarely been home.

I shoved the heel of my palm to my forehead. None of that mattered. Comparing the two wouldn't help a damn thing.

I made a quick stop in the kitchen to make a green smoothie filled with every disgusting green vegetable known to man, two scoops of protein powder. It smelled like dog shit, tasted not much better, but combined with my pre-workout mix, it'd kick the hangover thumping at the back of my head.

Gabby must have still been sleeping because the house was silent as I made my way through it and I squinted at the bright sun once I reached the patio.

We were scheduled to meet with a reporter later to sell our story, make sure it put the team and myself in a good, celebratory light. Interviews weren't uncommon, anyway, and since I'd had the hat trick that helped the team win, I would have had to give a few anyway.

I dropped my phone to the couch once I reached the gym and strapped on rollerblades. I'd installed an inline skating floor, half the size of an ice rink. Best damn investment I ever made because while I liked working out, skating, whether on wheels or blades, cleared my mind like nothing else. I worked on skills and drills until my ankles ached and my thighs burned before removing the skates and ran on the treadmill. After a quick break, I chalked up my hands, intent on grabbing the free weights and working my upper body when Gabby came into view.

She was dressed in a different bikini. Not the modest black one she wore in the hot tub. This one was emerald-blue, startling bright against her olive skin, the scraps of fabric left little to the imagination, and I'd been imagining a hell of a lot since I slipped into the hot tub last night with her. She was at the edge of the pool, brows puckered as she focused on the water, the length of the pool in front of her.

Then her hands rose, legs bent. She dove into the pool like she'd been doing it since I first stepped into skates. Her lithe figure was straight as an arrow in the air before hitting the water, and I lost sight of her, outside the minuscule splashes she made as her arms and legs kicked and pulled herself through the water like a fish. And then I lost my mind.

Because she was fucking gorgeous. Lithe but curvy with wide hips, a body that said she ate, loved doing it and didn't need to kill herself working out after, and yet there was strength in the body too, evident in the fact she reached the end of my twenty-five-yard pool, turned and swam back to the other end without pausing. Hell, I barely saw her take a breath as she started another lap. I stood there, gawking at her from my pool house like a fucking perv when she probably didn't know I had the perfect view of her—holding the weight bar in my fists, totally forgetting what I was supposed to be doing.

She finished three more laps, stopping on the wall of the pool and rested her elbows on the edge, arms crossed. Her head tilted back, rivulets of water fell down her skin as she gazed toward the sun, complete and utter serenity softening her profile.

I'd seen that look before. It wiggled into my memory, that vision of her, soft and at peace and yet so utterly excited once before.

Water surrounded us, the gentle rock of the boat swayed back and forth as we watched the riders snuggle up together. The sides of our bodies were so close we were practically fused together. After leaving the Flamingo, we stopped and refilled our deadly, lanyard hanging drinks. I should probably stop, it'd been years since I was this drunk, but there was something about being so close to Gabby that made me want to experience everything life had to offer, hangover be damned.

"Where do you want to travel to?"

Her grin stayed on the gondola ride, sweeping through the narrow faux waters of Venice. The customers kissed, his hands tangled in his lover's hair as they made out, missing most of the sights surrounding them and yet no doubt creating their own perfect memories. I only saw Gabby's profile, but for the first time tonight, she wasn't overly excited. She wasn't throwing her hands in the air and cheering and she wasn't exuberant, inspecting me.

She was at peace. My question softened her expression further until she turned to me with that mischievous gleam in her eye and the lilt of her lips I was beginning to crave. If I leaned in to kiss her, would she kiss me back, let me take my time tracing the outline of her lips with my tongue, teasing bites where the sting would wash away to pleasure?

God... I wanted her.

"Where do you think? If you could see me anywhere, where do you imagine I'd want to be?"

Right now I was imagining her in my bed, naked, beneath me.

I fought down the urge that glorious vision inspired and cleared my throat.

"I don't know. Rome or Athens? Fiji?" My teammates typically vacationed with their wives somewhere extravagant after the season. The wives' reward and thank you for all the work they sacrificed right along with us. Hell, I'd tried to talk Lenora into many over the years. When my season ended, her busy season was at its peak, so it rarely worked out, but there were always places I'd wanted to see. Scotland. New Zealand. I wanted to try surfing off the Gold Coast and see a hundred other sights.

"No." Her eyes gleamed with desire and while not directed at me, I didn't think I'd ever wanted anything more than to wish it was. "Not there. No big cities."

"No?"

She tapped her hands on the railing, pushed her lips to one side. The smile lingered, but she hesitated. "Have you ever had fudge from Mackinac Island? Walked through the streets of Helen, Georgia in their downtown that looks like a Bavarian Village during Oktoberfest?"

"Uh. No."

"I want to do that. Go to those places. The small towns and hidden gems. I want to go primitive camping in the Rockies, where I have to sleep with one hand fisting a can of bear repellent spray, go glacier sliding in August. I want to go sand dune sliding in Michigan."

She turned to me, eyes wide with wonder, and asked, "Did you know Michigan has a lake that they say is as blue as the Caribbean? Or that you can go to real-life cattle ranches in Wyoming or Montana and spend a week learning what it's like to be a ranch hand? Those are the places I want to go."

Her tone was wistful.

My dick was hard as a rock.

How had she made all of that sound like the most exciting vacation ever and we didn't even leave the United States?

"Why Michigan?" I asked, clearing my throat, trying to will my dick to soften before she noticed. Who got a hard-on over talking about flyover states in the Midwest?

"Coincidental." She laughed, shook her head, and turned back to the gondola ride. "You think it's lame, probably."

I wanted to tick off every single list of places she'd ever considered visiting and experience it all with her, just to see that look on her face over and over again.

11

GABBY

"You want to primitive camp in the Rockies. How do you feel about getting there by this?"

He spun his laptop and on the screen, a Mercedes van longer than any van I'd ever seen appeared in a matte, dark gray.

"What is this?"

"A camper. Sleeps four. But not much longer than a Suburban, so should be easy to handle through the mountains. We can stay in hotels, or campsites when we want, or just park this baby somewhere on the road."

"Um…" I was lost. Completely. "What are you talking about?"

"Your bucket list of places to see."

He flipped back the laptop without looking at me and might have taken my heart with him.

How had he…

"I told you? About that?"

He tapped a pen to paper next to him. "Hiking Antelope Canyon. The Delicate Arch Trail in Moab. Glacier sliding and camping in the Rockies, a week of wrangling cattle in

Montana... I found some places to stop on the way to Michigan where there are the sand dunes, Torch Lake is what that beautiful lake you mentioned is called. Looks incredible, by the way, and from there we can head up to Mackinac Island."

He glanced up, pen stilled, while my heart leaped into my throat.

"I told you."

"When we stood watching people go by on the gondola rides," he confirmed as if we'd been planning this trip for a year. He slid a notebook in my direction where I'd frozen as soon as I entered the kitchen. On it, a list of at least a dozen places I'd always wanted to see. "There are a few, like Antelope Canyon out of the way unless we hit it on the way back after Georgia, but we could maybe do it. What did I miss?"

My eyes burned. Beneath the list he made, he had them laid out in order moving from west to east, so we could start here and then travel across the country.

And beneath the locations? Length of stays. Driving distance to each, ideas on whether to camp or hotel stays. He'd thrown in an Amish Village tour in Iowa, a ferry that took you from Wisconsin across Lake Michigan, avoiding Chicago altogether.

"When did you do all this?"

"I remembered what you said while I was working out earlier."

"How long have you been awake?" I didn't see him before I went swimming dand I had no idea where his gym was. I hadn't seen one while I'd tried touring the home a bit more but given the fact there were multiple floors and more than one staircase, it was totally possible I hadn't seen it.

Then I'd showered, and I'd come back to the kitchen to find something to eat for lunch.

He officially rocked my world.

"I woke up at nine or so, headed straight to the pool house where the gym is."

The pool house, of course. I hadn't considered taking a peek in there.

"It's more of a guest house and gym, not that I need the extra guest rooms, but I like to have it."

"It's only two," I said stupidly, checking the time on the microwave behind him. "That's only a few hours for you to plan all this."

"Yeah, well... they're just ideas." His head dipped and he worried his bottom lip with his teeth. A move that made my stomach warm and twist. "Do you not want to do this?"

I wanted to take this trip with everything I had. But with Joey? How could I take my dream trip with my dream guy and not throw myself all over him?

"I see," he said and he might as well have dropped a bomb of disappointment onto the table. "I get it."

"No." I grabbed his hand, startled at the heat in his skin and how quickly it heated my own. "I want to do this. I'm surprised, is all. You did so much, so fast."

"Yeah? You in?"

I laughed. His grin widened and he joined me. "Are you asking if I'm *in* on my own vacation plans? Yeah, Joey. I'd love to go on this trip."

"Good." He nodded his head toward the seat next to him. "Then get your ass over here and help me out with where you want to stay so I can start making reservations."

"Campsites as much as possible," I said without thought, no hesitation. I could stay in a hotel anywhere, but it was summer. Most areas would be warm enough.

"Then camping it is."

"Are you sure?" I knew his life. His home alone was well

over a millions-dollar mansion. I could handle hotels, ritzy ones, even. Heck, there might be nights I'd kill someone for a hot shower if we did this.

"Hell yeah." He grinned, and it was so handsome, so sexy, without a hint of placating me, I almost threw my arms around him and kissed him.

"Why?"

I couldn't believe this. He was taking all my ideas and thoughts and dreams and *planning them*. Mom would like this. Someone who actually made plans.

"It sounds like a blast."

He made it sound like the most thrilling adventure ever. Problem was... "No, I mean, why would you want to do this? With me?"

His dark eyes turned molten. The pen in his hand tapped a wild beat on the table. Almost as frenetic as my heart was racing as he peered at me. The tip of his tongue appeared, swiped along his lip and I imagined that tongue, that slow caress of it against parts of me that shivered at the thought.

Oh God. A cross country travel trip with this man? I might not survive.

"Because you're my wife, and the next few days might not be easy, but it's the least I can give you for giving this marriage an actual shot with me."

"Joey—" He stole my breath. My sense. Pretty sure the only thing beating inside me was primal. The need to kiss him. Touch him. Press my lips to his and kiss away the nerves sparking in his eyes so he didn't realize...

I was no longer nervous about the idea of being his wife.

I was scared to hell I was going to ruin it.

12

JOEY

Gabby and I walked into the marketing offices at the Vipers' headquarters in a suburb of Vegas, her hand in mine. Not because she'd taken my hand, but because she'd been fidgeting so damn bad in the elevator leading up to the sixth floor, I'd taken hers.

However, satisfaction pulsed through me as she settled almost immediately.

"You'll be fine."

"Right. Because lying to millions on television is something I do all the time."

Okay, so technically we were lying. I preferred to call it stretching the truth a little bit.

"Alicia is a reporter our team respects. She'll do right by us and look on the bright side. At least it's not live."

"Bright side. Right," she mumbled, but her hand squeezed mine. Whether it was instinct or because she actually found comfort in me, I didn't know. With the way she leaned into me, allowing me to catch the fresh and minty scent of her shampoo, as she did, I didn't really care.

She came downstairs earlier, dressed like a snack, one of my favorites, and it'd taken everything I had not to cup her cheeks, kiss away her cherry red lipstick and muss up the thick curls she'd clearly taken time and effort to ensure were perfect. For a moment, I'd stumbled on my feet, over my heart and almost tripped over my tongue as I'd taken her in the elegant but simple, black wrap dress. The knot was belted off to the side, the collar was short, too short to fold over, the kind you saw on classical Asian style dress, and the V-neck of it dipped low enough to show off the barest, barely there hint of her cleavage. Ample cleavage I knew she had thanks to the visions of her in her bikinis now firmly imprinted into my mind.

The dress was sleeveless, showing off toned arms and the skirt of it ended just above her knee. It was the kind of dress my mom would wear to church, and it shouldn't have been so sexy given the modesty of it, but somehow, seeing Gabby in my home, in that dress, wearing equally modest and classy black heels made my chest swell with a foreign heat.

Goddamn, she was the most beautiful woman I'd ever laid eyes on.

And she was mine.

Doubts and hazy memories be damned... Gabby had agreed to be my wife and I wanted to make sure she never regretted a moment of us.

The growing click of footsteps and voices drew my attention off her before I could do what I wanted—which was to forgo my earlier self-control and say to hell with her lipstick and perfect curls. I turned as Alicia Gates, my agent Miles, and the team's PR rep, Brandon Mickelson, rounded the corner.

"Here we go," I muttered so only Gabby could hear.

"Yippee." Said with all the excitement of someone being walked to their death.

Still, I smiled. She was damn funny even when terrified. I led the way, closing the space between the people who wanted to help us and the woman I didn't want to leave behind.

"Thanks for meeting us today. I know you're busy." Alicia grinned and held out her hand.

"No problem, Alicia. We're happy to be here. This is my wife, Gabrielle."

"Hello. Please call me Gabby and it's nice to meet you." Gabby slid her hand from mine in order to shake Alicia's extended one. I introduced her to Miles and Brandon where similar hellos were exchanged and we were escorted into Brandon's office.

Cameras and lights had already been set up, a small couch I'd never seen in there before brought in along with a black velvet chair across from us at an angle.

Damn. They'd taken the time to ensure this looked like an actual interview and not someone out to save my hide and protect my image.

Relief flooded me.

In the span of thirty-six hours, I'd started to realize how much I actually enjoyed my wife, been splashed on the pages of all sport gossip blogs and social media pages, and like always, despite the concern, my team had my back.

Hopefully, Gabby would soon realize I'd always have hers as well.

"Is there anything we can get you? Water or a few minutes?" Alicia's gaze focused mainly on Gabby.

"I'm good," she croaked, her mouth dry even as she faked a smile. "We should get started."

And get it over with. She didn't say it. She didn't have to.

The look on her face, the wide darting eyes seeking an escape said it all.

"I do," I said to everyone. "A moment with my wife please."

"Sure thing." Alicia gave us a questioning look. Miles gave one that said not to screw this up and he slapped Brandon on the back.

Once they were gone, I turned to her. And fuck this.

I was attracted to this woman. I *liked* her. Sure it was a hell of a surprise, but that didn't mean it had to be a mistake. So far, I couldn't find anything I regretted about the decision to get married, even if I didn't remember everything.

"Gabby." I called her name softly so as not to startle her and she turned to me, those wide eyes glazed over with fear and uncertainty. Her pulse beat at the base of her throat so quickly it was a wonder she hadn't yet passed out.

"What? Is there something wrong?"

"Yeah." Please. Let this not be the biggest mistake I made. "There is."

Her brows puckered, along with her lips. "What is it?"

"This," I said and then I settled my hands at the sides of her throat, thumbs brushing her jaw. Her lips parted on a surprised, beautiful gasp and I pressed my lips to hers before I could rethink this decision.

As soon as I did, as I felt the softness of her lips, the hidden and soft taste of her, everything inside my chest expanded, exploded, and then clicked back together in the most perfect way. Her hands came to my wrists, and for the briefest moment, I feared she'd push me away, but instead, she gripped tighter. The tight posture of her frame relaxed and the soft exhale of surprise and acquiescence fell from her lips.

I kissed her softly, imagined kissing her so often I memorized every curve of her body and taste of her skin, and as I slid my tongue across her bottom lip, hers came out to meet mine.

"Shit," I gasped, and then thrust my tongue into the cavern of her mouth, sealing us together until our lips were locked, our chests pressed together and there wasn't an inch of space between us. I kissed her slowly, forced down the raging inside of me to *take*. It'd been months. Too damn many of them since I'd had a woman in my arms and pressed so tightly against me, all I could imagine was what a kiss like this would lead to.

Gabby's hands fell from my wrists to my hips where she gripped my suit coat in her fists and yanked me so tight against her she gasped as she felt my hard, thick length against her and God, what I wanted to do to her. In this dress. In this office. On this couch.

Lift her leg to my hip, spread her knees and trail my hand to her center, shove them beneath the panties she's wearing to her hot, throbbing sex.

It'd be good. So damn good. Combustible.

She moaned into my mouth and I swallowed it, pressing fingers tightly to her cheeks to prevent them from doing everything I envisioned and as another whimper came from her, the roll of her hips pressed against me and forced my own pleasured, needy groan from me, I slowed the kiss. Ended it with teasing nips and lips pressed firmly to hers. For a moment we stood there, lips together, breathing ragged and I gave us a moment to settle before I pulled back and stared directly into her whiskey-colored eyes—pupils blown with desire.

"I really needed to kiss my wife and know what it felt like," I said.

"Good." She huffed a laugh. "It felt good. Really good."

"Yeah." I kissed her softly, slid my hands from her throat and grasped both her hands in mine. "Really good."

GABBY CURLED next to me on the couch and I draped my arm over her shoulder. From the moment the interview started, I wanted us to present a united front. A picture of a couple newly married, in love, and not ridiculously trashed and making a rash decision like the blogs had questioned, and the social media videos had portrayed. I wouldn't confirm Gabby's worst fears of being seen that way. Not after that kiss.

Not after how good it felt to be around her.

She might be going along with this marriage reluctantly but that didn't make her any less mine to protect.

Alicia started with easy questions. She asked about the team. The playoffs. She asked me about the hat trick I had that won the game and final series for us. She asked us about the excitement over the parade the next day. All of the standard questions meant to get the focus back on my team and all the success we'd had together. While I answered her questions with the confidence of a man who'd sat in similar seats over the years and played this game, Gabby relaxed next to me. Eventually, her hand had settled on my thigh, a calm touch, but I'd still flexed my muscle beneath her.

I feel you. I want you. It'd scrambled my brain for a moment so when Alicia asked her next lead-in, it took me by surprise.

"But that's not all you're celebrating this week, is it?"

"No. No, it's definitely not." I entwined my hand with Gabby's and brought it to my lips, kissing the back of hers as she smiled softly at me. Gone was the terrified, deer in the headlights look she had. If she was still high from the kiss, I'd take it.

I sure as hell was.

I didn't know if I'd ever get over the way my body so hotly responded to the feel of her.

"So, from my understanding, you two have known each other a long time. Was there—feelings back then?"

"No. Absolutely not."

I'd been married for crying out loud. Although I could see how people would think that too. My divorce hadn't exactly been public fodder, but it did just happen less than a year ago. I could see how that looked to some people.

"No?" Alicia tilted her head. "So you haven't known each other for years?"

"I was married—" I started, but Gabby's hand gave me a gentle squeeze and she cut me off.

Whether she noticed my sudden pulse of irritation spiking at the insinuation *I* was the cheater, didn't matter.

"We've crossed paths," Gabby said, speaking directly to Alicia for the first time. "As most people probably know, my brother plays goalie for the Vipers, and one of his oldest friends is Joey's older brother."

"That's right. Jude Taylor, correct? He's with the Ice Kings out in North Carolina."

"Correct. They played together in Chicago in college and are still great friends," Gabby said again before I could speak. If she was now comfortable, I'd let her run this show. Save the slight tremble in her fingers, her face or posture showed no nerves. "And yes, like I said, we've crossed paths over the years. There have been times my family was invited to celebrate holidays with the Taylors, but like Joey said, he was married. And I was also younger. There was never anything going on, not even a small crush on my part, until recently, anyway."

She blushed at the admission.

I wanted to turn the cameras off, tug her chin so she had to face me and demand *when*. When did that crush appear?

Alicia beat me to it.

"A crush?" she asked, with all the leading of a sly fox.

"The hospital, earlier this spring."

"Yeah?"

I hadn't expected it. Hadn't expected she'd cut in, with her voice, lilted in a way I hadn't yet heard from her.

"Hospital?" Alicia asked, and Gabby bit her bottom lip, realizing what she'd said. Lizzie's scare hadn't been publicized at all, so no one knew and I realized the trap Gabby had fallen into.

"We had mutual friends who were in the hospital one night," I said, keeping Lizzie and Garrett's name out of it. The news of her pregnancy had broken since they'd posted on their social media months ago. "Gabby had helped them, and I stayed with her while they'd had some tests done."

It wasn't exactly a lie. Not a full truth, but it was enough to make sense.

Gabby smiled at me, a tentative, soft smile that was so damn sweet my teeth ached. "Yeah, that was when it started anyway, for me. You were great that night. So kind and patient. You comforted me when I needed it the most and, well, it was perfect. That was when I started falling for you."

That night.

The night I'd wanted to lean in and kiss her. She'd pulled away, breaking that moment and I was worried I'd gone too far. Read something that wasn't there.

Was it possible I'd been right, though?

I brushed hair off her shoulder, revealing that collar, the

slim throat of hers as she swallowed, lips parting at my touch. "That was the first time I realized how beautiful you were."

"Well," Alicia said, breaking the moment between us. "That is absolutely lovely. Isn't it? So, your wedding then... it's been being talked about as just another athlete doing something insanely stupid while drunk after a massive win. What can you say about that given what we now know?"

For shit's sake. It wasn't like I'd thrown a trophy over an open body of water. People had seen me carrying a woman in a bridal gown. For all they knew it could have all been an act. The double-edged sword of being known, especially considering the family I came from, was that every stranger assumed they knew my life better than I did.

I pushed down the frustration and flashed Alicia and the cameras a winning smile.

"What can I say, Alicia? Except that when you know it's right, it's right. What's the point in waiting when I could begin my forever immediately?"

Cheesy as fuck. But based on her satisfied gleam and the nods of Miles and Brandon behind her, it was perfect.

"And I think that's all I have for you." She grinned at us as the recording lights on the camera were cut. "Perfect. That was perfect and you two are absolutely adorable together. I wish you the best."

Me too, Alicia.

Me fucking too.

13

GABBY

My hand was firmly clasped in Joey's. Behind us, Garrett's rumble of disapproval was unmistakable. I glared at him over my shoulder. He'd been insufferable since he and Lizzie had picked us up on their way to the arena.

The team and their families along with the coaches were scheduled to meet up early due to road closures happening around the city but even then, hours before the parade would begin, there were packed crowds of fans swarming the streets, creating a forest of green and gold.

"It's seven in the morning," I mumbled as a group of three men well behind the barriers set up to keep the team safe bent over at their waists and shotgunned a beer. "They'll be passed out before the parade begins."

"One can only hope," Garrett said. "Fans like that turn into assholes later in the afternoon."

"Hopefully the heat will help them pass out faster."

Lizzie wasn't kidding.

"It's brutal," I agreed.

"I hear ya," she all but moaned and her hands settled at

the sides of her belly. She was wearing a maternity Las Vegas Vipers T-shirt that might have been glued to her stomach. Six months pregnant with twins and she looked like she could deliver at any moment. "I'm pretty sure I already have sweat in places where sweat doesn't belong."

"I don't know how you're going to last all day."

She laughed. "On a prayer and with an IV drip of water to stay hydrated probably."

"I'll make sure the bus has everything you need," Garrett assured her. "Trust me, there will be plenty of snacks on board so you don't get hangry, either."

"You try *not* being hangry when you have two demon souls sucking the life out of your body," she grumbled.

Joey laughed. "Demon souls," he snickered. "That's what I'll be calling your kids from now until eternity."

"I dare you," Garrett snapped.

To say he was still pissed at us for getting married would be an understatement. I still hoped he'd get over this, at least after seeing how well Joey and I were getting along. But he was toeing the line of being a massive jerk to his friend.

I'd feel guilty for creating this fissure if I didn't think Garrett would eventually get over it.

For now, Joey and I were both riding his pissy wave of protectiveness. I squeezed his hand still clasped to mine and he grinned down at me with an understanding look.

"He'll get over it," he murmured.

"Like hell I will." Garrett side-stepped us, tugging on Lizzie's hand and so they entered the lounger area first.

She shot me a sympathetic look as she passed.

We were stopped by security, needed to show our IDs for the third time since we pulled into the parking garage. The security even the team had to go through upon entering the arena was shocking. Our car had been stopped and searched before parking in the private underground garage. Then our bags went through x-ray before we walked through scanners. Now, as we reached the corridor that would take us to the Vipers' lounge area, we were all required to show our IDs and sign in electronically, our names previously given to security.

"You're all clear," the man said, barely glancing at us.

Garrett and Lizzie were quickly surrounded by a small crowd of teammates. Braxton and his wife, Sophie, first to reach out and give hugs and handshakes. Next to them, Paige, Seth McCabe's wife, was holding their three-month-old little girl, Ilsa, in her arms, all decked out in a gold skirt with a Vipers onesies.

To everyone else, Garrett was smiling, playful. But every time he caught my gaze on him, that smile dimmed.

I sighed. "I feel like I'm ruining what should be a really exciting week for him."

After all, he'd just gotten married too. Helped his team win by some ridiculous saves that were still being played on a loop on ESPN.

"It's not your fault if he can't look at all the good he's been giving in recent days and wants to focus on you. Frankly, I'm feeling pretty damn important to him for him to be so fixated on us."

He smirked down at me.

"You're a fool." I grinned at him, playfully shaking my head. "How can you make this all about you?"

"Because I'm awesome and everyone wants to be me."

I shoved him and he stumbled, letting go of my hand while he recovered. "Not nice."

"I'm plenty nice," I teased and stuck my tongue out. Inside, nerves were bundling together, creating a knot that grew by the second.

"I know you are. And I'm also wondering when you're going to let me kiss you again, just so you know."

My jaw fell. He hadn't brought it up. As soon as we left the interview yesterday we'd returned to his house. I'd laid out by the pool and swam for a bit, he'd said he had work to do in his office. I'd found him there later, on the phone, making reservations for our trip and we worked through the rest of the plans.

Then we'd ordered dinner from a local Italian restaurant, had some wine, and I'd eventually gone to bed.

I hadn't caught sight of a single, lingering look from him that told me he was interested in a repeat. Almost as if the kiss had never happened.

Oh, but what a kiss it'd been. Hell, my body had lit up like a live wire so quickly I was terrified one small spark from static with my shoes on the carpet would burst the room we'd been into a massive fireball. I'd gone to sleep last night, down the hall from him, in a bed that carried the softest hint of his scent somehow, and it'd taken all my self-control not to slide my hands down my stomach, beneath the yoga shorts I slept in.

"I... I didn't know you wanted another one," I said lamely.

His lips curled into a wicked smile. "Every single second I'm around you, I want that. I wanted you to be sure."

"Oh."

He laughed, kissed my temple, and dragged me toward the crowd of players, and I veered off to Paige McCabe. Her husband Seth was a second line right winger but more importantly, she had recently given birth. I stole Paige's little baby, Ilsa, from her in a second, and oohed and awed over the tiny fingers and listened to her rattle on about poor sleep schedules and needing to eat so often Paige was starting to feel like a dairy cow.

More than once, I caught Joey glancing at me, then Ilsa in my arms with a soft expression that made my limbs sizzle.

He wanted to kiss me and based on the way he looked at me holding a baby—he wanted a hell of a lot more than a kiss.

The answer to the question I had to figure out was whether or not I was ready for more.

"OH MY GOSH. LOOK!" I grabbed Joey's hand and pointed to a woman standing near the front of the crowd-lined streets.

She had blonde hair, a Vipers jersey bearing Joey's number six in gold on the front that matched the one he'd made me wear to the parade, but that wasn't what held my attention. It was her sign. *"If I can't have Joey Taylor, show me how he kisses!"*

She caught sight of me pointing at her sign and jumped up and down. Even over the raucous noise, her shouts cut through the mayhem like a whip. "Kiss! Kiss! Kiss!"

Joey laughed, his arm settled at my lower back where he'd placed it once we stepped onto the top level of the double-decker bus an hour ago. "That's insane."

I hadn't forgotten what he'd said earlier. I flashed him a wink, as others in the crowd caught wind of her chant—hard to be missed with her high-pitched voice. What the hell. I already knew his kisses curled my toes, and if he was waiting for my sign... "You might as well give the fans what they demand."

"Yeah?" But his hand was already moving, resting at my

jaw, thumb brushing the soft skin of my throat. He felt my swallow, dropped his gaze from my eyes to my mouth.

"Yeah," I agreed, and closed the gap between us, pressed to my toes. He met me before I reached him and sealed our mouths together. The kiss was soft, teasing, and if he was putting on a show for the crowd that roared with approval as we passed, he could have won an Emmy.

Because dear God, Joey Taylor could *kiss* and the heat of it reverberated through my limbs, more powerful than the rumble of the bus along the pavement.

He tilted my head, slid his tongue against my lips, seeking entrance and I opened for him, got lost in him, and felt the tension from holding himself back in his grip on my jaw and my hip, pressing me to him while we lost ourselves in the crowd's demands and our own desires.

"I might have just come," Alix said right as he bumped into Joey's shoulder.

The jolt and his words broke the spell and Joey pulled back, glaring at Alix before glancing back at me. His gaze swept over my face. "You okay?"

"Yeah. I'm *great.*"

"Good." He kissed me again quickly and then slung his arm over Alix's shoulder. The three of us stood at the edge of the bus, Alex holding a drink high in his hand as Joey shouted, "Champions!"

The crowd went wild with cheers.

It was insane. Absolute madness, and yet sharing this with Joey was one of the best experiences. The city *adored* their hockey, something that surprised me given the natural climate, but the desert dwellers were just as riotous as Chicago would have been. Or Minnesota or Detroit, where I was certain the love of hockey was embedded into every infant's DNA.

Paige and Lizzie tugged on my shirt, pulling me out of Joey's hold.

"This is wild!" Lizzie shouted, because we all had to shout over the echoing noise. "And I'm so damn hot."

She had a water bottle in one hand, a wet towel in her other that I'd seen her use frequently at the back of her neck. She was absolutely adorable with her swollen belly but she had to be miserable.

Paige, now wearing Ilsa in a carrier, appeared equally miserable.

I was sweating too, the afternoon sun beating down on us. So much for the *dry* heat not being as bad as humidity. I was practically boiling, and like Lizzie said earlier, there was sweat dripping down my body in places sweat never belonged.

"I hear that," I told her and reached into the nearby cooler a team staff member had been keeping stocked. I grabbed three icy cold bottles and handed them out, grabbing a fourth for Sophie coming at us as she pushed through the players at the rear of the bus.

"Thank you." She twisted it open and took a huge gulp. "Man, I've always wondered what these parades are like but I had no idea it was this insane."

We murmured our agreements, turned a corner, and apparently the crowd calling for kissing must have traveled down the line because as soon as the bus made the turn, Joey was once again pulling me from the small group of women and into his arms.

"Again," he said, right before he pressed his lips to mine.

14

JOEY

We fell into the house, tripping over shoes and whatever else we kicked off.

I couldn't get enough of her. Hours. It'd been hours of the parade, Gabby next to me, the frequent calls for the newlyweds to kiss and we'd done it. Every single time someone shouted *kiss* at us, I'd taken her, laughing. I took her deeply, gave her pecks on the cheek, quick nips at her bottom lip.

The entire time, we'd laughed. We'd smiled. We'd hugged teammates and we'd held the Cup above our heads and shouted for the masses there to celebrate with us while we stood on the second level of buses meant for city tours.

Gabby had been whisked away at points by Lizzie, laughed with other wives and teammates she'd already met earlier. But we'd always found our way back to each other.

Now I *needed her*. Based on the way she clung to me, tried ripping my jersey off over my head and almost tripping over my ankle, she felt the exact same.

And damn if I didn't want to give my wife everything she asked for.

The doorbell rang, and Gabby froze. My jersey was gone but the undershirt beneath remained, wrinkled from her fisting it and yanking it from the waistband of my jeans.

Her makeup was smeared, eyes glassy and both of us cursed.

"Who in the hell could be here?"

"I don't know," I replied. "Let's ignore it."

And I would have, until I heard the beeping of the door being unlocked and a spike of surprise hit the back of my neck.

"You have to be kidding me."

"What?" Gabby asked, but I was already on the move. No way. No fucking way she was here.

And more—*why* was she here?

"Lenora," I said, and next to me, all the lust and desire that'd been turning her cheeks pink vanished in a blink. "Don't. Don't worry about this for a minute."

"Why?" she asked but I couldn't answer because Lenora was turning the knob and walking into our—*my*— home like she still lived here. Like she hadn't left her key the day I kicked her ass out, like she hadn't spent hours getting ready trying to look good for me.

My ex-wife was gorgeous. That couldn't be argued. She had to keep her body toned and tight and in one hundred percent condition at all times. Add in the weight she had to carry from all of her costumes and there wasn't a single ounce of fat on Lenora's frame. Tall, nearing six feet, her legs were well over half of her height and dressed down, in cutoff shorts, a top that could have passed for a sports bra, and her hair and makeup done like she was headed to a rehearsal, she was absolutely beautiful.

And fake.

Because I knew of the Botox and the lip fillers and the

augmentation she'd had done two years ago to make her already large breasts fuller and larger, because she'd spent a month whining about how much they were already beginning to sag. Her skin was always tan from a spray, not the sun, and she spent more on extensions and her hairstyle than I'd ever spent on anything for myself, hockey skates and sticks included—and that shit was expensive.

Now, I saw the woman who didn't love me enough, the woman who couldn't be bothered to be honest, and the woman who'd never shown a genuine interest in my life or my passions.

Hell, in a drunken, barely remembered conversation, Gabby had shown more understanding and knowledge about my life than Lenora ever had.

"What are you doing here?" I glared at the phone in her hand, the app she had pulled up that allowed keyless entry with our—*my*—security system. I'd never wanted to rip a phone out of someone's hand and smash it until then.

How *dare* she enter my home.

Next to me, Gabby had frozen. Her white shorts were unbuttoned, the Vipers jersey I gave to her before the parade was a pile on the floor next to mine and her tank top beneath was wrinkled where I'd fisted it. Barely coming up to my shoulder, she was petite in contrast to the woman who closed the door to my home like she still had a right to it.

I slid my arm behind Gabby's back and dragged her against me until my hand was at her hip and my thumb could slowly rub against her.

She tightened against me, straight and cold as steel.

She had absolutely nothing to worry about.

"You haven't returned my calls," Lenora said, dropping her phone into her purse. "Or my texts."

Icy blue eyes met mine, the color of the ocean—fake due

to her contacts because her true eyes were what she'd always called a muddy brown.

She glanced at Gabby then, her first acknowledgment of her, scanned her face, took in the disheveled hair, undone buttons and squinted. "Am I interrupting something?"

"With my new wife? Yes."

Gabby flinched in my hold, tried to push off.

I held her tighter.

"No. It's okay—I should um—just... you know... go get cleaned up." She glanced at me, chin tilted high. With her gorgeous eyes narrowed, her skin was pale. There was pleading in those eyes, in that expression. "Or something. Please."

"She's not staying." I slid my hand from her back and grazed her hand with mine.

"I would just like a few minutes," Lenora said, and for the first time since I'd kicked her out of our home, the infrequent lawyer visits where we'd sat across from the table from each other, she looked contrite. Uncertain and if I wasn't mistaken, sad.

"Please let me go," Gabby whispered, and her voice was so pained. My body burned to kiss her, to kick Lenora out and finish what we'd started. I couldn't. Not with her looking so upset and shaken.

"Five minutes," I said, loud enough for both to hear. "This won't take long," I said only for Gabby and brushed my lips over her cheek. "Go on up. I'll come find you."

Her gaze slid toward Lenora and she rolled her lips together before scooting between us and hurrying up the stairs. I waited until I heard the echo of her door closing upstairs and crossed my arms, turning back to Lenora.

"Five minutes. Talk."

"I've been trying to reach out to you. I texted you… before your games."

"I saw." I would give her nothing. In her texts, she'd just told me good luck or that I played great. I'd deleted them all as soon as I saw them during the playoffs. So inconsequential I hadn't remembered receiving them until she brought it up.

"You, um… you never texted back."

"I know." I crossed my arms over my chest.

Her lips pushed to one side. I'd never been cold to her. I'd sought her out, pursued her. I gave my relationship with Lenora everything I had from the first moment I saw her at that coffee shop and I never quit until she had made it clear it was over. No doubt she was surprised to not see me being more open, but whatever she came for, she wouldn't get.

Not only because of Gabby, but because of her own actions.

"I'm sorry," she whispered, and her chin wobbled.

So help me, if she cried… my jaw tightened.

"I'm sorry for everything, but you never gave me a chance to explain. You were so angry that day, and then the divorce went so quickly. I wanted to talk, but you kicked me out."

She had to be kidding me. Based on the earnestness in her blue eyes, she wasn't.

"That's semantics considering I walked in on another woman fucking you."

Her head tilted, curious, micro-bladed brows tugging inward. "Is that the problem? That it was Rhianna and not a man?"

I laughed, but it was cold and brittle. I would have handled it differently. A man would have had my fist in his face. I'd given Rhianna the decency to gather her clothes and scurry around our room without looking at her naked body.

"No." At one time, it had been part of it. Along with my bruised ego. But then I realized that had never mattered. She'd betrayed me and our wedding vows and the life I'd thought we were building. It didn't matter if it was man, woman, or a fruitcake for fuck's sake.

She'd ruined all the trust I had in her in a moment, a glimpse of her body connected with another.

"I'm sorry. She's not you and I was so lonely. It was a mistake, though. Rhianna and I aren't together, and she's quit the show. Please, Joey."

She came to me quickly, the palm of her hand at my chest, and with her height, I barely had to dip my chin to see her.

Which meant I caught the flash of irritation as I took her wrist and flung her hand off my body and took two steps back.

"I can do better," she pleaded. "I'm so sorry. It was stupid, and I've regretted it for so long, but I didn't know how to reach out to you, but once I saw those pictures of you the other night, I knew I had to come talk to you."

My brows rose. "You saw that I was remarried and *then* decided to make your move?" Did she realize how absolutely insane that was?

"Well, you were drunk, obviously, so it's not like it was real..."

My hand flew up between us, palm out, stopping her. I was over this. Over seeing her plead for something she'd destroyed and had no chance of having again. "I'm going to tell you this once, and then I'm never going to see you again. There was no hope of us *ever* reconciling as soon as I caught you. That I'm married again now, plays no bearing on this. It isn't even the largest factor. Your behavior, on the other hand, showing up here and walking into a home that is no longer yours, thinking you're *owed* whatever time you demand *is*, Lenora. Life is not about you and if you're unhappy, if you're searching for something, that is a result of your own actions. But they will no longer, ever, have any bearing on mine."

"But... I miss you. And now that it's off-season, we can spend time together."

Off-season? Was she *high*? "So what happens in September when I'm back on the road? What then? Will you get bored again?"

Her lips pinched, selling her out before she could hide it.

"Jesus, Lenora. *Who* are you?" And how had I missed out on this part of her for so long?

She straightened her spine, jutting out breasts I didn't bother glancing at. There was a time I couldn't keep my hands off them, now I saw her using her body as a weapon. Bile rose in my throat. "Why did you even marry me?"

It couldn't have been love. Was it the money? She'd never acted like she cared about any of the *fame* such as it was from being with a pro athlete. Hell, I was rarely recognized. Did she like being able to use the name? Impress people?

"Because I loved you." Her chin shook, but there was no change in her expression. Fake. Just like the rest of her. "I can fix this. I can fix *us*."

She couldn't. She wouldn't. And I knew the kill shot to prove it. "Will you give me children?"

Her lip curled.

God. This was like finding her cheating on me all over again except now, I just... I didn't care.

Exhaustion settled onto my shoulders and I shook my head. "Get out, Lenora, and go home. We're done here."

"Rhianna kicked me out and I have nowhere else to go."

I laughed. Holy shot shit, how was this my life? "I don't even care," I said, still laughing. "You make money, go take care of yourself for once."

"You don't mean that. You can't. You're too nice."

The urge to slam my head against the wall hit me hard and fast. "You're a piece of work. I don't know if you just don't *care* about how big of a fool you're making of yourself right now, but this is my house and you're no longer welcome in it."

I moved around her and opened the door, stepping back so I was out of her reach. This was... hysterical. And truly, the perfect closure I didn't even need anymore. In a minute, she showed me more of her true self than she ever had and it was all... ugly, despite the pretty outer wrapping.

"If I ever see you anywhere close to this property, I'll be calling the police. We never would have lasted. We wanted two very different things long-term, so get out, before I force you to."

"You miss me. You missed being married, that's the only reason you got married again. I know you, Joey."

"You don't know shit," I hissed, and my feet had moved, in front of her and sneering down at her before I took a breath. "My relationship with Gabby is none of your damn business and never will be. And if you think so little of me that I'd be that *stupid* to get married because I was lonely— well, I suspect that rings more true to you than it does me. Get out before I call the police and have you arrested for trespassing. Now."

Her eyes narrowed, fury sparking in them, and at one time, her angry look had started a hell of a lot of hot angry sex. She was every man's dream woman, at least in body, but she was absolutely no longer mine.

"She will never give you what I can," she spit.

Oh, how fucking wrong she was.

"You're right. Because I know Gabby will give me *everything* I've always wanted, and that's something you were never capable of."

It was more than wanting kids. Or a family. It was the understanding and the compassion and the caring, genuine caring, about my life. Lenora had lacked in all of it.

My arrow hit its mark and she flinched.

I raised my brows, impatience licking its way up my spine.

"Five minutes are up."

She wrinkled her nose, again, adorable and it did nothing to me, but my wife knew how to work a crowd. Knew how to work men into a tizzy. It was her career and she was damn good at it. For once though, I felt nothing.

She left, gaze never dropping from mine until she reached the front patio and turned around.

I shut the door on her. Locked it, and then heaved a sigh and scrubbed my hands through my hair.

What a damn mess she'd caused. But I hope she heard every word I spoke.

Hell, I hoped Gabby overheard it.

Because if I thought for a second there wasn't a reason Gabby and I were meant to be, had done what we had, I would have gotten the marriage annulled yesterday, or the day before. I wouldn't be going through the effort to save something for ego alone. Lenora should have known that.

And if Gabby didn't yet, I'd soon prove it to her.

I found Gabby in my movie room. She'd changed out of the jean shorts and tank top and her hair had been pulled back into a loose braid. Face free of makeup, she was curled into one of the reclining, leather movie theater-style chairs. Short, black shorts, so tight they might as well have been painted on her and wearing a sweatshirt that draped off one shoulder and revealed a light purple bra strap, I couldn't decide how I found her sexier. Wearing a dress I could untie, my jersey declaring her mine for all to see, or this… Gabby, free from any façade, simply, perfectly, her.

"I'm sorry about that," I told her, and entered the movie room where she was flipping through a streaming service. "Lenora left."

"What'd she want?" She didn't look at me, kept scrolling, clearly not focusing on anything she flipped past. But her voice was dull, and my chest pinched with pain. I'd done that.

No. Lenora had. I'd handled it.

"Me." I rocked back on my heels, shoving my hands to my hips. "She wanted me back."

"You loved her." The sadness in her voice slayed me, cut right through my chest with a knife.

"Of course I did. But that 'd' at the end of the word is the most important part of it. Past tense. Not now."

Had there been any question before today, it was clear now.

"You loved her and married her. And then you married me."

If she was looking for declarations of love, she wouldn't get them. Not then. "You're right. Which means there's a reason for it. Don't pull back or push me away because I want to find out why."

"Is that what this was then?" She flipped her hand back and forth between us. "You testing out our chemistry?"

"No." Goddamnit, no. She wasn't even close. "Me being unable to keep my hands off you is because you're sexy. You make me laugh. Every time you touch me I get hard and that's not because I haven't fucked a woman since Lenora, either. It's you, Gabby. It's everything I feel when I'm with you and it's the fact that for hours today I kissed you and held you and laughed with you and all I could think about was all the different places I wanted to fuck you when we got back here and all the different positions I want you in as I do it."

Her eyes widened with every word, cheeks flushed as I continued.

"Don't you dare think I'm using you just to get off, either. I could have that anywhere, but I'm not that *guy*. Lenora's the third person I've been with. That's it. I don't fuck and dump like other guys and I wouldn't. This shit *means* something to me."

You mean something to me. What it was, I couldn't exactly tell her. I hadn't figured it out myself. But that didn't mean it wasn't there, a living, pulsing need and desire for her that itched beneath my skin.

God, my chest burned. I *wanted* this woman. So damn bad.

I reached for her to hold her, to comfort her and reassure her I meant everything I said but as I did, she pulled back, shaking her head and practically cowered in her chair.

A chill traveled down my back, pulled at my shoulders.

"I'm not... I'm not the girl my mom thinks I am."

"I know that."

"No, you don't get it." She laughed, but it was cold and brittle. Blinking, she slid her gaze to the windows, the pool and my yard beyond. "My mom, she has this idea of who I should be."

"I don't give a fuck of your mom's opinions. I like you as you are."

"I'm not the girl she says jumps without looking or is too stupid to make a plan. She thinks I live in my head, but it's not that."

I. Really. Did. Not. Give. A. Fuck. Nor did I want to be discussing her *mother* of all people.

She glanced at me, pain in her eyes and in the grooves of her forehead. "I've never been the daughter she wanted."

"Gabby—"

She jumped from the couch then, flung her arm straight out. "So what happens once we do all this, continue this insanity and you realize I'm not the wife you always wanted." Lenora. She meant Lenora. "You should consider that."

I didn't need to.

What I got from her distance and her pain was that she needed to believe I'd done just that.

"We can take a step back," I told her, doing exactly that by stepping backward toward the hallway. "But you should know I don't need it."

She pushed her lips to one side, eyes filled with doubt.

I wanted to pummel her mom for destroying her daughter's self-esteem instead of building it up. Rail at Garrett for not doing more to stop it, even if it wasn't his responsibility.

"Joey."

I stopped at the threshold and looked at her over my shoulder.

"You should know, what you said... all this means a lot to me too. I don't want to mess that up."

Sex. Marriage. She meant it all the same as I had.

At least we were on the same page about something.

A foundation—based on shared beliefs. She didn't realize she'd just proven why it was possible we could work together forever, but I wouldn't push her now.

"I'm going to go shower," I told her instead.

And on the way—I made a plan.

I was going to seduce my wife. And I wouldn't quit until she decided to stay married to me.

15

GABBY

I gave up trying to find a movie. I hadn't paid attention to the screen as I'd flipped through channels and I didn't even realize I'd wandered into his movie room until I was there, curled on a couch in the dark room. I'd just wanted to escape and hide, from Joey, from the feelings he was pulling from me every time he touched me.

And God. His kisses. They were more addictive than strawberries dipped in chocolate, more addictive than a perfect red wine, or an early morning, cloudless sunrise. I could devour every single one of them and even while hurting, be desperate for more.

That was how I was starting to feel around Joey.

Desperate. For his touch, his kisses, his presence.

Stupid. Stupid me. I'd married a man I barely knew only to find myself falling for him in two days.

I was sharing too much with him. Being too vulnerable. For some ridiculous reason, I was diving headfirst into a situation I'd end up hurt from, I knew it.

The problem was I wasn't sure how to stop it. The avalanche had already started and was growing, steamrolling its way through me, and tomorrow, we were supposed to be hitting the road, traveling the country in a van meant for lovers.

How in the hell was I going to stop this madness?

Antsy, irritated and still tasting Joey on my lips and in my mouth, I tossed down the remote and shoved out of the chair.

I hadn't eaten all day, the parade lasted hours and with traffic, we'd been gone since early this morning. I needed food. Thankfully, Joey kept his fridge stocked with all manner of food and I quickly found something I could make for dinner.

I had already prepared chicken breasts, the oven was preheated and I was finishing chopping up vegetables for a simple sheet pan dinner meal when his footsteps echoed headed down the back stairway and then he was in the kitchen.

He'd showered, like he said he was going to do and his hair was still wet. And his shaved scruff, thick and short... what I wouldn't give to feel the scrape of it beneath my fingertips or in other, more sensitive places.

Gah! I turned back to the vegetables, lest my fingertips ended up mixed with the zucchini, and tried as hard as I could to kick that errant thought out of my mind.

It was useless. The way we'd torn at each other still had me worked up and I hadn't been smart enough to relieve that ache when I'd run and hid earlier.

"This looks great," Joey said, scanning the baking sheet where I drizzled avocado oil over everything, seasoned with garlic and onion powders, some paprika and a dash of chili powder for a kick. "Do you like cooking?"

"It's not my favorite hobby." I couldn't bring myself to look at him, too terrified of what he'd read on my face.

Would he see the woman falling for him way too fast? The stupid little girl who acted on impulse? Or would he just see *me* the daughter and sister and hairstylist who was just trying to find her place in a world of billions and floundering like everyone else?

Worse—would he see me still so damn turned on I'd risk jumping him and climbing him like a tree?

"What is it?"

"What?"

The refrigerator closed and he stood, popping open a bottle of beer. "Your favorite hobby. What is it?"

"Oh. Um." I slid the sheet into the oven and set the timer. Hell if I knew. I worked. In the last year, I hung out with Kurt and his stupid friends constantly talking about the stock market and the housing boom and the bubble that would surely pop soon. Blah blah freaking blah. No one ever cared enough to ask about the training I did. New balayage techniques or eyebrow threading or eyebrow shaping. "Being outside. Doing anything."

"Yeah." He chuckled and grabbed a wineglass from one of his cupboards. "Want a glass?"

I shouldn't. I was already twisted up enough. But because I was reckless, I grinned. "Definitely. What'd the *yeah* mean?"

He smiled, that panty melting and too sexy it shocked my libido smile as he poured me a glass of white wine from his wine fridge in the island.

"Everything you want to do or see involves being outside. It didn't take a genius to figure that out."

Huh. In truth, I hadn't even thought of it. I just thought the places looked cool and why not see what the country has to offer outside museums and pavement. "Right," I mumbled and thanked him for the wine. The first sip tasted like lime and fresh air, and I inhaled the sweet citrusy scent before setting my glass down.

"What's yours?"

"Besides skating?"

I laughed. "Yeah. Something that isn't related to your job."

"I can't help it. I love my job. I don't know though, really. There hasn't been a lot of time in the recent years to spend time doing *hobby* type things, outside reading while I'm on the plane. And I'm not a big reader, either."

I imagined him, dressed in a suit, noise-canceling headphones on. The tie would be gone, the top collar of his shirt unbuttoned while he settled back with a paperback in his hand, a sole light on the airplane barely giving him enough to read clearly.

A shiver rolled down my spine and I swallowed thickly to shake it away. Was there anything Joey could do and not look devastatingly handsome doing it?

Doubtful.

"What about the off-season? What do you do then?" Garrett always spent time golfing. He played in tournaments all over the country that donated the proceeds to various charities. He'd also frequently rented a boat on Lake Michigan and would take teammates out for weekend trips, sleeping on the water. I'd gone with him once and spent half the trip bent over the tailing, puking up everything I ate.

"Ah. I forget you don't know."

"Know what?"

He broke out into a full smile. The kind of smile I'd tripped over my own feet earlier when I saw it. Delightfully happy, built like a man who could go *hours* and would enjoy every moment of it—no wonder why I was falling so quickly for him.

He was perfect. Absolutely perfect.

"I run a youth baseball league during the summers."

"Baseball?"

"Yeah." His smile turned shy and if I wasn't mistaken, color darkened his cheeks. "I bought this bar a couple years back—"

"A bar?"

I couldn't see it. Couldn't envision Joey owning a bar. A club? Sure. He had that modern vibe and based on the way he'd moved us early while we'd been superglued to each other, he obviously knew how to move his body, work those trim hips of his.

"Yeah." He cleared his throat and took another pull of his beer. "Malley's. It's this place a few miles away. Some of us guys found it after we were kicked out of the playoffs a couple seasons ago. We wanted to wallow, didn't want to go anywhere we'd be recognized so we stumbled on this small local place. Jerry, the guy who owned it, knew us as soon as we walked in, but the man didn't say shit. We could just tell, you know? Said something later on in the night about how we'd had a good run and should be proud. Anyway, we kept going, but then he got sick last year and was too afraid his life's legacy would be bulldozed and turned into part of the nearby strip mall. So I bought it from him."

"You bought it."

Because normal people went around buying up bars and buildings like it was nothing.

"Yeah. See, Jerry and some other local small businesses started this baseball league for underprivileged kids. He was worried if he lost his bar, the other businesses wouldn't have the money from him to keep everything going. They pay for everything, jerseys, gear, field time, refs. The whole shebang. They were barely scraping by before and hadn't been able to find more businesses to help out, so without them, the whole thing could have crumbled. So, I bought the bar, chipped in extra, and now all the kids get all brand new gear and uniforms every year and we were able to install lights in a few fields for night games."

Wow. I'd already known he was a great guy. With this revelation, given so simply, stated like it was just another thing he did during the day like some people mentioned vacuuming, my heart swelled until it hurt.

"How do you manage it all?"

He shrugged like it was nothing. Maybe it was. Everything came easy for him, it seemed. And he probably had a team of people making it easier. I know Garrett did. Personal shoppers when necessary, financial managers being only two of the people he considered his "team."

"Bar had a great staff up and running already. I approved one woman to manage and she runs it all. I just sign the checks and help with issues every once in a while. Jerry's now retired, but he stops in for a drink occasionally. Comes to the games that'll start soon." He paused and took a drink. I followed his lead, but my wine did nothing to my over-heating body. If possible, he was sexier while talking about this bar and helping people than he'd ever been. "And at the risk of bringing her up, Lenora's busiest time of performances are in the summer, so that didn't leave a lot of time for traveling like most guys do."

"I don't mind you bringing her up."

"No? Because when I say her name, you flinch."

He had me there.

"Outside hockey, she was the largest part of my life. I can't wipe that away."

"I know." I got it. I totally understood. But I didn't relish the fact that he might still end up thinking we'd screwed up.

I was the rebound after a woman he loved with his entire soul. Not a comfortable place to be wedged into.

"Can we go?"

His beer paused at his mouth and his brows pulled in. "What?"

"After dinner—can we go to Malley's?"

"Yeah. I know some of the guys were going to stop by later. They might be ready to pass out by the time we get there, but we can go if you want."

See the place where Joey admired a man enough to run his sports league and ensure his legacy stayed standing? What better way than to further get to know my husband. "I definitely want."

His look heated.

The doorbell rang.

"That fucking bell," he muttered and stepped back. "I'll go see."

Thirty seconds later, he shouted, "Get your sexy ass out here! You gotta check this out, Gabby!"

Sexy ass?

Damn.

He wasn't playing around. He might have said we'd slow this down, but I was beginning to think Joey didn't know what that meant.

Mach two versus Mach ten?

Still, I quickened my steps and met him on the front cement porch, jaw dropping to the ground.

"Holy shit." My hands flew to my mouth as I gaped at the Mercedes in his driveway.

He grinned at me, arms flung wide out to the sides. "Looks like they dropped it off early."

It was black. Matte. So much more *perfect* than when he'd shown me pictures.

Tears pricked my eyes. "I can't... it's..."

After a second hesitation, I rushed into the RV that only felt slightly larger than a Suburban but was so much *more*. The back had two couches, a small table between them. To my left was a small counter and sink, a fridge barely larger than a wine fridge beneath. To my right was the even smaller bathroom. I slid open the door, cringed at the size of the shower. How in the world Joey would be able to fit much less actually clean himself would be magic I'd let him figure out, but the necessities were there. We'd have water, a sink, and toilet. At the front of the van were two oversized chairs. They could recline enough to sleep in.

I spun in a circle, my grin stretching my cheeks so badly they shook when Joey stepped inside, ducking through the doorway.

"You like?"

"I love. Absolutely love." I bounced on the balls of my feet. If only we could take off now.

He had his arms crossed over his chest, stretching his sky-blue T-shirt over his muscles, straining the cotton and seams I was certain, but as he scanned what would be our living quarters for the next few weeks, his grin was almost large enough to match mine.

Holy shit. I was getting my dream vacation. If I wasn't mistaken, Joey looked equally excited as I was.

"Let me show you what I had included in the delivery."

I clapped my hands together. "Yes. Please."

He took his time opening the overhead cabinets as he told me he'd called a sporting goods store, told them who he was, what he needed and the RV rental had stopped there to load everything up.

Paid to make millions, I guess. But I wasn't knocking it,

not when he opened up the storage beneath the van and jam-packed in there were camping supplies.

"I think everything came we ordered," he said. There were sleeping bags and air mattresses. A tent for four so we could share but still have space. There was firewood and a gas stove.

This was happening.

My dream vacation. I turned to Joey. "We're doing this."

"Hell yeah we are."

And maybe, just maybe, I wasn't only talking about the trip.

16

JOEY

I opened the door to Malley's, allowing Gabby to enter first. As soon as the door shut behind us, all the guys on the team threw their hands in the air, beer sloshing out of many filled glasses.

"The hat trick king is here!"

"We're not worthy!" Kane shouted, sweeping his arm straight out as he dropped into a full bow at his waist.

"Holy crap, they're wasted." Gabby laughed.

"They've been drinking since the parade. I'm surprised there aren't more passed out in the booths."

As it was, while drunk, most seemed relatively in control of themselves.

Thank God. It wasn't uncommon for professional athletes to make front-page news on the day of championship parades or in the days after. It was a time to party our asses off after long seasons, regardless of sport, but our team didn't need any more front-page news.

Mine and Gabby's attention was enough.

Mostly, I didn't need Malley's Bar in the background of any said drunken photos. It'd become our home, in a manner of speaking, over the last couple of years and more since I took over ownership.

Since I'd closed down the bar, having the manager put a sign out front saying Malley's was closed for a private event, I didn't have anything to worry about.

"These guys can handle their alcohol. Trust me."

We stopped at the bar, where Gabby asked for a red wine and I got a double scotch on the rocks. I wanted to enjoy the night, especially with us hitting the road in the morning. Hangovers wouldn't go well with the drive we had in front of us, but a couple drinks wouldn't hurt anything.

"Come on. You know most, I'm guessing?"

"Yeah." She scanned the small crowd and a line dipped in between her brows. "There aren't any women..."

"Single guys night out. I can guarantee all the taken and married men are back home right now celebrating their own way."

She pressed her lips together, fighting a smile. "Nice."

We could have been doing the exact same thing. Had it not been for Lenora. Gabby's insecurities. This entire messed up situation.

I pushed away the doubt trying to claw its way in. It was my own insecurities.

Maybe Lenora's visit rattled me more than I let on. It wasn't like I'd forgotten what she said—or what she implied she wanted. No way in hell that was going to happen though.

Not ever.

Didn't mean trust would come easily and there I was, married to a woman I barely knew.

What a recipe for an epic disaster.

"Yo Dubiak!" Alix swooped into our space, wrapping his arm around Gabby and twirling her in the air.

She was gone and out of my reach, wrapped up in Alix before I could stop him.

"Hey Alix," she said, leaning into him. The move was friendly. A typical reaction.

I gripped my drink tighter and glared at his hand that was much too low on her hip. "Hey. Watch the hand, yeah?"

Because he enjoyed pissing me off, his thumb brushed against her and Gabby stepped back.

"Easy killer. I'm taken." She hitched her thumb in my direction with a smirk.

"No harm, no chickens, yeah?"

"Foul. Alix. Jesus."

"I know. Just giving you shit." He pointed at me, dipped his finger toward my drink. "You are not drunk enough to be fun yet."

"I'm plenty fun." He was right. The bar was loud. The guys were wasted. The only thing on my mind was getting Gabby alone, rewinding to when my door opened and having it *not* be my cheating ex-wife.

I took a large swallow of my drink, hissing at the heavy burn in my throat.

"Sorry to interrupt. Can we talk for a moment, Joey?"

I turned to Bonnie, my weeknight manager. She had the office iPad in her hands, stylus shoved through the band at her ponytail and a frown.

Awesome. "What is it?"

"We've had an issue with one of our barware suppliers. Sorry to interrupt your party and everything, but can you help me with this?"

Shit. "Yeah."

"Great. I'll be in the office then. Come grab me when you have a few minutes."

She left as quickly as she arrived and I faced Gabby. "You okay alone for a few minutes?"

Alix threw his arm over her shoulders. "I'll take good care of her. Promise."

Gabby shook her head, smiling. "I'll be fine." She narrowed a playful glare in Alix's direction. "I'm sure Alix knows if he does anything inappropriate I don't just have a brother who will kick his ass, but a husband, too."

Husband. My chest swelled until it ached. It sounded so *right* coming from her.

Alix threw his hands in the air. "Point taken. Point taken. Come and hang with us while boss-man gets to work." He spun and headed back to where Arlo, a rookie who was called up earlier this winter and got his formal spot two weeks later, was standing next to the pool table, cue in hand while he waited for Kane to take a shot. Near them were other guys, including Max... and to my utter shock, Dominick.

Dominick Masters, best defenseman in the league hands down. Out of all the guys on the team, I knew the absolute least about him, which meant I knew nothing. He *never* hung out with the team. I shook off my surprise. Maybe winning the Cup had finally broken through whatever wall he'd put up with the rest of the team.

"You sure you're okay? I'd put this off but with leaving tomorrow, I need to get some things taken care of anyway."

Things I probably should have thought about, like emailing the managers earlier. Planning for payroll and all the crap I kept a loose grip on.

"Of course, go." She flipped her hand in the direction.

"Thanks." I reached out, caught a hair that was stuck to her glimmering lip gloss and pulled it back. As I did, her lips parted, eyes softened.

Damn. One single touch was all it took for me to feel that warm beat in my veins, that steady thump of desire for her. Based on her look, she felt it too.

"Joey," she whispered my name like a prayer. Maybe a plea. I stepped in and brushed my lips over her cheek, settling my hand at her hip and holding her tight.

"I promised you earlier we'd go slow if you need that, but don't for one second think that I'm not going to be waiting for you to be ready, thinking of all the ways I want to strip you out of the clothes you're wearing." I brushed my lips down her throat, reveling in that hitch in her breath I caused as I moved and pulled back before I pushed too far. "I'll be back as soon as I can."

And before I swung her over my shoulder and ignored all my responsibilities and pushed her too far, I stepped back.

To my utter delight, her lips were still parted and that soft look in her eyes had darkened—no, heated.

Yeah. She might think she needed slow, but it wasn't what she wanted.

That, I could work with.

As soon as I was done in the office, I grabbed another drink from the bar and immediately found Gabby.

She was sitting on her own side of a booth, two unlikely brutes sitting next to each other on the other side.

Dom was all quiet, aloof, and wore a constant scowl, distancing himself from everyone. I wasn't sure what his problem was, but I was convinced he was the reason why the reminder "there is no I in team" started—guys like him who thought they were alone instead of learning how to work together. Sure, as a teammate, he did his job. He was a hell of a defenseman. But he played angry, like every game was a reason to throw a punch. He learned the plays, executed them perfectly but when it came time to celebrate, be there for their teammates off the ice... as soon as the skates came off Dom, so did his teamwork.

Which was the exact opposite of Max who lived like life was one huge party and he was the master event planner. Hell, I was surprised he was even here. He was the guy who'd take the Cup on his time with it to every dance club in the city, or hell, this time zone, for the sole purpose of getting pics taken with puck bunny after puck bunny, probably hoping to fill the cup with numbers of all the single women he came across. He lived for the adventure of the game, the excitement of the travel and the constant attention.

He was also our other first line defender with Dom, but outside practice, I wasn't sure I'd ever seen them hang out.

Now they were sitting on the same side of the booth like they were besties.

More shocking—Dom was smiling. At least, that's what I figured it was but given his thick dark beard and the fact I'd never known a look on him outside a scowl, I wasn't entirely certain.

And he was doing it with that smile aimed at my wife.

Who had her head thrown back, laughing her ass off as she took a sip of beer.

"You're such a cheating asshole," she exclaimed, pointing at Dom.

His grin widened—a look so out of place on him I almost ran right into the chair in front of me.

"Sticks and stones, Gabrielle. Sticks and stones."

She shook her head like he was a stuffed teddy bear and not the grizzly he showed all of us.

What in the hell happened while I was gone? It was possible I'd entered an alternate dimension.

"Room for more?" I asked, already sliding into the booth next to Gabby. She fell into me, resting her head against my shoulder, still laughing at Dominick.

"Yeah, and this cheater should be kicked off your team. Can you have him transferred or something? To like, I don't know... Alaska."

"Alaska doesn't have a team," Dom said. "And just because I'm better than you, doesn't mean I cheat."

"Nonsense." She slapped her hand on the table, making the half-emptied glasses rattle. "I'm the best at this. Always have been. Always will be. You sir, are a cheating McCheaterson."

He shook his head with a laugh and I took a drink of the beer I'd poured for myself on the way back to the table.

Bonnie had a handle on our supplier, who was threatening a three percent increase in cost to us over the contractually agreed on price. I made a note in my phone to call them first thing tomorrow before cell phone access got sketchy on the road.

This had happened before, once businesses we worked with found out who had taken over Malley's. Shady dealers and suppliers who assumed because I could afford the increases weren't shy about asking for it but fuck that. I might have been an athlete but I wasn't some dumb jock.

They didn't ask twice. If they did, they found themselves with a disputed contract and the lack of our business along with others considering since I became a business owner, such as it was, my network expanded across the city.

"You good?" Gabby asked, peering up at me. The desire

in her eyes was gone, replaced with a glassy, tipsy expression.

She'd never looked more beautiful. Not touching her was painful, but I managed. Barely. She smelled like peppermint and beer and somehow, it was my new favorite scent.

"I'm good. All things good here?" My gaze hardened on Dom on instinct as I asked. I saw him this morning in the lounge area, off in a corner with headphones, scowling at a spot on the carpet like he'd just lost a family member instead of won a championship with his team and left him to it. He must have ended up on another bus because I didn't see him for the rest of the parade.

"We're good," Max said, and grabbed the quarter from Gabby, sliding it toward me. "And it's your turn. You're behind."

I spun the quarter on the table. "Quarters like we're college freshmen? Whose bright idea was this?"

Both Max and Dom pointed at Gabby. She rolled her lips together and shrugged. "It's Dom's fault."

"How was it *my* fault? I was sitting here, minding my own business."

Typical.

"Exactly! And your team just won the Stanley Cup! You're here, out with the guys. You should be partying and laughing and giving each other shit and instead, you were here... brooding."

"I was not brooding." His black brows tugged in and he crossed his arms over his chest. I swore he slunk down in his seat too.

Max snorted and shook his head while Gabby pointed at him and yelled, "You're doing it now! Maybe you're not Cheater McCheaterson. You're Pouty McPouterson!"

"I'm not pouting." His brows arched.

I'd seen men wither under that look and instead, Gabby laughed it off like he was a puppy. "McPouterson," she said back, with all the sass I'd ever heard in the world.

Dom's shoulders shook and he ripped the quarter out of my hand. "Game on, Gabrielle. But you better fill that drink up first."

He didn't wait. He flipped the quarter—chose the drinker—Gabby—and that was how the rest of the game went. She made the call, Dom drank. He made the call, Max or she drank, but mostly it was her. I could have been jealous, the attention they were giving each other, but the more drunk Gabby got the more she leaned into me. She rested her hand on my thigh until her touch burned through my denim and hardened my dick. Max and I were essentially left to take our time on our drinks, laughing at them, and mostly, I was in awe.

In moments, it seemed, she'd thawed Dominick's rough and *get the fuck away from me* vibe he portrayed—a vibe our entire team hadn't been able to get through in the three years he'd been on the team.

I didn't care the two were basically playing the game against each other. I'd somehow unwrapped another mystery about my wife—how she could get anyone to open up to her in minutes.

She was magic, and I realized as I sat back, laughing with Max, that I was falling under her spell.

"Do you need help?"

Gabby stumbled around the front of my Audi R8, hand sliding along the engine, leaning on it for balance. "I'm good." She frowned. "I think?"

I laughed, and leaned forward, taking her hand in mine. "Maybe think a little harder next time you decide to go drink for drink with a guy at least one hundred pounds heavier than you."

She snickered, rested her head against my shoulder as I led her through my garage and through the butler's pantry. "Dom is funny."

She had to be more drunk than I thought if she believed that. "He's a loner."

"Not tonight, he wasn't. Tonight he was funny."

She was right. Max and I sat in that booth and watched Gabby challenge Dom to game after game of quarters. She got her ass kicked, happily so, but it never once stopped her from backing down.

At some point, Dom had gotten a phone call, his typical scowl slammed back into place and he practically shoved Max to the floor to get out of the booth. "Gotta go. See ya around."

And then he was gone. I'd been baffled, Max pissed considering it was his ass that hit the dirty floor.

Gabby had just shrugged, taken another drink, handed me the quarter and proclaimed it my turn.

Considering I'd stopped drinking to ensure I was okay to drive us back home, I declined. She'd climbed out of the back of the booth and went to find Alix and Arlo and before long, was beating all the guys left at darts.

"You're right. Tonight, Dom was funny." For a brief time anyway, and even then, he wasn't necessarily funny, but *nice*.

Strange enough.

"Let's get you to bed. Early morning tomorrow."

"I'm not driving first," she declared, feet slowly trudging as she gave me more of her weight.

"Deal." I wouldn't let her, even if she wasn't looking at a

raging hangover.

We trudged up the stairs, her feet growing slower with every step and we were almost at her door when she started giggling.

"What?"

"It's nothing." Little liar.

"Then why are you laughing so hard you're crying?"

"It's just," she hiccuped and covered her mouth, which only made her laugh harder. "It's just, I always knew you Taylor boys were so sexy and nice, but I didn't think you were all so perfect, either."

She tried to tug away from me, but I stopped her. Ignoring the fact she included all my brothers in that sexy statement, I brushed hair off her cheeks that had gotten stuck to her tears. "You think I'm sexy?"

"Like you need me to tell you that," she scoffed.

"Maybe I do. Maybe I want to know my *wife* finds me sexy."

She gazed up at me, eyes glazed from all the beer she'd drank, but there was a light in them too. A spark of desire hidden behind it. "Yeah. I think you're pretty damn sexy."

She'd been drinking. I should have been a gentleman, set her in her room and left her to sleep.

The pull was too strong. I'd been wanting to taste her since Lenora ruined everything.

"Gabby." A whispered question. A plea.

She didn't answer with words.

Her hand lifted, slid to the back of my neck, sending a shock of fire in her wake, and then she pulled me to her. Pressed her lips to mine.

My hesitations broke on contact. I'd spent all day with her body against mine. That first kiss had been for the fans, a show to get them more excited, to sell that what we'd done wasn't a mistake. The rest had been for me, because I couldn't *stop* kissing her once we started.

Tonight, this was for her, and I kissed her with all the banked desire I had, all the passion I felt for her. Passion that had grown and expanded within days, moments even.

I kissed her until she was pressed to the wall and her leg was hitched over my hips, until my hand slid beneath her shirt and my palm was at her skin. She was hot, chest heaving, tiny little whimpers sliding down my throat as soon as they left hers.

I kissed her until she pulled back, shoved her forehead against my throat and in a harsh, heaving breath, whispered, "I don't know if this is a mistake or not, but I want it."

Slipping into an ice bath after a brutal game couldn't have chilled me faster.

I cupped her cheeks with my hands, stepping back, giving us space until her foot was back on the floor and she had her balance.

"Then we'll wait until you're sure it's not. I can't do that, Gab. I won't take you the way I want to so damn badly only to have you wake up in the morning with regret."

"But—"

"No buts." I kissed her cheek to soften the blow. "Sleep well and I'll see you in the morning."

When we set off for an adventure across the country.

The two of us. My wife and I—living out of a van for fuck's sake.

How in the hell was I going to keep all my desire for her contained?

I brushed my lips across her forehead, stealing one last taste of her, and reached around and opened her door. She rolled her lips together, blinked, almost surprised I stopped it when I did, and she ducked into her room.

17

GABBY

My bloodshot eyes were hidden behind sunglasses. My embarrassment over last night tucked firmly into a corner of my brain I didn't have the energy to think about.

I was so hungover, we didn't get on the road until seven, when we'd meant to be up and moving before sunrise so we could get to camp early afternoon. I hadn't slowed us down long enough we wouldn't still be able to enjoy the afternoon, maybe get in a quick hike near the campground Joey had found, but it wasn't making a good impression on how well I'd travel.

For his part, Joey took it all in stride.

He didn't mention the kiss last night, the heat that swirled between us and the desperate *need* I'd had for him while I clawed at his clothes and his shoulders, rolling my hips into his hard length. So desperate for him, too ignited by his touch that was far from gentle, the perfect side of rough.

No, this morning, he came into my room, woke me up and set down a mug of coffee. He gently brushed hair off my cheeks until I blinked at him through blurry eyes and pressed the heel of my palm to my forehead.

"Headache?"

"Maybe," I'd grumbled.

His chuckle had warmed the room and he held out pain meds. "I let you sleep in, any longer and we might hit traffic later. Still want to take off this morning or do you need sleep?"

He hadn't seemed bothered by my foolish behavior in any way, but I was. What an impression I'd made over the last few days. From getting so wasted I didn't remember my wedding to getting so drunk we couldn't leave on time for a vacation he'd insisted on footing the bill for.

That reminder—and the fact I wanted to prove I not only wanted this, but him, and it wasn't for his money like my mom believed I mooched off my brother for, got me moving.

"Thirty minutes. I'll be ready."

Surprise, probably doubt, made his brows arch. "Really?"

I'd laugh, despite the headache. I'd drank way more than that before, although Dominick gave me a good run for my money. "I just need a shower and have some eggs and I'll be good to roll."

I'd packed yesterday, finished anyway since I really didn't have that many clothes, and Joey had ordered all of our hiking clothes that came pre-packed in the RV sitting in his driveway.

"I can get your breakfast going." He'd stepped back, eyes roaming my face until I sat up and took that first sip of coffee.

"Delicious. Thank you for this, and yes, breakfast would be great."

"Good. Then I'll leave you..." He opened his mouth to say something.

Probably about the kiss. My regret.

He closed it, nodded once, probably more to himself like he'd made a decision without voicing it and then left. As soon as the door clicked, I'd hurried out of bed, swallowed down a slight shriek when I caught my reflection in the mirror, smeared mascara, bloodshot eyes, and purple moons beneath them and ducked into the shower. The brutal cold of the spray sparked me to life and the heat that quickly followed finished waking me up. Fifteen minutes later, I was downstairs, packed, wet hair in a braid and my face makeup-free, shoving eggs into my mouth and washing my dishes while Joey loaded my things into the van.

We were on the road exactly thirty minutes later and outside the GPS giving directions and our murmurs of awe as we made the trek toward Moab, we didn't speak much.

There was so much for me to say, not enough courage to give voice to it.

The view was breathtaking. The interstate took us around Dixie National Forest, red stone and rock and dirt created a wall of wonder we drove through. To our benefit, the sky was bright blue, cloudless, making everything feel bright.

I gawked at it all with fresh-eyed wonder. Had my trip ended that night, I would have seen enough to have a summer's worth of memories.

"And we're just beginning."

I hadn't realized I'd said it out loud until Joey asked, "What?"

"Nothing." Embarrassment tinged my cheeks. Thank God my shades were massive and could hide it. "I was just thinking how incredible this view is, and we're only on the interstate."

"I've always wanted to hike Moab. Some of the guys have done long weekend trips out here before but I was never able to make it."

Because of Lenora. Because he'd been married. I forced the truth of his past not to bother me—we all had one, even if mine hadn't made an appearance in our lives—and pushed forth.

"Well, I hope I'm as good of company as they would have been."

"You will be."

And he sounded so certain.

But that was all he said before his focus returned to the road and the view.

"I wouldn't have regretted it," I blurted.

Yup. Smooth, Gabby. Real smooth.

"Excuse me?"

I shifted in my oversized leather chair, fully reclinable if we wanted to sleep in it and adjusted my seat belt over my shoulder. We needed to face last night, move on from it.

"Last night. I wouldn't have regretted it." It was all I'd thought about since last night. Perhaps, before he gave his reply and stopped us as soon as I doubted myself, I would have. When I replayed those brief moments while I ate breakfast, though, I'd considered how he'd behaved. How he handled it.

He stopped immediately. Respected me, and yet was still kind and still sweet.

There would never be a moment I regretted anything happening with this man next to me, even if it ended in heartbreak.

"I told you last night I was worried about that."

He nodded once, grip tightened on the steering wheel. "You did."

"I wouldn't have. This morning, I wouldn't have regretted anything."

He glanced at me then, a slow, sly smirk curled the corners of his mouth into a smile... only more wicked. It sent a shock to my core, that look.

"Good."

Joey turned back to the road, and that was it.

Good.

But that look said a whole lot more.

HOURS LATER, after a quick stop near a lookout point we spotted where we stopped for a quick bite to eat of sandwiches and chips, we pulled into our campsite near the Arches National Park. We'd already decided to ease ourselves into the primitive tent camping, and since we had this crazy awesome RV, I was looking forward to spending some time enjoying it. And even though it was June, and it was hot during the day, the nights could still be cool.

After checking in to our reserved site, we followed the narrow dirt lane road past other sites already set up with travel trailers hitched to trucks, RVs larger than ours, and tent camping only sites. Most people were dressed for the day, hiking boots and thick socks and clothes for the hot sun, and my knee bounced wildly, anticipating what this trip would bring.

For someone who'd always traveled, taken off for weekend trips on the spur of the moment with little to zero planning, all of this was new to me.

So was having a travel partner I was attracted to.

Joey backed into our spot so we could hook up the electricity and water, and as soon as the gear shifter was in park, his seat belt was off and his hands were at my chair, flipping the lever to spin the chair toward him. His hands braced on the armrests, I could only gape in surprise at his sudden movement.

"What?"

Oh. He was bent over me, eyes aflame, black hair dipping down over his eyes. He was shadowed, blocking the sun, but there was no mistaking the heat coursing through him, the restraint making his arms shake and a map of veins appear, twisting and trailing up the backs of his hands until they disappeared beneath his short-sleeved black shirt.

"Did you mean it?"

I wasn't connecting the dots he was drawing. "Mean what?"

"That you wouldn't regret what happened with us?"

"Yes. I meant it."

Dear Jesus, he was scrambling my brain, making everything else inside of me thick with need and *want*.

"Do you want this?"

Him. Did I want *him*?

I barely nodded before he lunged. His mouth was on mine, his hand at the buckle to my seat belt. He wrestled it over my shoulder, grunting, grabbing, and then his hands were at my armpits, pulling me out of my seat and we were moving.

My back hit cold leather—the couch, I realized as my eyes flickered open in surprise and I saw the upper storage cabinets right before Joey's face, that dark thick hair and his newly shaved and close-cropped beard came into view.

"Do you want this *now*?"

As if he needed to make certain I understood the innuendo, he rolled his hips.

His dick, hard, nudged against my center, sending my eyes rolling to the back of my head. "Yes," I groaned and grabbed his shirt, the waistband of his hiking shorts. My fingers slid into his belt loops and I pulled him against me, arched into him.

Holy shit.

We needed to be naked. Immediately.

"That's the plan, wife," he said against my mouth.

I laughed against him. "I didn't realize I said it."

"I'm glad you did." He grinned down at me with that gleam in his eyes, the twist of his lips that set my body on fire for him.

In a blink, all humor vanished, as he kissed me again, dug hands into my hair with one hand and clasped on to my hip with his other. His hips rolled again, hitting that perfect spot, pulling a groan from my throat as he kissed me like he'd been dying to do it for so much longer than a few days.

I returned the kiss, hands sliding to the button of his shorts. I undid it easily and then shoved my hands beneath his shirt and met his rock-hard stomach and heated flesh.

"Fuck." He groaned into my mouth as soon as my hands began exploring his body. He was ripped, and his muscles quivered where I touched, flexed, and eased as I shoved his shirt higher to press against his chest.

Joey ripped his mouth off mine, staring down at me with harsh breaths and tore his shirt off him. He was straddling me, and sat up, giving me the full view of him in all his glory. The hair that spattered over his chest, trimmed short, and perfect.

"Wow." He was just...

"Same," he said, and climbed off the couch, leaving me

there, laying down, shirt askew. "We need more room." He held out his hand and his brows rose. A silent question, waiting for consent. He stood there patiently but in the blink of an eye, I knew—if I stopped it, said this couldn't work or happen, he'd drop his hand and walk away.

He would do that for me to ensure I was comfortable and ready.

Which made it so easy to place my hand in his, let him pull me to my feet where I kicked off my sandals, and with my gaze on him, I gripped the bottom of my shirt and pulled it off, only briefly losing eye contact with him, until my shirt joined his in a pile on the floor.

His dark eyes flared with want, sending a shiver of delight dancing down my spine. "I want to touch you everywhere," he said, and his gaze fell, scanning every inch of my exposed body and the still clothed areas, mapping out his plan of attack with his eyes.

I felt that gaze like his touch, which would be firm but tender, confident and comforting.

I lifted my hands to my sides. "So do it."

And then he lunged.

18

JOEY

In all the ways I wanted to get my hands on Gabby, in all the things I'd already thought about, having her right in front of me, naked save her shorts and a satin pink bra, scrambled every plan I had.

My plans to seduce her slowly, to give her time to come to me when we hadn't been drinking. When we'd gotten to know each other more. A ridiculous thought, considering we were *married*, but I'd been content to wait.

Until she told me earlier she wouldn't have regretted last night.

All the plans I'd made flew out the window and I reacted like a beast, and even now, as I slid my hands to her cheeks, tilted her head and kissed her, she took it. There wasn't enough damn room in this RV to do all the things I wanted, but first and foremost I needed to make room for us, to recline the couches into the bed so I could take her the right way, not rushed on the too-small couch.

My body was burning up and all the passion I'd banked over the last few days roared to the surface so brutally fast it almost scared me how much I wanted this woman.

"Couches," I gasped into her mouth. "We need them lowered."

"How?" she rasped against me and we both turned to them.

A low laugh left me. "Hell if I know." I shoved a hand through my hair, tried to inhale a breath that would hopefully give me a clear head for the time it would take but then—

Fuck it.

I needed her too badly. I flipped open the storage over one of the couches and grabbed the blankets and sheets that had been stowed there. With quick work, I threw them to the floor, creating our own bed.

"We'll figure out the couches later." When I had brain cells that were above my waistband because right now, all my blood and sense was beneath my shorts where my dick was still hard, pushing against the seam of my zipper and flung my hand to the mess of blankets I'd created. "This okay?"

Her hands, clear of the green and gold nail polish she'd worn earlier in the week, went to her shorts. To her button and her zipper. The *zip* bounced off the walls in the RV and I moved to do the same to mine but she shook her head as her shorts fell to the floor. "Let me," she said, her voice throaty, *wanting*.

Yessss.

I stayed still, soaking in the curve of her hips, the sway of her breasts and her center hidden beneath a matching pink thong as she came to me. She was beautiful. Curvy in all the perfect places with hips I couldn't keep my eyes off of and a plump, round ass I wanted shaking as I took her on her hands and knees.

Not today.

Soon.

As her hands touched me, a ripple of pleasure shot down my spine and with unhurried, sure movements, she trailed a hand down the center of my chest. I couldn't keep my eyes off her, couldn't have paid me to miss the way her eyes flared with desire, and the lick of her lips as my muscles rippled in the wake of her warm, soft fingers.

"You're going to need to speed this up," I murmured, and earned a quick flash of a smile before her hands went to my shorts, the button already undone. I stood still, not touching her. I'd let her run this show for a few minutes, but then her hands were sliding inside my shorts, against my hips and in one firm push, my shorts and boxer briefs were sliding to the floor.

I didn't have time to step out of them before her hand wrapped around my hard cock, pulling a moan and string of curses from me.

"Shit." My knees shook from the pleasure of her touch. The first woman's touch I'd had in way too long. Far too long, but so fucking worth the wait to watch Gabby's expression heat, her cheeks burn and her lips part as she slowly continued learning the feel of me.

A soft twist of her hand at my tip unraveled me, shoved me into action and I whipped out an arm to her hip and yanked her against me, kicking out of my shorts and underwear pooled around my ankles.

"Play later," I said, as my mouth went to the crook of her shoulder and she let out a surprised breath. "I haven't... it's been a while for me. You keep doing that and I'm going to embarrass myself."

Her hand slid down my shaft and let go. "Then I'll wait to see that another day."

God, she made this fun. So damn fun. I slid my hands up

her back, unclasped her bra and then I picked her up, laid her down on the makeshift mattress that still wasn't good enough for her. As I did, she wrapped her legs around me, until I was sliding my dick along the center of her soaking wet thong.

Fuck. She was *drenched.* The heat of her made my balls draw up and I kissed her again, slipped my tongue into her mouth and devoured her while I tried to control the need to release. How fucking embarrassing.

There was more to do. More to explore and touch, but first, I needed to ensure this was good for her. I ripped my mouth from hers, her lips wet, parted, and breath heaving as I slid down her body, I trailed my tongue along her collarbone, earning me a shiver, before moving down to her breasts where I gripped one in my hand, learned the weight of her and the mewls she made when I pinched her nipples.

"Please." She bucked into me as I twisted one, sucked the other into my mouth. "Oh. Shit. Yes."

Her hands dug into my hair, nails scraped my scalp, and I drove her wild with need while I played with her cherry pink nipples, hardened into sharp round buds.

"You taste so damn sweet. Like candy. I could do this all day long."

"I might die," she huffed, and her abs contracted, showing me gentle mounds of muscle ripple across her stomach.

"You won't." As I assured her, I continued sucking her nipple into my mouth, switching to the other while I trailed down to her stomach with the palm of my hand. She arched into me with every whisper-soft touch, groaned as I settled my hand at the crease of her thigh and held her down. My thumb was so close to her center, she writhed beneath me, seeking my touch.

Finally, when she seemed as needy and desperate as I already was, I slid a finger into her. And holy hot shit, she felt fucking *divine*. A goddess, as her body clung to me, gripped me, and so damn wet. I added a second finger, moved further until my mouth was added.

Her hands flew to my hair, gripping and tugging. She urged me on with her sounds and the slight tremble of her thighs. But hell if I needed the encouragement, I hadn't been lying. I could eat her every day. My new favorite meal.

She came suddenly, arching her hips and her sex into me, thighs clamping and shaking. Her sounds rattled the windows in the RV and I kept going, kept swirling my tongue over her clit, making her gasp with pleasure.

"Oh shit," she chanted. The sounds only made me harder because if she could explode so gorgeously like this —what would she do when I was inside of her?

"Stop," she rasped, fingers lightening their grip on my hair and playfully shoving me away.

I wiped her off my mouth. "You sure? Because I think it wouldn't take much at all to get you there again."

She shook her head, smiling at me, sated, cheeks flushed, hair a mess, and I ran a fingertip over her clit just to prove it.

"Stop." She laughed, grabbed my wrist. "When I come again, I want it to be with you inside of me."

"Then I should probably get to that." I bent over her, kissed her stomach, the space between her breasts and then brushed my mouth over hers. "You know what they say— happy wife, happy life."

Something that looked like uncertainty flared in her eyes right before her smile turned soft. "Yeah." A tiny frown, and then... "Um. Do you have condoms?"

I shoved up to my knees, intent on getting to my feet.

"I might have included that in the packing list."

"You did?" She barked out a laugh.

"No." I kissed the tip of her nose as she grinned at me and climbed off her. "I bought some the other day while you were swimming, before I started planning the trip."

It took me seconds to find them in the small bag I'd brought into the RV and I grabbed the box out of the side zipper. Tearing it open, my hands were still shaking—with need, with satisfaction.

I'd thought about Gabby every minute since I saw her dive into my pool, how soft she'd feel, how she'd react to my touch.

So far, she'd blown all hope and expectation out of the water. As I managed to tear open the condom, my nerves were shot with anticipation, but my body was primed to deliver in all the ways I'd imagined.

"You ready?" I asked as I laid down next to her. I was on my side and bent down to kiss her.

Immediately she responded, clinging to me again and pulling me to her as if the first orgasm I gave her barely took the edge off. I needed it slow, *wanted* it slow. She wasn't just a fuck and I wanted to take my time to prove that to her, to ensure she knew how much this meant to me, but we moved frantically, her legs parting as she pulled me over her.

She was sexy laid out beneath me, glorious when she took what she wanted.

I had a moment to pause before my dick rubbed against her still wet sex before her hands gripped my ass.

"Oh God," she moaned, head thrown back, eyes closing as I pushed into her. "Shit. That feels..."

Perfect. "Yeah." It was almost too perfect—the way our bodies aligned, the way she responded to me. The desperate need I had to claim her, to finally make my wife *mine*.

The thought alone was almost enough to send me over the edge. I was fucking my wife for the first time. And it was absolutely, one hundred and ten percent amazing.

Her body took to me like we were made for each other and I braced myself on one elbow as I slowly pushed in, pulled out. I took my time, held a hand to her hip to find the angle that would make her whimper. And as she did, her fingers tightened on my hips.

"Like that?"

"Yes. More."

More indeed. I couldn't get enough of her. The way every emotion, every sensation splayed across her face and how her body responded.

I moved my hand at her side, into her hair, tugged so her eyes met mine and then I moved. I snapped my hips against her, kissed her as she cried out, I swallowed every one of her pleasured cries and relished every sting of her nails digging into me. And hell if tugging on her hair, holding her down didn't seem to turn her on anymore.

A million ideas raced through my mind, things I'd always wanted to try. If she liked it rough, while restrained, I would give her all of that.

A vision of my wife, tied, at my mercy dripping wet and with her full breasts heaving, needy for me, flashed in my mind and it was the vision, the feel of her body beneath me as she began to lose control that shot heat down my spine, tugged up my balls and sent a rush of lust straight to the tip of my dick.

"Oh God," she cried out. "Yes!" She came, clenching my dick and I gritted my teeth to keep from coming, but I couldn't stop it.

As her body pulsed around me, sucked me deeper into

her, I slammed into her one more time and came, burying my own groans and curses into the crook of her neck.

"Holy shit," she gasped, hands finally loosening on my ass to run up my back.

"I'm sweating and probably crushing you but fuck if I can move anytime soon."

My first time having sex since my ex-wife left me, and now I was fucking my new one.

The comparison wasn't fair—and it wasn't close to being in the same ballpark.

Gabby was incredibly responsive and so into it, I could become hard again just thinking about it.

"I need to get rid of this, clean you up."

I lifted off her enough to kiss her, run my hand through her hair. "Was that... too rough?"

The last thing I wanted to do was hurt her. Physically or otherwise.

"No." She pressed her lips to my throat, my jaw, her hands still trailed up and down my spine, causing sparks to follow in her path. "It was incredible."

19

GABBY

He stepped out of the tiny bathroom, a washcloth in one hand and nudged me on my hip with his toe. "Are you going to move?"

"Not anytime soon." To prove it, I stretched, arms straight above my head and smiled up at him.

That was possibly, the best sex I'd ever had. The hard floor beneath me wasn't even a deterrent. Joey could fuck like a god, or an immortal, with unending stamina. And the way he touched me? Pleasure zinged down my spine as I remembered his hands on me.

Chuckling, he scanned my body slowly, almost like he was remembering the same things I was. Based on the smirk that curled up one corner of his lips, he was pleased.

"I think you broke me," I admitted. Ruined me at the very least, for other men.

"That's too bad." He stepped around me and grabbed a bottled water from beneath the kitchen sink. We hadn't had room to store them in the small fridge. When he came back, he was pouring a small amount of water onto the washcloth.

I froze as he bent down, squatted in front of me, and ran that cloth over the crease of my hip.

"Oh!" I jumped, the water cool enough to force goose bumps to the surface.

"Sorry," he said and proceeded to clean me.

Dear God, could he get any more perfect? "Sorry to hear I broke you." He leaned down, kissed my navel, trailed his lips over the sensitive skin on my hip bone where he lightly bit.

I flinched again, hand going to the back of his neck.

"But I hope you recover soon. I have more plans for you."

Suddenly... "I think I'm all better now." I widened my knees, rolling my hips where he continued to trace with the tip of his tongue, those gleaming eyes meeting mine, and sighed.

"Damn," I panted.

He chuckled against my skin, and moved forward, up my stomach, to the tops of my breasts and then his lips brushed over mine.

As he moved, our van swayed a bit. "It's a good thing our site is private. We were probably rocking this van quite a bit."

Joey snorted, nipped my bottom lip with his teeth. "Why do you think I chose it?"

"You—"

"Hoped." He shrugged. He had no shame.

"Well, good thinking on your part."

"I have lots of good thoughts," he teased me with more kisses, priming me. I couldn't believe I was getting turned on all over again, but there I was, arching into him, desperate to get as close as possible. At my lower stomach, he was hard again too and I reached between us and felt his desire for myself.

"We need to get the site set up," he muttered, choking over the words as I began to stroke.

"Say it more convincingly and we will," I teased, tightening my grip.

"Fuck it." He dropped to one elbow at my side, pulling my face toward him where he slid his tongue inside my mouth and kissed me like we hadn't already had the most mind-blowing sex. As he did, his hand slid down my body, finding my sex, wet and swollen and already throbbing with need for him. He found my center like he'd memorized my body and pressed two fingers in.

My eyes rolled back at the pleasure of him, his firm strokes and my hand matched his rhythm until we were kissing, the sounds of my wetness and our grunts took over. He played my body perfectly, not like it was the second time we'd done this, but we'd known each other for years.

And I responded the same, until my thighs began shaking, he added a thumb to my clit and his cock swelled in my hand.

"Yes," I chanted as he hit that spot inside me that sent shocks to my limbs. "More."

"Harder?"

"Yes." I could barely speak as he listened, learned what I liked and continued fucking my hand. I came quickly, powerfully, clawing at the floor with my free hand and increasing the speed wrapped around his dick.

He yanked his mouth off mine, shoved it to my neck and as his hot seed expelled onto my stomach, all over my hand, the sting of his teeth hit the side of my throat.

His groan was guttural as if I'd pulled it deep from his

core and rattled the van. "Shit," he rasped against my heated flesh. "You are fucking good at that."

I couldn't believe we'd just made each other come again, and so quickly.

But hell if I couldn't wait until we could do it again.

And again.

And again.

EVENTUALLY, we climbed off the floor, both of us stretching our backs and limbs. We cleaned up the mess we made all over the floor, figured out how to get the couches turned into the bed.

While Joey went outside to set up the hook-ups, I stayed in and made the bed, straightening the sheets and blankets we'd already laid on and made us a quick meat and cheese board for a snack.

There were plenty of hours of daylight left, so after we ate, we dug out the camping chairs and set them up outside near the fire pit and Joey dug out the hiking clothes he'd had delivered for us.

"I hope this all fits you," he said, as I opened the box of hiking boots. I'd given him my sizes for everything.

"I hope so too." I laced them while he took care of his, filled his small hiking pack with waters for us, sunscreen, and other essentials.

"Perfect." I wiggled my boots back and forth.

"Yeah." His tone made me look up and once our eyes met, I realized he wasn't looking—or caring—about the boots. His entire focus was on me.

"We should go," I said, but it came out breathy.

"Before I toss you over my shoulder and take you again, yeah, we absolutely should."

He grinned then and held out his hand. "Let's go see what kind of fun we can have together, Gabby."

A challenge I'd have no problem completing.

We walked through the campground, rowdier and busier than it'd been when we pulled in a couple hours ago. The sun was brutal, the heat almost unbearable, but I forced myself not to complain.

We had days of this heat, and thankfully, it would only reach the midnineties this week.

Somehow reading my mind with his superpowers, Joey glanced down at me. I was unable to see his eyes behind the sunglasses he'd thrown on and the Vipers hat he had pulled low on his forehead. "Our group hike starts at seven tomorrow morning. Hopefully we'll get through most of it before it's this painful outside."

I squeezed his hand and nodded. "I was just thinking the same thing. It's so damn hot right now."

"Shade will help."

He wasn't wrong. We found an entrance to hiking trails right off the campground and chose the three-mile "easy" trail.

As soon as we were hidden in trees and walls of red rock, the light breeze we'd had earlier picked up, cooling me even as I heated from the inside out. Most of it, solely true to Joey's presence next to me.

"Tell me something about you." He'd picked up a walking stick discarded on the path once we started and then found one for me. The clunk of the stick on the dirt path and the crunch of dirt beneath our feet were the only sounds.

"What kind of things?"

"I don't know. Anything. Favorite movie. Foods. What do you do after work? Do you like what you do?"

He rattled off the questions quickly, and it took me a minute to realize he'd been nervous in asking.

A laugh bubbled in my throat and burst free.

"What? Why are you laughing?"

I covered my mouth, still giggling and shook my head. "It's nothing. It's just... I just had sex with my husband for the first time and you don't even know those things about me. And we're married."

I stumbled over the words, my laughter getting the better of me until I was roaring with glee.

How in the hell did I get myself in these situations? Not that I regretted it. Not yet, anyway.

Joey laughed with me and nodded before his smile turned softer. "I like hearing you call me husband."

Oh. *Oh.* I'd meant it as a joke, but he was no longer joking.

I cleared my throat and focused on the trail. Ahead of us was a group of six, but we were far enough back they couldn't hear us.

"Let's see." I recalled all the questions he'd asked. "*Mean Girls* is a classic. I'm a huge pasta lover. Give me all the carbs, all the time. Usually I zone out to something on Netflix with a glass of wine while I do laundry and clean. And I *love* what I do for a living."

"*Mean Girls*?"

"It's the most iconic girl's movie of all time. Are you telling me you've never seen it?"

"Considering I'm not a girl—"

"I'm teasing. But it's good. And funny. It came out when I was young, like first grade or something. I was probably too young to watch it, but I've loved it ever since."

"And pasta?"

"I can eat it every day, it's only better when it's pasta stuffed with cheese like manicotti or ravioli. Tortellini soup..." I trailed off, my stomach rumbled. Just thinking about my pasta made my mouth water.

"Chicken parmesan is my favorite meal."

"Yeah?"

"My mom made the best food. Did you know she's Italian?"

I hadn't. Although his coloring would have made me suspect even if his brothers were blond. They'd gotten their looks from their dad, but it was clear Joey favored Sonya.

"No."

"Her great-grandparents immigrated here from Sicily in the early 1900s. They opened and owned a tiny restaurant in Little Italy when it was filled with Italian immigrants."

"That's... that's incredible. Is their restaurant still there?"

He shook his head and gestured at a sign for a lookout point. We headed that way, staying in one line as hikers leaving passed us on the narrow trail. Once we reached it, my mouth dropped.

The heat no longer bothered me.

All my worries about where I was going with my life vanished.

"Holy shit," I breathed. We were at a higher elevation and beyond and beneath us, as far as the eye could see were budding red rock walls and landscape, filled with valleys. It went off into the distance, until the red stone met blinding blue sky.

"Damn," Joey whispered next to me. So quiet, as if speaking would shatter the enormous glory in front of us.

The group of six that had been in front of us were there

too, all of us whispering if bothering to speak at all. Tears pricked my eyes.

"You okay?" Joey asked, slipping an arm behind my back and settling at my waist on the other side of him.

"Yeah." I rested my head against his shoulder. "It's overwhelming and so beautiful."

We stood there for several minutes, until we grew restless from standing still and the glaring sun had sweat dripping down my spine.

Once we were back on the trail, alone, Joey answered my earlier question. "My family's restaurant is still there, however, my grandparents sold it in the early sixties, so it has a new name and everything. But my great-great-grandparents' picture is still on the wall above the bar. My older brother John and his wife, Kara, go there occasionally especially when her family comes to town. They love to do all the touristy stuff which is what Little Italy is now."

"I've been there too. I think it's charming. Where do they live? They're still in the city, right?"

"They have a home near Central Park, near Kara's school."

Outside of seeing Jude and Joey occasionally, I'd had very little contact with his family. And yet—

"Oh my God." I clasped my hands over my mouth and pulled to an abrupt stop, gaping at Joey.

"What?"

"I just... I just realized that your family is my family. Which means Katie is my sister-in-law."

His brows jumped right before a beautiful, slow smile stretched wide. "Shit. Garrett's actually my brother now."

I fell into him, hand hitting his chest. "This is weird. So weird." When would it sink in that we were married, and actually trying to make it work? I had no doubt he wasn't still with me because of his image. The team's PR could have smoothed this over somehow. And yet he was still here, fucking me like he needed it, laughing with me, taking me on the adventure of a lifetime…

"This is one hell of a honeymoon," I said, still laughing, the hits still coming in waves.

"You're just now realizing all of this?"

"It's weird," I repeated, now matching his wide smile and laughing.

"Bad weird or good?"

He swallowed thickly, his hand at mine on his chest, thumb brushing over the back of my hand. The humor diminished.

"Good," I breathed. "I think it's a good weird."

"Me too."

He leaned down and kissed me. "You're also right. This is going to be one hell of a honeymoon."

20

———

GABBY

"We should get married," Joey said, as we both watched a newlywed groom and bride traipsing happily down the street, arm in arm, her bouquet in her hand like she'd never let go of it.

"What?" He had to be joking.

"Marry me." His hand slid into my hair until he was cupping the back of my neck. "I feel more connected to you than I have any woman, ever, including my ex-wife. Marry me."

"That's... that's crazy." He wasn't joking. His eyes were steel, unwavering.

I'd had the best time with him I'd ever had with anyone. I understood exactly what he meant. From the moment he saved me at dinner, we'd been on the same page with everything. Kids. Family. What was important in life.

But marriage? Did you get married because you could talk to someone easily?

"It's the best kind of crazy."

"I..."

He leaned in, brushed his lips over my cheek and at that first, soft touch of his body against mine, mine responded. Holy shit. A *barely there kiss from Joey and my entire body awakened with a desperate need to feel him. But still... marriage?*

"We'll have forever to figure out the rest. But we'll make it work."

"I..." I could hardly think clearly. He'd moved us, walked us backward until I was pressed against the stone building outside the Venetian. We hadn't even been inside yet to see his team and party with them. But this? Marry Joey Taylor? It was insane.

As his body pressed to mine, as he trailed his lips down to my jaw, the soft flesh behind my ear, all hesitations I had fled.

He got me. More than anyone else. We finished each other's sentences after a few hours of drinking and exploring. Hell, until I realized where we were, I'd totally forgotten we were supposed to go find his team, we'd been so consumed with each other.

"Yes," I whispered, my hand in his hair and at his side. "Yes, I'll marry you."

I woke with a start, my heart racing and sweat dripping down the back of my neck. It took a moment, more than several breaths to sit up and realize where I was.

I was sleeping on the bed. I was in the RV. Shit.

I'm in Moab.

I turned to look for Joey and instead I found a present. Joey —sleeping without the sheets on, wearing nothing but his boxer briefs and even in sleep it looked like he was smiling. His hand was settled at his abs, fingers splayed over all those bricks of muscles. The waistband of his briefs were low, showing off the V-muscle I'd spent so much time tracing last night before we fell asleep, before we did so many other things first.

He hadn't been joking when he'd said there were a lot of positions he wanted to fuck me in and after the last day, it seemed he was in a race to try them all.

I stretched my legs, the pleasant ache at the apex of my

thighs reminding me. I'd been on my knees, he'd yanked me so my back was to his chest and while he'd pounded into me with long, hard thrusts, his fingers had worked my clit until I'd almost drawn blood from biting down to contain my screams.

But it wasn't the memories of our sexcapades that had my heart racing.

"He'd proposed to *me,*" I said, itching to reach out and touch him. Wake him.

It hadn't hit me until that dream I hoped to hell was a memory.

"What was that?" Joey grunted. His head shifted on the pillow and one eye slid open. "What'd you just say?"

"I didn't mean to wake you."

"I'm glad you did. You look..." His other eye opened and they both squinted. "You look upset."

"I'm not." And I wasn't. Relieved, maybe? "I dreamed you proposed to me, like a memory."

A tiny frown marred his sleepy face. "That makes sense since we're married."

"I guess." How did I explain this? I grabbed the hair tie Joey had torn out of my hair last night and thrown to the floor. Wrapping up my hair, I said, "I guess, considering I'm prone to foolish things, I thought this was all my idea. But it wasn't."

He propped himself up on his elbow and I had to fight the urge to grab my phone. Take a hundred photos of him posed like this, with all that sexy, sleepy hair messed up, the slow spread of his smile and the rhythmic rise and fall of his chest. "I don't think you're foolish."

"Well I'm not," I teased. "Since this was all your idea."

"But not a bad one."

He'd said almost the same thing to me yesterday on our hike. Good weird or bad. Good idea or bad.

I ran my hands through his hair and kissed his forehead. "Not bad, I guess I'm surprised. Getting drunk and thinking it was *funny* to get married does seem like something I'd do. But you wanted this. You—"

"Don't." He reached up and covered my mouth with his hand. "Don't tell me. I want to remember it on my own."

"But..." What if he didn't?

"I will." How did he *do* that? He dropped his hand and smirked. "Now, do you want to know what I dreamed of last night, because it was similar to this... us, in a bed—but you were wearing nothing but a smile. I could show you... in fact, yes, I think it's better if I did."

He reached for me and I smacked his hand away, shoved his chest so he fell to his back.

"You're insane." I laughed and climbed out of the bed. "And we need to get ready for the hike."

"Later?" I'd had my back to him and when I turned, I forgot everything. My name. My reason for pushing him away.

He had his arms bent, hands behind his head, and his arousal, thick and large—and now I knew how good he tasted—was tenting his briefs. Unashamedly ready and spread out for me.

And dear God—that smirk twisting his lips. I wanted to take back my words just so I could kiss that look off him.

Instead, I bent down and grabbed his shirt and flung it at his face. I could focus better with it hidden.

"I'm using the restroom."

"Later then?" he called out.

"Obviously yes," I replied, and closed the door to the bathroom, such as it was.

His laugh reverberated through the van.

That man. Sex with him might just end up being the death of me. But what a perfect way to go, with all that passion, all that thickness, and all that smile and body being the last thing I'd see.

"WOULD you like me to take your picture?"

I smiled at the woman, close to my mom's age, and then held out my phone. I'd been trying to take a decent selfie of Joey and I and the canyons in the background and we'd failed.

"Thank you, that'd be wonderful."

Joey kissed my temple, wrapped me in his arms.

The woman, with her thick, blonde hair piled on her head and wearing army green khaki shorts and a cream tank top, smiled as she took several pictures, telling us to smile each time. Behind her, a handsome man gazed at her in that way he knew everything about her but couldn't stand to stop discovering more. He looked like he spent his time in an office with that slicked to the side hair, only a hint of gray at his temples. His green eyes crinkled at the edges as he rolled his eyes at his wife, possibly her over willingness to help, like it annoyed him and he thought it was the cutest thing at the same time.

Wow. Their love was tangible, and I'd only seen the way he looked at her with her back turned.

My heart pinched as she handed me back my phone. "Thank you," I told her.

"No problem. I'm Andrea and this is my husband, Corey." She shoved her thumb behind her and started walking, like she knew we'd follow. Like she was used to people following her lead.

I did, because there was something about her sweet smile and the fine lines at the corners of her eyes that made her so approachable. "Are you two newlyweds?"

Had I fallen into a time warp where everyone could read my thoughts?

"We are," Joey said behind me, and like me, he'd simply followed Andrea like there was no choice to refuse. He and Corey introduced themselves. "This is actually our honeymoon."

"I thought so," Andrea said and turned to him. "And you are...?"

"Joey Taylor. This is my wife, Gabby."

"Lovely to meet you. Corey and I are out here celebrating our twentieth anniversary, aren't we dear?"

She barely glanced at him. But I looked harder. His lips curled and that same glimmer in his eyes sparkled. "Best twenty years of my life."

She didn't scoff, like he'd said it teasingly. Instead, her hand went to his heart and she grinned at me. "Best man I ever met, knew it the moment I saw him on our college campus."

He kicked a stone out of the path. "Please don't tell them this story..."

It was too late. Andrea was already starting. "See, I was in a sorority, and we were having a house party. I saw this guy" —she nodded her head in his direction— "on the main quad on campus. He was talking to some friends, laughing, had a frisbee in his hands like they were getting ready to waste time on a Friday afternoon instead of heading to class."

"That's because it was Friday and we *were* skipping class to hang out."

She shook her head playfully. "Anyway, I had a few invites left, and I wasn't quite so sure what it was about him—"

"Besides the fact I was the sexiest man you'd ever seen."

"There was that." She nudged me with her hip playfully. "So hot. Best looking man I ever saw, but I think it was the smile that made me go to him. It was so... open. Not cocky like other college guys, you know?"

"I do." I hadn't gone to college, but I knew the look. The bars were full of guys with that look, like the world owed them something just because they'd been fortunate enough to be born with a decent strand of DNA.

"So, I walked right up to him—"

"In front of my group of friends."

"Because I had no shame and he was that good looking," she finished, shooting him a playful glare. "So I held out the invitation and told him I wanted him to come to the party, and do you know what that jerk did?"

Behind me, Corey chuckled, shaking his head as if he was remembering that moment, and was still embarrassed.

Joey's brows rose. "What?"

Andrea settled her hand on my arm and gave me a quick squeeze before letting go. "He told me that he hated the Greeks and wouldn't step foot into a house if his life depended on it."

"You did?" I turned, asked Corey.

He shrugged. "Just wait. It gets better."

"What'd you say?" I asked her. Why I was so invested in their story, I had no idea, except Andrea had an aura about her that pulled you in. And I was hooked.

"I held out the invitation and told him then it was a good

thing I was French and English, and if he didn't come to see me, it'd be his biggest regret and I didn't think he looked like a fool, but if he didn't want to get to know me, he was one. He made no move to reach for the invite, so I dropped it, let it fall to the ground and I left."

Wow. The confidence in this woman. I barked out a laugh. "Did you go?" I asked him.

"No he did *not*," Andrea answered for him. "And I didn't see him again for weeks on campus which really fired me up because I had the perfect speech planned for him if I ever saw him again."

Based on the fire in her eyes, I had no doubt. We reached a narrow path on the trail, where we had to go single-file again and as we moved into a line, Andrea reached behind her and took my hand.

"So how'd you two get together?"

Behind us, Corey bringing up the rear as Andrea and I squinted at the bright sky filtering down the narrow canyon, red rock walls so high they seemed to go on forever, said, "I went up to her in the student union a few weeks later. First time I'd seen her in two and I couldn't resist."

"Really?" I asked.

"This *fool*," Andrea started. "Sat right down across from me, tossed his bag on the seat next to him. He leaned forward like he had a right to be in my space after he blew me off, and said, without a single hesitation, '*I haven't been able to stop thinking about you. You're right, I'm a fool and I regret not going. So how about you let me walk you to your next class and take you out to dinner tonight?*'"

My eyes widened with surprise. "And that worked?"

She shrugged, like it was nothing, like they weren't still living their happily ever after all these years later. "I'd told him he'd be a fool not to get to know me, and I figured I'd be one too. So yeah I went. Never regretted it for a single moment after."

"We were married eight months later," Corey said. "Everyone thought we were too young to be married at twenty-two years old, barely knowing each other. Our friends—"

"Your friends—"

Corey chuckled. "Fine, my friends placed bets on how soon we'd be divorced."

"But here we are, twenty years and four kids later."

Tears pricked my eyes. Their happiness was almost as blinding as the sun.

"That's a beautiful story," Joey murmured. "Incredible really."

Andrea grinned at him. "When you know, you know, and I knew the second my eyes landed on him across that quad he was meant for me. Sometimes life is crazy and happens that way." She gestured to the two of us, her smile widening. "Like you two. You two remind me of us. All your sweet smiles and holding on to each other with those lovey-dovey looks. That's why I wanted to take your picture so badly, so you can remember how you feel together right now. Whatever you feel right now, don't lose it, because daily life will try to tug at it until you've forgotten this feeling."

I turned away to wipe away my tears. Maybe she wasn't clairvoyant with other people like she'd been in her own relationship. We weren't them. We couldn't be.

I couldn't find the words to explain and I wouldn't. No way would I pop her happy little bubble with the truth, and besides, I'd most likely never see this couple again.

Although I had no doubt the impression she left was something I'd remember forever.

"Thank you," Joey said, his voice gravelly like he was thinking the same as me. As the path widened, he stepped to my side and took my hand, giving me a gentle squeeze before settling his hand at my lower back. "That's sweet of you."

Andrea shrugged again. "It's the truth. And hey, since we're staying at the same campsite. Want to join us for drinks later? I have bottles of wine in our cooler that need to get emptied before the ice melts."

She had me at drinks. Wine was a no-brainer.

I glanced at Joey for confirmation.

"We'd like that," he confirmed.

The rest of the hike lasted two hours. We spent the time walking with Andrea and Corey, laughing. Eventually, Corey asked Joey if he was the Joey Taylor he thought he was. Turned out Corey grew up in Michigan, a huge hockey fan, before he and Andrea met in college at Purdue. We talked about our upcoming trip, our plans for Michigan and he gave us restaurants to stop at and enjoy at Mackinac Island and Grand Rapids.

By the time our hike was done and we trudged back to camp in need of a wash-up and food before meeting them later, Andrea and I had exchanged numbers, she'd followed me on TikTok, and I felt like I'd known her forever.

I WAS tipsy on wine and high on life as Joey and I stumbled back to the RV. We'd spent hours with Andrea and Corey, and despite the twenty-year age differences between us, I'd decided she was my new big sister and I wanted to be her when I grew up. With them currently living in Minnesota, I had no idea when our paths would cross, if ever again in person, but I had no doubt Andrea would keep in touch.

I was still laughing at the stories she'd shared of her children when we reached our van.

"I like them," I said, still giggling as we stepped inside.

"I do too. They're good people. But mostly, I like you," Joey said.

I spun slowly until I faced him. His tone was so serious, his expression so intense, I immediately sobered.

I wasn't quite sure *like* was what he meant.

"Good." I nodded. "I like you too." I tried for aloof, but based on the predatory gleam in his eyes, I failed.

"Do you?"

"Yep." I backed up as he prowled closer. Already my body was responding. It didn't even take a touch from him. One look and I was ready. Willing. Wanting. Desperate for his hands and mouth on me, inside of me.

Andrea had given me a dream to shoot for—*never let this feeling fade*.

I doubted she meant *this* particular feeling, but if I could feel like this forever, I'd never be sad again.

Or alone.

21

———

GABBY

The first hotel we stayed at was in Milwaukee. Tomorrow, we'd board a ferry to take us across Lake Michigan. Yesterday and the day before, we'd slept in the RV in truck stops, able to use full-size showers and enjoy running water for a change of pace, but nothing could beat an actual hotel.

I stood outside the door, a bag over my shoulder, two at our feet, as Joey used his phone to electronically unlock the door. At the click, he opened it, kicked one of the suitcases on the floor into the doorway so the door didn't close on us as we entered.

"Oh my God," I groaned as soon as I saw the bed. Even better, there was a hot tub in the corner overlooking the lake. It was early afternoon and had taken us five hours on the road to get there after we left the Amish Village in Iowa where we'd stayed last night and spent the day visiting.

I could now say I had experience building a barn, but no joke—the Amish could *party* when the work was done.

Joey and I both woke up with the headache to prove it, eased only by the way he slowly slid into me from behind on the bed. He'd woken me slowly, aroused me at a much quicker pace, and by the time we both orgasmed, my headache was a distant memory.

But now... a *bed*.

"A king-sized bed," I muttered. I could weep with joy.

Behind me, bags thumped to the floor and the door slammed shut. Joey was at my back in a second, his arms wrapping around my front. I was still gazing at the bed like it was heaven-sent and Joey must have had the same thought.

"I have loved every night I've spent with you in tents and the RV, but I am fucking hard at the thought of finally being able to have you in a real bed."

He proved it by rocking into me, his thick hardness I knew so well pressed against my lower back.

Oh yeah. I wanted that too. Wanted it in a way I wasn't sure the desire would ever die.

But first things first.

I turned to face him and stepped closer to the bed. If I didn't get my eyes off it, I might fall face-first into it and collapse. We had plans later to explore the city, go out for dinner. I would even be able to wear one of the few dresses I'd brought on the trip.

Granted, it was probably a wrinkled mess from being jammed into my duffel bag, but that's why irons were invented.

Joey followed my steps until he was almost leaning on the bed. He reached out his hand, brushed the fluffy, thick white cover looking as soft as clouds.

"Do you want that? Because I have ideas for you—bent over this bed. On your knees on it. Riding me without the fear of burns on your knees."

I smirked at that. Needless to say, the bed in the RV

wasn't the *softest*. More firm leather we'd learned the hard way more than once.

I pointed a finger at him and scowled. "Keep that thought alive, then, handsome, because I would shank you right now for first dibs in the shower."

"We could do that together."

I shoved him in his chest, hard enough he fell to the bed. Laughing, he pushed up to his elbows, one of his hands reached down and he groaned as he rubbed his erection, obvious beneath his athletic shorts.

Hot damn—my husband had the best dick on Earth. I couldn't lose focus, though. I tore my eyes off one of my favorite parts of him and met his gaze. "I need to shave... *all* the important places." I should have had a wax done before we left. If only there was time.

Joey waggled his brows. "Will I get to see the final results?"

"Only if you're good."

"What if I want to be naughty?"

A shiver danced down my spine. One he noticed that made his fists curl into the covers of the bedding. The shower *could* wait. He hadn't seemed to mind the hair I was growing *everywhere.*

"How naughty are we talking?" And dear God, when did my voice turn that... husky?

Joey's eyes narrowed and he licked his bottom lip slowly before pulling it into his mouth. "Go shower and after we've both cleaned up, I'll show you how filthy we can get."

My knees almost buckled, but I made it to the bathroom, overheated and wet before I ever stepped foot into the hot water from the shower's spray.

That man—he was deadly.

"DAMN YOU," I rasped.

Joey hadn't been kidding. As soon as he got out of the shower and dried off, he dropped the towel and lunged straight for me.

I'd been at the windows, my back to him although I'd caught sight of his naked reflection in the window right before he grabbed my waist. I was tossed into the air, limbs spread wide on the bed and Joey didn't give me a moment to move before his mouth was at my sex.

Gone were the tender, quiet moments of exploration like this morning. Joey dropped to his knees, grabbed my hips and yanked me to the edge of the bed, devouring me like he hadn't been eating me every day for a week now.

I was so close, my hands fisted into the covers beneath me where he'd commanded I leave them. His arm was braced over my hips, pressing me to the bed. I could do nothing but take his mouth driving me to the brink of insanity and two of his fingers shoved deep inside of me, fucking me slow but hard with every thrust, twisting them in a way that made me squirm beneath them.

I was so damn close. My body was electrified. Nerves were on fire when he pulled back and stood.

Naked, his dick rising up to his stomach, he took himself in hand.

"You hurt your husband's feelings earlier." He feigned a pout that would have had me rolling my eyes if I wasn't considering all the ways to currently murder him.

"What?"

"I wanted to watch you shower."

"You can do it now. Just please... finish this." I reached

down, removed my hands from the covers and ran a finger over my slit. "Holy shit," I groaned.

I was *drenched.*

He smacked my hand away. "That's mine. And I told you to keep your hands on the bed."

"You're cruel. A sadistic bastard, you know that?"

But hot damn, why was his bossiness making my sex pulse and throb with need? "I want to taste you too." I licked my lips, mouth gone dry at the sight of his hard dick, proud, so thick, sticking straight out from him.

He tilted his head to the side and smirked. "Do you?"

"Yes. Please." Who was this woman I was becoming? I couldn't remember ever begging for sex, or to give a blow job. Yeah, I liked sex, even liked taking the time to pleasure a man. But this desperate need? Never.

"On your knees then, facing me."

A shiver whipped down my spine, making my fingertips tingle. Hot damn, this bossy side of him did crazy things to my body.

I listened, dragging my body to the center of the bed and I lifted up on my knees. "Like this?"

He stood still, all that naked and hard flesh on display for me, driving me insane with lust, but his expression wasn't faring that much better. I drifted my own hand over my breasts, down my stomach, and I was about to reach my slit when Joey arched a brow.

"Didn't I just tell you not to do that?"

"Technically, you said it was yours." I dipped a finger inside, lips parting on a whimper as I felt my own heat and need. "So take it."

A feral gleam reached his eyes before he pounced. He moved so quickly, adjusted us so I was arching over him, and he yanked me down to his mouth with one hand while his other went to my shoulder blades and pushed me forward.

I collapsed onto the bed, my hands hitting right outside his hips to brace myself and then everything I was lusting after was right there, in front of me.

I took him into my mouth right as he speared me with his tongue and both of us elicited groans so deep and loud they might have been illegal in at least thirteen countries. My thighs were already shaking and my spine shook with desire as I took him deeper, wrapped a hand around his base and tried—oh, I tried so hard to stay still while he devoured me, but it was useless.

As soon as Joey got his mouth on me, my body was primed and ready for the finale.

He added fingers and I swallowed him as deep as I could, until he bumped the back of my throat and I tried to open to take him further but with him driving me absolutely mindless, his finger at my clit, his mouth on me, his tongue driving me absolutely insane, focusing on him was useless. My orgasm hit me so fast, took me by surprise, I tore my mouth off him to cry out, my body shaking as I came, dripped juices down my thighs, mixed with Joey's mouth. All I could do was dig into the mattress covers beneath me until the first edges of the powerful climax began to recede.

"Shit," I gasped, my body alive and sated, and yet still, there was more. A pulse deep beneath me that craved more of this, his attention and his strokes and the way he worked me so expertly.

I was just starting to come down, and I settled my mouth at his tip, licking him, wanting to make it as good for him as he did me, when his thumb brushed through my slit, and then... up to the rear of my creases until he hit me *there*.

I jumped, startled, and looked at him over my shoulder.

"You ever?"

"No." And holy shit, who had stolen my voice and replaced it with some husky, porn star voice.

He pressed again, gently but firmly and shoots of excitement spread outward.

"Oh…"

My eyes flared wide at the sensation.

"Do you want to try it?" As he asked, he licked his lips. He wanted this. But he was patient, waiting, even as he teased me there before gathering more moisture and slowly sliding his thumb back to my other hole.

Did I? The sensations he was creating scrambled my brain.

He pulled back. "It's okay—"

"Yes," I gasped. I wanted it. Him. In all the ways and everywhere. Hell, I could trust him with this. "I do want it."

As soon as I gave him my answer, he grabbed my hips, yanked me back toward him. He shoved his tongue into my sex, making me cry out. My fingernails dug into his thighs, making him grunt and I lost total concentration on his dick as he trailed his tongue up my crease, toward the back, and then his tongue was *there.*

"Oh my God!"

It was wet. Strange. And yet as he prodded my hole back there, it felt so damn *amazing* I wasn't sure if I should jump off him or suffocate the poor man.

"I need you lubed," he muttered, and dragged his finger down to my opening, gathered the juices running down my thighs and then one finger brushed over the tightly puckered ring.

I burrowed my face to the base of his cock, licking it as an animalistic groan was yanked from my throat.

"Good?"

"I don't…"

And then he pushed. Gently. His finger prodded my entrance and as I let loose a guttural sound, I cried out, "Yes. Oh my God. So good."

"Good. Now get back to sucking my cock before you come again."

"I can't—"

"You can."

How in the hell did he know? I went to ask but he stole my vocabulary, pushing his finger deeper inside me, his mouth back at my sex. I was strung so damn tight. I did what he told me to and wrapped my hand around his base, lifted enough until I could suck his tip into my mouth.

"Fuck," he grunted, his own groans vibrated against me, drove me wild and then there was more pressure, another finger I realized, entering me there. It stung, burned like a dozen bee stings and then it was…

"Fucking amazing," I muttered around his dick.

He thrust his hips harder, shoving him deeper into me. I was held steady by his fingers in my ass and his mouth sucking my clit, and I was absolutely *losing my mind.*

This orgasm was different. It hit me slowly, started where his fingers were and then tore out from my center to my limbs until I was mindless, shaking with desperation and satisfaction. I sucked him all the way as I came, past my gag reflex, breathing through my nose even while sounds still tried to escape my throat. As I swallowed around him, I reached down to grip his balls.

He came on a wild shout, thrusting into me until my eyes watered and his seed shot straight down my throat. He came in long bursts, emptying himself while my orgasm continued to roll through me, until we were both breathless, until he gently moved me off him. He rolled us onto our sides, my head on his hip.

He propped on his side while trailing the line and curve of my body with a calloused fingertip. The delicious scrape of his rough hand over my soft skin elicited another shiver.

"I take it you liked that?"

For a moment, he looked nervous, right before he wiped it away with a cocky smirk.

"I'll let you know when I can think again."

He leaned forward, kissed my hip bone and I climbed up onto the bed so I was next to him. He immediately took me in his arms, held me to him and kissed my forehead.

"I think you're incredible, Gabby. Everything I learn about you makes me want you more and it's not just because of all the things we just did."

I wanted to answer, wanted to respond with something witty and equally impactful, but I blinked heavily, closed my eyes and was asleep before I'd figured out how to string words together again.

22

JOEY

I woke to sunlight peeking in through the curtains. It was late afternoon, and my limbs were loose as well as sore from the exertion earlier. Next to me, Gabby was still curled into me in the same position as she'd fallen asleep.

I'd managed to throw the covers over us, keeping us both warm. After I'd made sure she wouldn't wake up cold, I joined her in a nap.

Now, the scent of wild sex from earlier still lingered... in the air... on our skin. Gabby's quiet puffs of breath were the only sounds around other than the muted car traffic outside.

We'd planned on a night out, managing to actually have a reason to get dressed up nice and go to dinner and while I'd already mapped out several restaurants I wanted to try, more than anything I wanted to order in, spend the night alone.

The more I got to know Gabby, the less I wanted to share her.

I wouldn't do that to her, though. As much as she obviously loved camping and being in nature, she'd talked about her excitement for having a reason to get dressed up and do her hair and makeup for days now. She was definitely looking forward to this stop before we returned to the camper lifestyle on the beaches of Michigan's western coast. We'd be there three days before heading north to Torch Lake and then traveling east to go to Mackinac Island.

From there, we were supposed to head south to my brother in North Carolina.

Our trip was over a week from ending before we grabbed Route 66 and heading back west toward Vegas. We'd figured by then we'd be ready to get back, so while we were staying in camping areas, there wasn't a lot of sightseeing planned. We'd be on the road three days to get back after our stop in Georgia and the Bavarian Village only a few hours from Jason and Jude, but already it felt like it was coming too fast.

Too soon, I'd be back to off-season training, spending my days in the practice arena with the team, and my nights and weekends at the baseball fields. I'd be back to making sure Malley's ran smoothly. I looked forward to the slower pace all season, especially this summer since our time off would be drastically reduced.

But right then, with Gabby next to me, I wanted to extend the trip. Keep traveling. Keep staying off the radar and social media. Neither of us had looked, the benefit of camping in mountains and national parks and Amish areas with little to zero cell phone service. Hell, I hadn't even checked in with my family yet, something I figured both of us should do while we could. At least let them know we were alive, and when Jude should expect us.

I wanted more time with her before I had to share her. Before we had to face the reality of returning to Vegas and the uncertainty of what she'd want when this ended.

As for me, it'd been nine days with my wife. She might have been a woman I barely knew eleven days ago, but now, I couldn't imagine not being with her every day, all day long. She made traveling fun and easy. She made it easy to laugh. She tempted me with every sway of her hips and every excited expression she had when she saw something on the road she liked.

Gabby brought life back to me when I needed it, but she gave me so much more—so much I didn't realize had been missing before either.

How in the hell would I let her go at the end of this if she asked for it?

I was falling in love with my wife, and I had no idea if she felt the same for me.

Falling to my back, a heavy sigh escaped, enough that Gabby's hand on my stomach jolted.

"That didn't sound like a happy sound," she murmured, and her eyes fluttered open. "How long have you been awake?"

"Few minutes." My fingers found her hair and ran through her thick, silky locks. "Sleep well?"

"Like the dead. How long was I out?"

"Couple of hours. I think we both probably needed a decent bed."

"Especially when it came with all that before stuff."

I chuckled. "*Before stuff?*"

"You know what I mean. I don't think my hips will work right for a week."

"If you expect me to feel bad about that, I don't. I'm going to replay earlier in my mind forever."

A slow shiver rolled through her, making her curl into me.

She'd gotten off on all of it. And holy hot damn, it'd been some of the hottest sex ever.

"I'd never done that," I said, softly, wanting her to know. "I don't know where that came from, but I want you to know that. I just... I needed to claim all of you."

If she was surprised by my admission, she didn't show it.

Instead, she kissed my chest, wrapped her arm over me more tightly. "I liked it. A lot. And I'm glad we shared that experience."

My heart thumped wildly against my rib cage. She understood. Good. I'd hoped she knew how much it meant to me, that she trusted me with the most private parts of her, but it wasn't even that she was willing or trusting, it was how vibrant she was, how much she enjoyed everything we did.

Beneath the soft brushes of her hand, coupled with the memories, my dick started to harden and I shoved a hand beneath the covers to cover myself. "We need to get out of this bed before I take you again." She had me harder faster, more often than I'd remembered being in years. "I think both our bodies need a rest."

"Yeah." She laughed softly, her warm breath skating over my skin. "That's probably a good idea." She stretched and groaned, flinched in pain and then faced me. "I'm going to need to start working out to be able to handle all your stamina."

"Get up." I laughed. "If we don't get out of this bed, I won't be taking you out for dinner. I'll be *eating in* instead."

I let that linger, eyes heating with my thoughts until Gabby laughed and climbed off me, jumping out of bed with another cringe.

I'd feel bad for hurting her, for making her sore—but I kept thinking of how she came when I had my fingers lodged in her ass.

What would it be like if she allowed *all* of me there?

I grabbed my dick and squeezed, painfully so. Seriously, when was the last time I thought about sex this much? I might have been in my prime, but I'd never felt this desperate desire for someone—couldn't ever remember this intense feeling even with Lenora.

"I'm going to shower," Gabby said, standing naked at the edge of the bed, completely confident in how my gaze trailed over her body. "Want to join me this time?"

Hell yes I did. Absolutely.

I TOOK a sip of my old-fashioned, while across from me at The Grille, the restaurant Gabby had ended up deciding on, she scanned the menu. She'd taken time after our shower to do her hair, curl it, and put on makeup. I'd become so used to seeing her beautiful when she was natural, the effect of her all done up and wearing a sexy, skimpy little black dress and heels almost undid me.

She looked how she'd done the night we were married, the night I'd sat next to her at dinner and put a stop to her mom's questioning. It was no wonder why I wanted to marry her that night.

She was sinfully beautiful, mouthwateringly sexy all done up, but I now knew she was even more perfect without any of it. She carried herself with a grace, even while perusing the menu, tapping her freshly painted fingernails to the stem of her wineglass.

I could have stared at her all day and never once grown bored. I discovered something new every time. Tonight, there was the faintest purple mark at the base of her neck— caused by me in the shower when she'd wrapped her hand around my hard dick and gotten me off while insisting she was too sore for me to return the favor. She'd dropped to her knees, right before I came, opened her mouth and took all of me like she craved it as much as I was craving the taste of her.

I'd hauled her back to her feet, slammed my mouth to her and kissed her so passionately, all over, I'd left more than one bruised marking.

I didn't even give a shit. Hickeys should stop being cool in high school but I liked the fact she not only didn't cover my mark, but I swore she kept draping her hair off her shoulder in order to show it off more. More than once, I'd caught her running her finger over that area, grinning at me like she was definitely remembering me leaving it.

Fun, yes. My wife was made for me, perfect for me in every way. And I knew so little about her.

She glanced at me, caught sight of where I'd been staring and a slow grin curled her lips at the corner. "You're awfully proud of yourself for this, aren't you?"

"I'm proud to be the man who gets to sit across from you, enjoying your company."

Her eyes widened in surprise. I wouldn't take it back. From this day on, I wanted her to know everything I felt for her, all the time, so there was never a doubt in her mind that when it came to us, this marriage—I was all in. Not because I didn't want to be twice divorced before I was twenty-seven, but because I wanted this with her.

"Joey—" she rasped, and then stopped, taking a sip of her wine. "I'm happy to be here with you too, you know. And it's because you're *you*, not some hockey player or anything." She blinked rapidly several times, like she was embarrassed, or said the wrong thing and I went to ask her about it, but she continued. "I just think you should know that. That I like *you* and it has nothing to do with your money or anything like that."

"Thank you, but for the record, I never considered anything else. It's nice to hear though."

"Good." She flashed a tentative smile and went back to the menu.

My tongue burned to ask where that came from, but as our waiter strolled to the table and we placed our orders, I let that go. I knew there were women out there who chased professional athletes for their money, for potential fame or whatever, but to be honest, most of the guys I'd met in pro sports had met their wives in high school or college. Before we became famous. The vast majority were more firmly planted with morals and ethics than I think people imagined.

I'd known Gabby's family too long to think she'd be anything different. Knew her so much better now, but still not enough.

Once the waiter left, I took another sip of my drink and leaned my forearms on the table. "If you could do anything in your life, professionally, would you change or do anything different?"

I knew she did hair. Based on how she could make herself up, I had no doubt she was successful. But I'd never fully learned why she'd been in Vegas for so long.

She sipped her wine, smiling around the rim of her glass. "No one's ever asked me that."

I raised my brows, waiting.

"No." She shook her head. "I love my job. I love taking care of women, making them feel beautiful. I don't provide a service that people dread going to, but it's the highlight of their week, month sometimes. I get to make them feel like the most special woman in the world and I think a lot of women, moms especially, don't take enough time for themselves, so it's my honor when they trust me to do it."

"I'd never thought of it like that." And yet, I was stunned at her truth of it. I suppose she was right. Lenora had always had a bounce in her step when she returned from the salon. Like she felt freer. I'd never quite understood why until then. "So are you working in Seattle? Because..."

"No. I was pretty much forced to quit shortly before I came to Vegas."

"Why?"

She sighed, ran her fingernail along the stem of her wineglass. "It's a long story but mostly it was simply due to construction. The road around where I'd been working had been under construction for so long we lost foot traffic, clients who were traveling into the city to see me started finding parking difficult. We lost a lot of business and the construction kept getting pushed back. Eventually, the owner decided to close, look into moving until it was done but that would have meant for me, losing even more clients, so I told them all I was leaving and I'd let them know where I landed."

"So you were fired?"

"No. Estella owned the salon. She rented out the stations. So I'm mostly self-employed, I just have to pay rent to use her space."

"And now that you're not working?"

"I have money," she said, too quickly, too harshly. I jerked at the tone, the fierceness of it.

"I wasn't implying you didn't."

"Shit." Her eyes squeezed close and she blew out a breath. "I'm sorry. It's that money is a big source of contention in my family." She paused, pushed her lips to one side. "Garrett paid for my apartment."

She shot me a wary expression I didn't understand.

"If that's supposed to mean something to me, you're going to have to be more clear."

Fingers tapped on the table, another drink... a flip of her hair over her shoulder. "My mom hated that he took care of me. Said he should have let me figure things out for myself, but he offered. And then insisted. I was just getting done with school and only nineteen. I didn't want to be working full-time and living with my mom but I didn't have the clientele to move out yet, so Garrett went and rented me an apartment."

"I still don't get why that's a bad thing."

Our server appeared, sliding salads in front of us and brought us both a second drink. All the while, Gabby looked like she was ready to bolt, to not endure another moment of this conversation even if I still didn't get what had her so upset about it.

Once the server left us, Gabby speared her salad with her fork and then sighed, setting it down.

Whatever was bothering her, had been eating at her for a while.

She leaned back in her chair, cupping her wineglass like a safety net. "My mom got pissed I agreed to let him lease my apartment for me, even though I'd told him not to and even though he did it without me knowing. It wasn't even a lavish place or anything, like, had I been a bit more settled, I could have easily afforded it on my own—and I could now, except Garrett always insisted he wanted me comfortable. But my mom never let me live it down that I was taking advantage of him. So, I don't know... I want something of my own. My *own* salon. I'm tired of leeching off Garrett and I'm tired of blowing away the rent money." She took a large swallow, cringing as she swallowed. "To your earlier question, I would never choose to do something different, I *love* what I do. What I want though, is something of mine. Something I own through my own hard sweat and hard work. I want a small, full-service salon with just one or two other stylists and then a staff for massages and facials and nails, but I want it to keep a small-town feel. Like the old-time barbershops you see in movies where someone walks in and everyone knows them."

Her eyes lit up as she explained her dream, and hot damn, she was as passionate about her career as I was mine. So damn sexy, the way her eyes glistened and she got choked up. I wanted to reach across the table and kiss her and promise her I'd give her all of that just to see her living her dream every day.

"So, what's stopping you?"

23

GABBY

What was stopping me?

Me.

For as much as I could sit across from Joey and tell him all the things I wanted, I was a dreamer. Not a doer. I loved the idea of all of those things but I'd never once sat down to figure out the logistics and make a plan.

Most likely I had some serious mommy issues. Refusing to follow and chase my goal and dreams because in doing so, I'd have to do exactly what she'd always told me to do.

Make a plan. Stick to it. See something, for God's sake, through to fruition. And every time I started researching, disappointment set in.

I didn't have the equity to purchase something. I didn't have the age or experience or down payment for a small business loan.

I had nothing but dreams and wishes and wants.

"I don't want to stay in Seattle. I'm tired of the constant clouds and dreary weather. Don't get me wrong. I love the Puget Sound and being close to the mountains. Every year I act like a tourist and get in some whale watching, but I want something slower. Something brighter. I want warmth and sun and I want to have my own community. I haven't found that there..."

A look flashed in his eyes I didn't recognize, and he asked, "Do you know where you want to be then? At all?"

Las Vegas. With you. The realization slammed into me so hard I almost jolted from the truth. But that couldn't be, could it? I couldn't know that so desperately in my soul so quickly. It had to be another rash thought, high on the insane sex and his broad shoulders with all that dark hair sitting across from me, so tempting.

Yeah... I'd want to stay with Joey. What woman wouldn't?

But wouldn't that mean I was just jumping from having one man take care of me to another?

So I opened my mouth, and I lied.

"I don't know yet."

"I see." He stabbed at his salad like it'd personally offended him, but I knew the truth. It wasn't the food. It was me, and I longed to rip the words back, tell him everything I was thinking.

I might have always been a look before you jump kind of person, but this time, I was certain I jumped right into someone who would always catch me.

But wasn't it time I started trying to catch myself first?

I couldn't bear to stand the way his expression had tightened, shoulders tensed. Much less face what I was only now learning about myself.

I wiped my mouth with my napkin and resettled it in my lap. "What about you? If you weren't playing hockey, what would you do?"

His eyes narrowed for a moment, before marginally relaxing.

Thankfully, he gave me the out and moved on. Apparently he wasn't interested in dissecting my statements either. Thank goodness. I was far from ready.

"I just finished my master's degree last year in Kinesiology and Exercise Science."

"What?"

"Yeah. I've been taking online classes for a while now, doing lab work in the off-season. So last winter, I finally got my degree. A back-up, you know, in case I get injured."

"What would you do with it?"

"Sports trainer for a team, professional, I'd hope. But I also think college-aged athletes would be a blast to work with."

"That's... that must have been a lot of work."

He shrugged like it was no biggie, but I was impressed. I'd always struggled in school, never wanted to go to college only to struggle for four more years. I'd been nervous enough knowing I'd have to take a certification exam after finishing cosmetology school. But to have the demanding job he had and *still* manage to get his master's?

Impressive. Like so much else about him.

AFTER DINNER, we walked around Milwaukee, ducked into a piano bar where there were dueling pianos driving the crowd crazy with excitement and taking requests.

We laughed and danced, had another drink, but still weren't nearly drunk and by the time we got back to the hotel, both of us were exhausted.

Which meant when Joey woke me up again, it felt like it was only twenty minutes later, and I was a grumpy, grouchy wife.

"We need to get going," he whispered in my ear.

I swatted him away like a pesky fly. "Go away."

"Can't." He kissed my cheek and then the delicious scrape of his cropped scruffy beard followed. "We need to be at the ferry by five-thirty and it's a twenty-minute drive."

"We just fell asleep." If he wanted me out of this bed, he'd have to carry me. *Finally* I was in a comfortable bed that hugged me while I slept and the covers were so soft, so cozy. I didn't care it was a bed in a hotel in the middle of Wisconsin, it was my new home. Maybe I could open a salon here.

"We fell asleep six hours ago." It sounded like there was a smile on his face as he said it.

"So tired. So sore—and it's all your fault."

He chuckled and footsteps fade away. "I'll give you five more minutes, but we need to get moving."

I was an early riser, surprisingly since my job never started before ten in the morning, but a week of camping and bright sunny mornings and hard as rock beds had done me in. I might as well have been in my sixties, for as much as my bones ached.

Or rather... that could be blamed on Joey too.

I rolled to my back, stretching, still unable to open my eyes. "I need *sleep*. So much sleep."

Firm hands gripped my ankles through the thickness of covers.

"Don't even think about it," I warned, but I wasn't sure my tone carried heat.

Partly because I cracked open an eye and my grin twitched.

His eyes laughed at me and his grip on my ankles tightened. "Throw off the covers or I'm going to do it."

"You would—AH!"

He did. He tugged. Hard. So fast and hard my ass was on the floor, my ankles still in his hands and my head was resting against the hotel's bed mattress before I felt him move.

"You're an ass." I laughed, threw covers off my face, my body, and kicked at him until he let me go.

"At least you're out of bed."

Joey stepped back, arms crossed over his chest. Good Lord, it should be illegal to look that good in the morning. His shirt, plastered to his chest, biceps only made more bulging from the way he stood. Damn it. Even his legs were sculpted to perfection, visible beneath the light blue khaki shorts he wore.

"You look too damn pleased with yourself."

But I knew one way to wipe the smirk off his face. And since I was wide awake now, albeit unhappy about it...

I untangled from the covers he'd yanked off the bed with me and scrambled to my knees. As I did, I ended up right in front of him, on my knees, peering up at him as I ran a hand up his legs.

"You need to get ready."

"I already am," I whispered, my breathing already labored. In front of me, behind his zipper, he swelled and I caught sight of him licking his lips.

Smirk gone.

My hands went to his shorts. The button there and then the zipper.

"Gabby—"

"Are you saying no?" I curled my hands into his waistband.

He cleared his throat, Adam's apple bobbing as he did and then his shoulders fell. "I'm saying you need to be quick about it."

"I can do fast."

24

JOEY

"**I**'m so glad we woke up early for this."

I turned to Gabby and handed her the cup of coffee I'd gotten for her when she went to the restroom after boarding.

"*We* woke up early?" I took a sip of my own strong, hot drink. The sun was shining but it was still early, the sun rising in the east ahead of us over Lake Michigan. We were on the bow of the ferry, watching it with the other passengers. She was right.

It was a beautiful sight, although far less gorgeous than the way Gabby looked this morning when I'd attempted to wake her. There hadn't been a moment since the morning we woke up married where she hadn't been gorgeous, this morning was different. I'd left the dinner last night uncertain where we stood, if she was planning on us staying married. I'd pushed the worry away while we explored what little we saw of Milwaukee, but this morning, I wasn't certain anything could hold me back from her.

The way she'd frowned before her eyes had opened, that pucker of her lips she pushed out into a pout when she refused to get out of bed. Last night's makeup remained around the rim of her eyes and lashes. It'd taken feats of strength to pull myself away from her and not burrow beneath the warm covers and delay our departure time.

She harrumphed and cupped her mug in both hands. "Perhaps I was a little too grouchy but in my defense, that bed felt like heaven."

Heaven was the way she'd curled into my body all night long, her breasts pressed against me beneath the thin tank she slept in.

Wind, which had been nothing more than a gentle breeze when we boarded the ferry to take us to Muskegon, thirty minutes south of our next stop, now whipped through the air, making tendrils of Gabby's hair fly in the breeze. She shivered from a sudden burst of wind and gripped the railing to steady herself over the choppy waves.

"How long will this ride take?"

"Three and a half hours. Probably four by the time we depart and are on the road again." The van was safely stored with all the other vehicles beneath the ferry. The ride was only saving us a couple of hours of driving time, but when I'd accidentally come across the ferry option in my search, Gabby's eyes lit with excitement.

I'd give her anything to keep that look on her face.

"We'll drive almost another hour north to get to the campsite and B&B we're staying at. Can't check in until later this afternoon but we should be able to find some things to do while we wait."

"We're on the beach, right?"

"Camping right on the sand."

I'd been lucky to find an old bed and breakfast that had beach-facing campsites. We'd camped in the mountains, the red rocks of Moab. We'd stayed in our van in a truck stop and on the outskirts of an Amish village. Camping right on the beach, on the water, was what I was most excited for even if the late spring weather would most likely make the water frigid.

She shivered again, dressed appropriately in a long sleeve shirt with thumb cutouts and a pair of leggings that molded perfectly to the curve of her plump backside, but even I was getting cold outside.

"Want to go play UNO?"

We'd packed a few card games and board games in case the weather didn't cooperate on our hikes but hadn't yet had to break into them.

She blasted me with a bright, full smile that was almost as bright as the sunset in front of us. "Game on."

∼

"You cheated."

"I did not."

"You cheated eight times."

I threw my head back and laughed. "Just because I *beat* you doesn't mean I cheat." The night we'd spent at Malley's playing quarters came back to me and I frowned. "Do you always accuse everyone who beats you of cheating?"

Gabby huffed, sitting across from me in our chairs in the main cabin and crossed her arms. "No. Of course not."

"Then how can I have cheated at UNO?" I flipped the cards in my hands, shuffled them and reshuffled and dealt another hand.

Behind Gabby's chair, a young girl with tow-headed hair tied up into pigtails appeared, her light blue eyes narrowed on the cards in my hand.

"Lilly, come down." Her mother glanced over the chair

and I gave her a polite grin as she tugged the child back to her lap.

Gabby bounced from the movement of the seat behind her and turned back that way, smiling at the girl as her mom tried to get her to be seated. "Would she like to play with us?"

"Yes!" the girl said. "Please, Mommy."

"No, let these nice people play their card game, sweetie."

If I wasn't mistaken, disappointment danced across Gabby's eyes before she turned back to me. "One more hand, and this time, don't cheat."

This woman. "You are the sorest loser of all the losers I've ever met, Gabrielle Dubiak."

"Isn't it Taylor?" She winked.

Did that mean she was planning on taking my name?

We hadn't talked about it. Hell, after last night and Gabby saying she still wasn't certain where she'd end up and open her dream salon, I'd doubted she was starting to feel the same way as me.

Maybe she was just teasing, didn't mean a thing by it, but before I could ask, two sets of shoes appeared in my line of sight next to the table where my head bent to shuffle the cards.

"Excuse me, I'm so sorry." I glanced up as the woman, *mom*, rather, held the little girl gently with her hand on her shoulder. "But you two happen to be playing my daughter Lilly's favorite game and she's bored as the dickens. Is there any chance..."

"We'd love to have her join us," Gabby said, and she patted the seat next to her.

The mom bit her bottom lip, glanced to her husband watching me with eagle-eyed precision. "You're welcome to sit and join us too," I offered her.

She glanced at the man I assumed was her husband, back to me and Gabby. "Um. Maybe in a bit? I have a hungry baby who needs to eat but if it's really not too much trouble…"

"It's not," Gabby assured her. Lilly was already climbing into the seat next to her. "She'll be safe here."

Most of the seats on the ferry were lined like an airplane, but we'd sat in the center section with chairs in groups of four facing each other with the table between us. The ferry had a rather light load this morning and our row of seats was completely empty. The family, if they wanted, could easily join us with plenty of room to keep an eye on their daughter and us, but the mom must have been assured by Gabby because she kissed her daughter on the cheek and told her. "Dad and I and Landon are right behind you if you need anything, okay?"

"I won't," the little girl confidently declared and held out her hands waiting for her cards. "I'm good."

The mom chuckled, brushed her hand over her daughter's hair and returned to her seat as I redealt the cards.

"How old are you, Lilly?" I asked.

"Six." She fumbled with the cards in her hand, trying to fan them out and peered at me over the top. "How old are you?"

Gabby hid a laugh behind her handful of cards.

"Twenty-six."

"Not so old then," the little girl muttered. "Mom says I'm old for my age. My teachers say I'm smart as a whip." And then, to prove she'd been paying close attention to our earlier games, she glanced at Gabby. "If I beat you, are you going to call me a cheater, too?"

I burst out a laugh and threw my cards on the table.

This little girl was awesome.

Three games later, Lilly's parents called her back to her seat to get some food. She'd won one of the games, and I doubted either of us had let her. Her teacher was right. She was whip-smart and I tried to recall my nieces and nephews and how they'd acted at her age, but I was certain none of them had this girl's quick humor.

After she was gone and seated, I leaned my elbows on the table and made sure I was quiet and couldn't be overheard as I asked Gabby, "Is there anyone you meet who doesn't fall in love with you in moments?"

The truth of what I revealed came out unintended and yet there it was. Somehow, in a manner of moments or hours, I'd fallen in love with the woman across from me, like Andrea had on the hiking path. Like this little girl who behaved as if she'd known Gabby her entire life.

Gabby licked her lips as her eyes widened. "I'm a hairstylist and I like talking to people. It comes with the job."

She could blow off what I'd essentially confessed. I'd allow it, but I wouldn't let her diminish her gift with people.

"No." I shook my head and shuffled the cards in my hand. "I think that's purely you."

"Enjoy your stay at Portsmouth, and please, if there's anything you need from us, don't hesitate to ask."

The brunette, one hand on her swollen stomach looking like she was ready to have a baby at any minute handed us the registration to our campsite with a smile.

"Thank you, Haley," Gabby said. "And from what we've seen, your resort here is absolutely gorgeous."

Haley's smile stretched across her cheeks. "Thank you.

It's been in my family for generations, so it's always such a pleasure when people love it as much as I do."

A guy entered from the back room, barely scanned his eyes over Gabby and me before going right to Haley and settled his hand at her back. "You were supposed to let me handle this."

Her hand at her stomach reached up, fiddled with the metal choker she wore at her throat. I'd noticed it as soon as we checked in. The heavy thickness of her choker wasn't just a choker, but declared ownership. "It's one check-in, honey. I can handle it." She grinned at us. "You'll have to excuse my husband Jensen. He's overprotective with our baby coming. Even if it's our third."

"That's because you work yourself too hard and don't listen," he said. There was a playfulness to his tone, yet his eyes settled at her hands at her throat and that look turned to something deeper.

Next to me, Gabby cleared her throat. "Well, thank you, anyway, for everything."

The man, Jensen, focused on me. "Need any help setting up the water or electricity hook-ups?"

"I think we're good." I'd done it enough in the last week to be an expert by now.

"If you change your mind, come find me."

"Will do. Thanks again."

"Enjoy your few days and if you need restaurant recommendations or any sightseeing brochures, grab some on your way out. Portsmouth has something for everyone." Haley gestured to the stand near the door and we said our goodbyes.

Gabby had already grabbed the ones for sand dune sliding, the adventure we planned on doing tomorrow, but as soon as we stepped outside, her wide eyes, sparkling from the sun, peered at me with wonder.

"Did you see... that *collar*?"

"Collar? On Haley? Yeah, I saw that."

"You know what this is?" she asked, and a blush hit her cheeks having nothing to do with the heat.

I settled my hand on her back and guided us through the parking lot. We'd settled the van there earlier and spent the afternoon walking the streets of Portsmouth. We'd ducked into a coffee shop first, wandered through a few small touristy type shops where Gabby purchased a coffee mug, something she'd done in every place we'd stopped or stayed. By now she had to have enough mugs to fill an entire cupboard. I'd stopped myself from trying to imagine waking up in my house, heading to my butler pantry and filling my own coffee with one of her mugs far too often to bother dreaming of it now.

"I do," I told her. "Had a former teammate once involved in the kink community. Took us guys once to a club he visited and taught us all about it. Not really my thing, but it was interesting." As I explained, Gabby's cheeks pinkened and she bit the corner of her bottom lip. I'd been intrigued at first. I think as athletes, most of us liked control and being in charge. I could remember some of the scenes we watched and while whips and humiliation definitely weren't my thing, watching a woman get turned on being restrained or spanked had definitely made me hard that night. "I'm surprised you do."

"Well," she huffed, ran her tongue over her lips like she wasn't sure if she wanted to admit anything to me. "I read books and have watched a couple movies."

I opened her passenger door and as she climbed in, brushed my hand over the skin showing at her thighs. As soon as the weather had warmed, she'd ditched the long sleeve top and leggings she wore on the ferry for cutoff jean shorts that barely covered her ass and a crop top that showed off the curves of her breasts and the muscles at her abdomen.

She was testing my patience to wait until nightfall to take her again.

"You're going to have to share some of those books with me. Maybe it'll give me a few new ideas." If she was curious, I'd explore that with her. Hell, I'd already done more with her than any other woman.

Her cheeks flushed, goose bumps popped on her thigh where I trailed my finger in a lazy figure-eight shape and a shiver made her squirm in her chair.

"Not fair," she grumbled. "You can't turn me on *now*."

"It's fair, considering I'm always turned on when you're around me."

I shut the door on her as her jaw dropped and hurried around to the RV.

Nightfall and privacy couldn't arrive soon enough.

25

GABBY

I set down a bottle of wine on the table that popped out from the back of the RV. It had to be the greatest thing about the RV. A tiny table, perfect for two, and at the perfect height for our camping chairs, we'd shared more than one meal at it, but this location might just be my favorite.

"Do you want me to open the bottle?" I asked Joey who was inside, grabbing plates and silverware.

Bags of Chinese and sushi had been delivered to our campsite, and we'd chosen to eat at the perfect time. On the horizon, where the lake met the sky, the sun was beginning to set, casting an array of oranges of pinks and purple across the sky through the gentle clouds rolling in.

"I'll get it," he called out and reached into the drawer to grab the electric wine opener.

He crawled over our bedding, the couches never once been turned back into furniture to sit on and set everything on the table before leaning over the edge of the bed. His hand whipped out, slipped behind my neck and he pulled me to him, kissed me senseless and until I was breathless before he pulled back.

"What was that for?" I asked, chest already heaving and my core tightening.

"Because you're sexy. And every time I see you, I want my mouth on you."

"Oh."

"Also because now I keep thinking about all those books you read, all the things you could probably teach me."

I rolled my eyes and laughed. "Please. With the way you boss me around, I'm sure you have more tricks up your sleeve."

"If you're lucky, you'll see."

"I already am."

The truth surprised me as soon as it was out. I imagined I looked like Joey had earlier when he almost, kind of sort of, admitted to falling in love with me in moments.

"Gabby—"

"We need to eat before it gets cold."

Disappointment flashed in his eyes but he climbed over the edge of the bed and stood in front of me. "Right."

I broke something then, that fragile tendril we were building. Before I could repair it, he wrapped an arm around my shoulders, pulled me to his side and we faced the sunset.

"We've seen so many indescribable things this trip."

From sunsets to sunrises and cloudless skies and glacier-tipped mountain tops, babbling brooks that ran down the mountains and pebbled with bright yellow flowers budding at the edges. My camera roll was full of all the sights we'd seen. There were so many natural wonders we'd viewed, I didn't want to forget any of them. Nor did I want to forget the security Joey gave me, the happiness. The leap of joy in my chest every time he looked at me or I made him laugh.

"We've made memories to last a lifetime in some of the most incredible places on this planet."

He kissed the side of my head, hugged me tight and let me go.

"I will never forget them," I said to his back as he walked away.

"Good." He flashed me a smile, opened our wine and I set out our plates and opened the camping chairs while he popped the tops open on the food containers. We dug into sushi and Chinese food, beef and broccoli for me, and three different orders for him. At one point, he brought his chair around to my side, grabbed a beer he'd picked up earlier from the fridge, and we sat on the beach, shoulders brushing, drinks in hand long after the sun set in front of us.

"I almost don't want this trip to end," I admitted, resting my head on his shoulder. "It's coming too fast."

"So you like being with me?" he asked, but it was too heavy to be a tease, too quiet to not be laced with worry.

I'd done that, with my earlier thoughtlessness and last night's uncertainty.

"I like you a whole lot, Joey Taylor."

His grin curled at his lips and he leaned in, brushing his mouth over mine. "That's really good to hear, Gabrielle Taylor, because I think I like you a whole lot more than just *like*."

He lingered at my mouth, brushed his tongue over my lips and then slipped inside, kissing me while my heart fluttered at his own admission and honesty and I cursed myself for not being able to give him the same.

And for not the first time, I wondered what it'd be like to really be Gabrielle Taylor... on paper and permanently.

A WARM HAND trailed down the curve of my side, over my hip. Behind me, Joey's body pressed to mine. I was nestled in his warmth, my head on his bicep, while his free hand roamed my skin, pressing beneath my tank and slipping along the band of my underwear I'd worn to bed.

Soft kisses traveled along the width of my neck and his arousal was undeniable as he rolled his hips.

"If I wake you up again, are you going to be grouchy?"

Not sure it was possible to be in a bad mood when he was touching me like this, teasing me, waking me with hands and lips instead of whispered demands.

"As long as it's not before the sun rises, you're good," I mumbled and turned enough so I could kiss the soft skin on his arm.

"How awake do you want to be right now?" As he asked, his fingers dipped beneath the waistband of my underwear, to my lower stomach, and slid through my crease.

"Oh," I rasped, and jolted at his first, light touch.

Joey chuckled against my throat. "I want to fuck you as the sun rises, see the night become day right as you shatter."

Last night, we'd stayed outside until the bugs turned into pesky nuisances and he'd ravished me until I was spent. He'd held my hands at my sides, barked out commands I followed on instinct. This felt different. His touch was slow and soft, barely skimming the line of my body.

"I want that, too." I always wanted him. Everywhere. Any way I could get him.

His finger pressed inside, drawing out another raspy breath from me, and I settled my hand on his arm. Somewhere to hold him. Touch him. As he worked his finger slowly, my core heated, my body responded, rolling hips, seeking a deeper touch, trapped beneath his frame at my back.

His hard length sandwiched between us. I reached back, tried to find him but he moved out of the way.

"Uh-uh. You first."

His wish. My command. He added another finger, included his thumb at my clit until I was panting, writhing, gripping the sheets in front of me and biting down on my pillow to stay silent.

All the while he murmured his praise, kissed my throat, until I was so close and he stopped.

"What—?"

"Gimme a second." He kissed my shoulders, moved his body behind me and then his hands were at my hips, tugging down my underwear. I heard the crinkle of foil, the hitch of his breath as he rolled the condom down his length and he was back again.

"Yes," I sighed as he lifted my hip, held me open. And then he slid inside.

"Jesus. You feel so damn good. All the time. I could spend the rest of my life inside of you and tasting you and never want for anything."

The confession came too close to last night. Too close to my heart. I bit down harder on the pillow and whimpered as he adjusted the spot he hit inside of me.

"Please," I begged. I begged him for harder. For faster. I begged him for more pressure and every time I did, he chuckled and told me to be patient.

"You're beautiful," he whispered. "You're so sexy."

"Joey—"

"You can do anything you want. I'm so lucky to be yours."

My body was electrified. With every slow, deep thrust

inside me, every brush of his fingers at my clit, he whispered more praise.

My mind scrambled, my body overheated.

I clung to the sheets like a lifeline as his words slid deep into my soul and his body drove me to the edge.

"You can do anything. Anything you set your mind to."

"Oh God," I groaned, that familiar flare of heat sparking in my core and spreading outward. I was no longer sure if I was going to orgasm from the way he saw me or how he played my body like a master.

I wanted *him*. *This*. Forever.

"I want you," I pleaded, spreading my legs further apart, arching into him.

Right as the first wave crested, I turned to him, pressed my mouth to his, and I came, falling over the edge and yet feeling safer with the free will than I ever had in my life.

He loved me.

And I was certain that I'd fallen in love with the only man who I knew, no matter what, if I leaped before looking ever again... he'd always be there to catch me.

26

JOEY

My wife was a goddamn sex goddess. Whether she was dressed in cutoff shorts and a crop top, in jogger sweats and faded sweatshirts with no makeup, or in summer dresses with her hair and makeup done that showed her professional talent, she could enter my line of sight and steal my breath and make my dick go hard before she blinked.

Seeing Gabby in a modest one-piece swimsuit, all black, that was so much less revealing than the bikinis she wore when she swam in my pool or relaxed in my hot tub, had to be one of the hottest experiences.

Probably didn't help she grabbed men's attention with every sway of her hips, with every thrust of her hands in the air as she flew down the sand dunes, laughing her ass off and screaming with glee while most of the other women there acted too scared to attempt. In a move I was no longer surprised by, as I stood at the bottom and watched her fly toward me, she had two kids chasing her down the dune on their sandboards, instantly drawing people to her.

Yeah. Gabby was stealing the show and I didn't mind

observing her constantly grab hold of a new adventure and live her life to the fullest.

She rushed to me at the bottom, gripping her board we'd rented at a shop before we reached the national park area where we were sledding. Her smile was more blinding than the sun, her happiness an almost tangible aura dancing around her and as she stumbled, climbing to her feet, laughing at herself, it hit me deep.

I *loved* this woman.

I didn't have the memory of proposing or coming up with the idea like Gabby had said, but I also didn't care. I didn't need to know what happened that night that made marrying her seem like a great idea.

I knew. Right then.

Her contagious laughter singing across the sand and into the air, her happiness, and every single thing I'd learned about her, I had no doubts. What we'd done hadn't been a drunken mistake. It wasn't a mistake at all.

It was destiny. Hers and mine.

Her smile wobbled. "What? What's wrong?"

"Nothing." I picked up her board and held the two of them in my own hand while grabbing her hand in my other. "Absolutely nothing is wrong."

Everything was perfect.

I kissed her, a peck on her cheek to keep it family-friendly and we started hiking up to the top of the hill.

Tonight, I'd tell her. I'd tell her everything I was feeling. Everything I wanted to do for her and *give* to her.

Tonight I was going to lay all my chips on the table, take the biggest gamble, and hope like hell she felt the same. I was done with seeing her admit to liking me when it was so much more.

If she needed reassurance from me so she could be fully

honest about what was going on between us, I'd spread my heart out for the world to see.

And I hoped like hell, she felt the exact same way as me.

WE PULLED up to the restaurant, two miles down from where we were staying in an Uber I'd ordered. I helped Gabby out of the car and we headed inside. The sun was already setting, the night coming fast. We probably could have walked but even my thighs ached from the countless trips we made up the sand dunes. We'd fallen asleep after returning from the sand dunes earlier and woken with barely enough time to make the reservation I'd requested online. A quick stop to the Portsmouth Inn and Haley gave me a few names of some of their favorite local restaurants.

Since Gabby loved *all things carbs and pasta*, we were eating at an Italian restaurant overlooking the lake. The night was cool enough for us to sit on their rooftop dining section and her eyes twinkled as the hostess led us to our table. Lights were strung crisscrossed all over the area, making it almost impossible to see the stars that would appear later. The news said a storm was rolling in but would hopefully be gone by the time we reached Torch Lake in a couple of days.

We had one more day to relax here, and even if it was raining, I wanted to spend it with Gabby beneath me, on top of me, relaxing next to me on the beach, and laughing that infectious laugh of hers until our stomach muscles ached.

I held out her chair for her, allowed the hostess to hand us our menus before declaring our server, Stephen, would be here momentarily, and I took my seat across from her.

Our table had already been set with fresh lemon water and thin, crunchy breadsticks in a basket.

Gabby reached for one as soon as she was seated and snapped it in two.

She'd worn another dress tonight, this one more slinky, more revealing. Straps so thin they looked like they could snap at any moment and the black fabric held a shimmer to it every time she moved. The front draped loosely over her breasts, revealing cleavage that made my mouth water. The lights above us reflected off her, making her appear like an angel—a dirty, filthy angel who loved all the things I did to her in bed—but an angel all the same.

"You're giving me the sex look," she muttered, biting into her breadstick.

"My sex look?"

"Yeah." She spun the breadstick in a circle pointed at me. "Yeah, that dimple on your cheek pops out when you're thinking of sex."

I cleared my throat. "Of course I'm thinking of sex. You're in front of me, and all I can think of is dragging my tongue down that cleavage on display, sucking on your nipples until you're begging for more."

Her lips parted, cheeks flushed, and she huffed. "You can't say things like that to me in public."

"Why not?"

"Because now I want sex, too."

I laughed as her cheeks turned crimson. "You make that sound like a bad thing."

She rolled her eyes and hissed at me in a way that was much too playful to be serious. "Well I don't want to leave a wet spot on their chairs, so stop it."

I waggled my brows playfully, fighting against the urge

to make her do just that. "Have I turned you on already? Just thinking about how much I like sucking on you—"

"Stop." She tossed the remainder of her breadstick across the table at me.

I caught it easily and popped it into my mouth.

"You're horrible," she grumbled.

"That's not what you said this morning."

Our server appeared at the table, smirking at me in a way that proved he'd heard me. Gabby choked on her water.

We ordered, scallops and shrimp pasta for Gabby, a ribeye and lobster tail for me, and as soon as he left, I returned to the conversation.

Seeing Gabby's cheeks turn hot pink had become my favorite thing. "If I remember correctly, which I'm sure I vividly do, you called me amazing. Incredible. You said I was awesome."

As predicted, cheeks warmed, eyes rolled. She tipped her glass in my direction. "That's not what I said."

"No?"

"No. I said *it* was incredible. Amazing and awesome. *You* were not mentioned at all."

"Semantics. You wouldn't have had *it* if it hadn't been for *me.* Which makes them interchangeable."

Another eye roll but she said nothing.

I took that as a win.

It was after dinner was done. After we'd both had a couple of drinks. After we both groaned *absolutely not* when it came to our server's offer of seeing a dessert menu. The only dessert I needed was sitting across from me, a woman who I'd fallen in love with much quicker than I realized.

It was then, with the twinkling lights around us, the soft laughter of others at tables nearby, the breeze in the air and the sound of the lake in the distance I took my shot.

I'd meant to wait until we were back in our RV, bundled beneath blankets and curled up skin-to-skin, but Gabby looked so relaxed, so *happy*.

I wanted to help her stay that way forever.

Leaning forward, I set my drink off to the side.

"I'm going to say something, and I'm hoping you're ready to hear it, because I can't keep it to myself any longer."

She blinked, surprised, wiping away the relaxed gleam in her eye. "What is it?"

I reached across the table, took her hand in mine. She was soft, a slight chill to her skin and as I rubbed my thumb over her palm, she shivered.

"I love you, Gabby. I'm pretty sure I fell in love with you the night we were married, only I didn't know it truly until we came on this trip."

As I spoke, her lips parted, that shiver turned to a full body tremble. Her hand tightened in mine and she opened her mouth but no words came out.

I pushed on.

"I know when we woke up that morning, and since then, I've said there had to be a reason for why we got married, and I wanted to figure it out, that we owed it to each other to do that, but now I know why."

"Joey—" Her voice was a rasp, barely audible, as if finding words were difficult, but mine were easy.

They fell from my lips like rain fell from the clouds.

"You *love* life. You love finding the enjoyment and the beauty in the smallest things. You enrapture every single person you come in contact with. Your laugh is infectious, and your smile can light up a starless sky. Everything I learn about you makes me fall deeper under your spell, so we might be married already, but I'm asking you when this trip is done to move to Vegas with me. Permanently. Let me buy you your salon so you can chase your dreams. *Stay* married to me, Gabby, and I swear it, I will bust my ass to make sure you have everything you can possibly desire and more."

My heart raced and my grip on her hand didn't loosen. One breath passed.

Then two.

Another.

Tears swam in her eyes and she swallowed, opened her mouth, and I swore the words *yes* were going to fall from them as easily as her smiles came.

But then she said, "I... I can't."

No. She said no. It was possible my heart stopped, shriveled. A pain so severe ripped through me I was terrified of collapsing right there. My world imploded just as I'd hoped it was beginning.

"Why?" I could barely choke out the word.

"I think... no." She flipped her hand beneath mine and held on to me as I tried to pull away from her. "I love you too. I want you to know that and I would love nothing better to let you do all those things for me. But part of the reason why I always wanted to make this trip and see these things isn't just to see the country, but to figure out myself. I can't do that if I go from letting Garrett take care of me to having you do it. It's not right."

"I'm your husband. It's my *job*."

"It's mine to figure out how to take care of myself first, though. I need to know I can do that. My mom's right—"

"The hell she is."

Is that what this was about? Her *mom*?

"Please. She is, in a sense. I need to know I can be independent. I need to know I can live life on my own two feet. I need to know what kind of woman that makes me *before* I stand back and let someone else make my dreams come true for me."

She was killing me. Absolutely killing me. I wanted to plead with her, to get her to see that even if she had family who helped her, she'd already done so much for herself. She'd proven she could take care of herself. She held down a job, a career she loved, she lived on her own. She had the strength to leave a relationship after investing so much time in a man who treated her like shit—something not all women did. But there was something in her eyes, all light from our earlier adventure now gone, that told me she wasn't in the place to listen.

She wouldn't hear all the ways she took care of herself and had already proven her own strength.

This was something she needed to figure out for herself.

She needed to grow, and I loved her enough to know how incredible she was without doubt.

My heart flayed open, bleeding all over the floor, I reached for my glass of water to soothe the pain she'd torn through me.

"So, where does that leave us?"

27

GABBY

I f it was possible for me to feel completely torn in two, it was happening.

Everything in me demanded to reach across the table, smooth away the pain I'd brought to Joey's face, the way he looked absolutely shattered.

He had to know, though. He needed to know I loved him. That I wanted him.

I wanted to be *with* him.

I just needed to be whole first, and I couldn't do that, not with what he was offering.

I still had a life in Seattle to finish closing down. Hell, I'd been in Las Vegas for *months* and had never once even considered canceling my lease, moving out.

Joey sat across from me, offering me my dream on a silver platter, but I couldn't agree to it.

Not *yet*.

I spun my ring on my finger, a tear falling to the diamond as I blinked. "I'm not taking this off, and I won't." I glanced up at him. His gaze had gone to my ring finger while his thumb slowly turned his. Once he dragged those dark, sorrowful eyes to meet mine, I fought the desire to say *fuck this. Yes. I accept because I love you too.* "But I think I need to head home. I need to start working on me so I can return to you a woman who knows exactly what she has to offer a man like you, and then I hope... well, I hope you still want that woman too."

He closed his eyes, head fell. My mouth turned dry and I attempted to lick my lips but there was no moisture inside me, it was all streaming down my cheeks. I grabbed my water, barely able to get the glass rim to my lips due to the trembling in my hands.

"Please. Say something."

His shoulders rose and fell with a shuddering, shaky exhale. "I get it. I get what you're saying." Shaking his head, his gaze rose to meet mine again. "I don't like it. *I* don't think it's necessary when there isn't a single piece of you right now that isn't exactly perfect, but I get what you're saying. I do." A brief flash of a sad smile appeared and then slid right off his face. "I wouldn't be the husband I want to be with you if I didn't encourage you to chase everything you needed in life, even if that chase takes you away from me for a while. But, while you're gone, I want us to keep in touch, though. I want you telling me everything so I can share all of it with you. Okay?"

God. How could I be doing this to him? To us? And yet deep in my soul, beneath the pain, beneath the searing sensation of loss happening in front of me, there was peace. A tiny ember of confidence growing.

My smile shook as I said, "I'd like that."

I STEPPED out of the bathroom, makeup removed, trying to hold back tears. I was doing this. I was leaving the man I loved.

Only, that man I loved stood in front of me, dressed in only a pair of pajama pants with his bare chest on display and a sad smile pushing at his lips. My resolve started to crumble as Joey reached for me, took my hand in his and pulled me toward him, cupping my cheek with his other hand.

"I feel like I'm hurting you for no reason right now."

"You have a good reason." He took my hand, placed it at his back until his forehead pressed to mine. "It hurts, and it might keep hurting both of us for a while, but we'll get through it."

He was so certain. So understanding even if he didn't fully agree with this, but God... how could I leave him? How could I walk away from this when my body was already warming to his tender touch?

All the tears I'd tried so hard to force down since he paid our bill and made the sullen trip back to the RV made my chin tremble and my throat tighter.

"We'll be okay," Joey murmured, voice like velvet over rocks. Rough but smooth.

And then he kissed me. He pressed his lips to mine and inhaled, like he was trying to sear the memory of this kiss into his entire body and soul. I kissed him back, emotions still making my body tremble and curb to his back. The heat of his body suffused my hands, traveled up my arms and right to his chest before he started walking us back slowly. We made it to the edge of the bed where he guided me down and onto my back.

His kisses were so slow, so sensual, I widened my legs and let him fall between.

God. Should we even be doing this? This wouldn't take away the pain of what was coming and yet as he rolled his hips, pressed his hardening thickness against me, I arched into him.

"Is this smart?" I asked, gasping for one last tendril of common sense.

"I want to even if it's not." He pulled back, dark eyes blazing with lust. "Do you?"

"Yeah." I swallowed down my fears.

This wasn't goodbye forever. There was no way I could meet a man who ever made me feel how Joey did or respected me as much. What we'd done was crazy, what we had was intense, but it was something worth fighting for, even if that fight put us in different locations for a short time.

~

"Hey, sleepyhead." I rolled over as Joey jostled my hip until I was on my back.

My eyes opened slowly, squinting against the light and then widened quickly.

"What is it?"

He was crouched at the foot of the bed, fully dressed in khaki shorts and a short-sleeve T-shirt I'd picked up for him in Colorado. It was nothing special, a gray shirt with Rockies typed across in bold navy font. He'd shaken his head when I showed him my matching shirt. *Something to remember the trip by* I'd told him as he'd taken the shirt from me.

I don't need the shirt. I have you, he'd replied.

The memory burned my eyes, and I shoved my palms against them to stave off tears. Last night's decisions rushed back to me in a moment.

What if what I was doing was *wrong*? What if I was once again running from responsibility instead of facing it? What if...

I cleared my eyes to ask him, only to catch the dark circles lining his eyes, his messed hair. He stood, pushing off his knees until he was towering over me, head needing to be tilted down due to the lack of height inside.

"I bought plane tickets for us. We need to head to Detroit."

"What?" I scrambled on the bed until I was sitting. I'd fallen asleep naked, after he'd thoroughly used my body in a way there was a slight ache to my hips.

His gaze barely dropped to my breasts before meeting my eyes and I yanked the sheet over me.

This was it then.

I couldn't find even a hint of desire when he looked away, a playful tease of his smile I'd become so used to receiving.

"Tickets." He cleared his throat. "One for you to Seattle and one for me to Charlotte. I'm still going to head down to see Jude and Jason, spend some time with them. But I want you to call me when you get to Seattle and every day you're there, okay?"

"You didn't have to do this." Or so quickly. I hadn't... I hadn't considered what my decision last night would mean. Where it would leave us today.

He swiped a hand over his mouth and scratched at the back of his neck.

"I did. I don't think the drive back would create the memories our trip here did, and I don't want that for us. I've taken care of everything with the van and your mom knows when you arrive."

Oh shit. "You... you called her?"

"Yeah."

I could hear her now. *Don't worry, Joey, it's not your fault. This is just, Gabby being... Gabby. She does this. Takes off...*

My chest squeezed tight and I reached for the tank top I'd been wearing when I stepped out of the bathroom last night. It smelled like Joey but I tried to ignore his woodsy cologne while I tugged it on.

He'd called my mom.

"What'd she say?"

He worked his jaw side to side and then sighed. "I think, I think she was sad, and proud. I just told her you had some things you needed to handle back there and asked if she could get you."

"So you didn't mention I ruined our trip because I was being flighty?"

"No."

I was pulling on my shorts, fumbling to get my left leg through the hole when I found myself wrapped in his arms.

"I didn't tell her anything, but that we'd agreed."

"You didn't agree to this."

"And it's killing me to let you go but I think... this is the right thing. I'm not trying to hurt you."

"Seems like we both keep saying that."

"We'll be okay," he assured me with a tighter hug and stepped back, dropping his arms to his sides like he couldn't stand to touch me anymore.

What was I *doing*?

"When do we fly out?" I couldn't look at him, couldn't bear to see the pain in his eyes, pain I'd caused. "Tonight. I called a moving company. They'll bring the RV back to Vegas, all our stuff, so just..." He turned away then, reached for the door to the RV. "It'll take a few hours to get to the airport, so pack up what you need."

"Joey."

"I'll wait outside. We'll leave when you're ready."

I didn't think I'd ever be ready to leave him. Not like this.

But I couldn't stay.

IT WOULD HAVE TAKEN King Arthur's magical powers with the sword to slice through the sad, thick silence between us. For four hours we drove to Detroit, barely speaking other than when I needed to help him navigate. On the way, Joey told me more specifics about how the RV would get back to him. He told me he'd keep my stuff there unless I wanted it to go to Garrett's.

Yours. Your place. So I know it's safe, I'd replied.

Ours. Our place, was what I'd wanted to say. And *so it's there when I come home*. I couldn't bring myself to say either.

And like he knew, he'd nodded, thrown my carry-on bag over his shoulder and led me through security to my gate.

My flight left an hour before his, and both of us had received a handful of texts from our families.

Jude and Jason asking Joey if everything was okay. Jude would pick him up at the airport.

I had one from my mom: **We'll talk. Be safe and everything will be okay.**

One from Garrett: **If he hurt you, I'll kill him.**

That'd made me laugh, but when Joey glanced at me, brows rose in question silently asking what was so funny I couldn't bring myself to share it with him.

I wonder what Garrett would say if he knew this was my fault. My idea.

It was time to board all too quickly. Everything had gone

fast even if every painful minute of the day had lasted an eternity.

"Maybe I'm wrong," I said, panic slicing through me. "Maybe... maybe I don't need this at all. I can just... figure it out later."

"And regret it?"

He'd stepped close to me, my carry-on now in my hand and my phone lit with my boarding ticket like a bomb in my palm. If I used it, would everything I felt for this man explode?

"Don't," Joey said, and he slid his hand to the back of my neck. With a quick yank, my forehead was at his chest and he held me there, murmuring in my ear. "This is what you need. The next time I sit across from you, tell you I love you and want to be with you forever, I don't want there to be hesitation in your eyes. It's okay to *need* this. Everything's happened so fast, Gabby. I get it. I do, even if it hurts. We'll figure it out."

"I do love you though," I choked out. I couldn't bring myself to hold him back or touch him. If I did, I'd fall apart.

"I know." He kissed the top of my head, slid his hand from my neck to my cheek, and tilted my head up. "And when you tell me it again it will be with a happy smile on your face and not tears on your cheeks."

To prove it, his thumb swiped at my tears.

"Text me when you land. I should be landing about the same time anyway." Given the lengths of the flights and time differences he probably wasn't too far off.

"Okay." I bit the inside of my cheek to stop my tears. Around us, other flyers were lined up. Some gawked at us with their own sad smiles, acknowledging they felt whatever we were projecting with our whispered goodbyes and tears.

If only they knew I was walking away from the man I loved to find myself.

"I love you. Be safe."

"I will."

I squeezed my eyes closed as Joey whispered in my ear. "I will love you in every form of woman you come to me in." He swallowed, scrubbed a hand over his eyes and exhaled with a heavy whoosh. "We'll keep in touch?"

"Yes. Of course. Every day."

"I'll hold you to that." He winked, a sad smile flashing and he lifted his chin for me to get moving. "We'll see Torch Lake and Mackinac Island someday, but don't go without me."

"Never."

I didn't want to go anywhere without him, which is what made this so hard. I loved him, deeper and more intensely than I could have imagined loving anyone.

"Does this make me a fool?"

"No." His sad smile shot an arrow straight to my heart. "It makes you brave, honey. And it only makes me love you more even if this hurts."

28

JOEY

"I feel like our home is bad luck for your love life."

I shot Katie a grin as she joined me on the back patio.

Ironically, it was less than a year ago I was sitting in the same chair, moody and mopey, and it'd been Lizzie who had joined me. Back then, I couldn't imagine getting over Lenora.

Today, I just wanted to count down the days until I could see Gabby again.

"How'd Marissa go down?"

It was after dinner and at almost a year old, Katie had warned me Marissa was beginning to hate bedtimes.

"Jude took over. I wanted to talk to you."

I brought the beer bottle to my mouth and took a swallow. "I don't have much more to say."

After arriving in Charlotte late last night, Jude had waited until he got me to his home and handed me a beer before he and Katie grilled me on what happened. I'd told them everything. From what I remembered of getting married, why we went on the trip, about meeting Andrea and Corey, and then the way all the kids were magnets to Gabby sand dune sliding. I danced over our last night, but from what I'd explained, they both seemed to understand.

Today, neither had said much even if I'd brought their probably normal happy home down with my moroseness. Perhaps if I told myself I understood more, I actually would.

I got her need to be independent.

I just didn't think it had to happen *alone*. She could do all the things she wanted with me. That's what marriage was. Giving when you can and receiving when you needed it. But I'd grown up with privilege and money. Yeah, we'd been taught responsibility but we'd never wanted for anything and since we all spent so much time on the ice rinks, I'd never actually had a *real* job. I'd never had to worry about finding my path, paying bills. Hell, I had a financial manager who handled all that daily shit for me.

"I'm kind of all talked out," I told Katie and turned back to the scorching heat. Not as bad as Vegas, but it was brutal enough especially since Jude had forced me into a three-hour workout earlier and then a game of one-on-one basketball.

Jason and Tessa were supposed to head over tomorrow to spend the day swimming.

Which would mean more questions.

Perhaps coming to see my brothers wasn't the best idea given the circumstances.

In my hand, my phone buzzed and I glanced at it.

Almost all packed. Followed with two hearts, green and gold for my team.

The text included a picture of Gabby's now almost completely empty apartment.

That was it.

She'd called last night before she went to bed. We'd

talked this morning, three times this afternoon when she took packing breaks. Whatever plan she was working on somehow meant she needed to move out of her apartment her first day back in Seattle.

"Is that Gabby?"

"Yeah." I set my phone on the small table next to the lounger and closed my eyes, resting my head back. "She's packing up and moving home with her mom while she *finds* herself."

I couldn't keep the irritation out of my voice.

"You'll be thankful for this later."

I peered at her through one open eye. "Thanks for the pep talk."

She slapped my shoulder. "Stop being so grouchy. You know how I grew up. My mom? The world's ultimate hippie always trying to find herself? Do you know how hard that was on me? The kid who just had to follow along with her?"

I knew all of that. Katie had grown up living out of cars and never really attending schools until she'd forced her mom to settle down while she went to high school. She'd then gotten a scholarship to Chicago, a city she'd chosen because it seemed so *normal and plain.*

"I know how hard it was for you."

"Good. Then you know why this is good. If Gabby needs to have this confidence in herself, it'll only mean she's that much better for you when she comes home."

Home. To my house. In Vegas.

"Doesn't make it easier."

"I know." She squeezed my shoulder. "And I hate you're hurting again. I just don't see this as a bad thing. Besides, she'll be in Vegas in what... eight weeks?"

Lizzie was due in September with the babies but she'd already been warned she'd probably deliver early.

"Yeah. Something like that."

"So two months, at worst, until you can see each other."

"And then what? What if she's not more settled by then? What if she goes back to Seattle? What if…"

I stopped. The *what-if* game was useless. Always had been.

"Forget I said any of that."

"What if she's the absolute perfect woman for you and you two just met at the wrong time and everything will end up wonderful in the end?"

"You're teasing me."

Katie laughed and smiled out toward the distance. "I'm saying you two barely knew each other, got drunk and married, and now you're acting like it's unreasonable for her to need a minute to get her shit together." She glanced at me out of the corner of her eye. "No matter if you two love each other, you have to see that it makes sense from her perspective. I mean, at some point she would have had to get rid of the apartment anyway, right? Gone back home… packed…"

"Maybe."

She was making too much sense.

"So think of this as just her taking the time to close down what she needs to in order to start her life with you. Spin the perspective so it's more positive."

"Has my brother ever told you you're smart?"

"And sexy," Jude said, stepping onto the patio with a burp cloth still tossed over his bare chest. "And wickedly hot, and funny and hilarious and the best damn mom on the planet and the most incredible wife. Yeah… she knows."

Katie laughed.

I couldn't help but crack a smile.

"My wife get you sorted?"

He grabbed Katie, yanked her off the lounger.

"Hey!" she shrieked, but before she could stop, she was settled across Jude's lap where he'd sat in her spot.

"I think so."

"She's good at that kind of stuff."

Katie grinned at me, eyes filled with happiness that made my stomach curdle with jealousy for what they had.

"Don't forget, Joey. I had to close down my life in Chicago before I could be here with Jude. And I can guarantee you one thing."

"What?" Guarantees would be fantastic.

"If she loves you half as much as she says she does, she'll be busting her ass to get back to you sooner rather than later."

~

My weights slammed back to the squat rack and I stepped back, letting Dominick take my spot.

We'd been the only two who were in the training facility, but that had been common. I was working out three times more than usual since I got back to Las Vegas.

After three days in Charlotte with my brothers, their wives, and happy families, I'd headed home. But outside of checking in on Malley's and spending a weekend at our baseball league's opening season tournament, I'd had nothing but time on my hands *to* work.

I'd been surprised as fuck the first time I stepped into the facility at five a.m., needing to get out of my house and even my own gym to find Dom already there, busting ass by himself.

We rarely spoke at first but had started taking turns spotting each other when necessary.

It hadn't taken him long to figure out Gabby wasn't in

Vegas with me and it'd taken another week for him to ask about her.

"How's Gabby?"

"Busy. Working on things."

I kept my answers generalized. Mostly because I was starting to get concerned. All of Gabby's answers to me asking that same thing had been general. "Things are good. I'm working on it. Mom and I are talking. I have some meetings coming up I'm looking forward to."

What meetings?

I had no clue. She didn't offer up the information and even though I was dying to know, I was letting her guide the pace.

She'd tell me when she could. Hell, maybe she didn't tell me much because she wanted to do it all on her own. She didn't want my help.

Which was starting to suck. I kept trying to hold on to what Katie said, that this might not be bad, but every time I had another call with Gabby where she didn't tell me anything, a rock grew larger in my stomach.

It'd been fourteen days since I'd been able to touch her. To feel her. And every day that passed, I wanted her more.

"She coming back soon?"

"She'll be here for Lizzie and Garrett's delivery. I know that much."

Which was still well over a month away. She had an induction date set for thirty-seven weeks if she went that long. Apparently that was common with twins. From talking to Gabby, I knew Lizzie had wanted to do everything natural, give birth at a birthing center but once she had a scare early on in her pregnancy and then learned she was having twins, she'd decided to go a more traditional route.

From talking to Garrett, both of them were nervous as hell about it.

He, fortunately, had not murdered me when I returned to Vegas. Instead, the night after I got back, he showed up with half the team, cases of beer and whiskey and he'd thrown a party in my backyard.

"Talked to Gabby and then Jude called. Said you were down in the dumps. Get over your shit. Things will be fine." That'd been his hello. Then he shouldered past me and straight to my backyard like my home was his.

Fine. Everything was fine. It was all I kept hearing and the word *fine* was becoming my most hated four-letter word.

Dom finished his set and stood, nabbing a towel he'd dropped on the floor and swiped it over his forehead. "She's a cool girl."

It still surprised the hell out of me how much Gabby had gotten Dom to laugh the night before we left on our trip. Hell, him bringing up anything personal had shocked me.

Dom was an awesome defense player, but he lived alone. He never showed up for team events, except for the night Garrett had found out Lizzie was in the hospital months ago. I was still surprised as hell he'd been at Malley's the night before Gabby and I hit the road. Hell, he'd been playing on our team for years and I barely knew him.

"How about you?" I asked, taking the plunge. "Any women in your life?"

He usually had several. At least that's what social media sites and gossip bloggers would show.

"No time." He flung the towel down and grabbed his water. "Got enough shit going on in my life without needing that hassle."

"Like what?"

He glared at me like he wanted to push me, slam me into

the boards or something. It was the typical reaction I got from him when anything personal was asked.

Usually, he stomped away and left.

"Family shit," he finally muttered. "Come on. You can spot my bench."

I followed him, eyes wide. *Family shit.* "You have a *family*?"

I couldn't help it. He'd never... never once mentioned a family. Kids? A mom and dad?

"I didn't just pop onto this planet out of nowhere."

He gave me a look like I was an idiot and wrapped his hands around the bench press.

Conversation over—but so many questions left behind.

I knew better than to push.

"I miss Gabby," I finally said, standing above him, hands ready to catch them if needed but based on his weights, he wasn't pushing himself all that hard. "All the damn time."

"Based on the way she looked at you the night I saw you two together, you have nothing to worry about."

He clenched his jaw, got back to work.

I left the facility later, after finishing my workout, after Dom and I threw on skates and chased each other on the rink, eventually joined with Miko and Kane and played a quick two on two, just four guys fucking around for fun.

I left with a smile on my face, giving the guys typical shit, with two things on my mind.

Why had Dom chosen that day, of all people, to open up even if it was just a sliver—and why in the hell couldn't I squash the worry niggling in my stomach that something might not be right with Gabby?

29

———

GABBY

I hated lies. I despised keeping secrets and I knew as the days were going on, I was doing an incredibly piss-poor job of it.

However, it'd taken me approximately five minutes of being on the plane headed back to Seattle three weeks ago to come up with my plan.

By the time I landed, due to the time change, it was only six-thirty my time, and while the flight had been technically five hours, I'd spent the entire time writing up drafts and plans.

And oh man, did it make my mom happy when she saw me and I explained everything I wanted to do.

"This is a lot, Gabrielle. Are you sure?"

'Are you sure you can handle the responsibility?' Was what I was sure she meant, was certain that's what her true question was, but I'd looked at her with all the seriousness in how I'd thought everything out and told her. "Yes. I'm sure."

"Okay then." She focused out the windshield.

She was probably thinking of a thousand warnings of what could go wrong. Maybe I needed more time. Maybe I should...

"What does Garrett say?" is what she'd asked.

"He's refusing the money back."

He always had. Even when I tried to insist.

"You're my sister. I've got it easy. More money than I'll ever know what to do with. Invest the difference if it makes you happy, but over my dead body are you handing that money back to me."

That's what he had said to me years ago. The same thing he said as soon as I called him before even leaving the airport.

Fortunately, I'd taken his advice four years ago when he first leased my apartment. I'd taken my monthly rent money from every paycheck and invested it. The market had done well. Which meant *I* had done well.

Yeah, I didn't have enough money to buy a building, but I had plenty of capital to do exactly what I wanted.

My own salon.

The location was the only surprise of my plan.

Because I was going to move to Vegas, move to Joey, and follow my dream with him at my side.

There were just details to work out. I'd already filed for reciprocity with my license, but I still needed to sit for my state test exam in Nevada.

I'd spent hours studying over the last few weeks. After moving out of my apartment, back in with my mom, I'd taken a few days to finalize my plan and then I'd gotten to work.

I researched buildings, locations. I wanted a new area with high foot traffic but not so expensive I'd have to charge an arm and a leg for services to meet the lease payment. I wanted one or two employees to begin so we could open up shop, running as a full-service salon and spa.

Surprisingly, my mom had actually been excited about

my plan despite the worried looks she tossed my way, but I was trying to ignore them.

I could do this. I knew I could.

And hell, I was doing exactly what she always asked of me—made a plan and followed it.

It'd been anything but simple, but fortunately, since I'd invested so well, I didn't have to take out a small business loan to get the business up and running. I'd gotten ahold of Garrett's realtor, the woman who helped him buy his own place less than a year ago and she gave me the name of a commercial real estate agent she worked with and respected.

I'd called Christy, and then I called Kelsey Campbell.

Kelsey was the goaltending coach's daughter and she'd done Lizzie's hair and makeup for her wedding. She'd looked absolutely glorious and Kelsey and I had spent hours that day and night swapping shop talk.

I called her only to ask her for help, to get her opinions and advice on locations, but like on Lizzie's wedding day, we'd instantly fallen into a conversation as if we'd known each other for years.

She loved the area where she worked and the salon, but as soon as I reached out, she said she'd absolutely want to take on this adventure with me.

So after two weeks, and seeing tons of buildings, Kelsey seeing them in person and me seeing them via FaceTime, we'd signed our lease agreement. Now Kelsey and I talked every day, discussing the construction that needed to be done. My life was now spent checking and double-checking my spreadsheet, careful to stay within my budget, and twirling with excitement.

I was *doing* this, and all of it was falling into place so much faster than I could have predicted.

I also wanted it to be a surprise, even if I hated not sharing every single detail with Joey.

Which was why I was currently on the phone with Joey, his face on the screen in front of me, and my indecision with keeping this a surprise from him was killing me.

"How was your day?" He was sitting on his couch, shirtless, a protein shake he occasionally sipped from in one hand.

God, I wanted to be there, seeing all those muscles he'd been telling me he was growing in person.

"Busy. How was your workout this morning?"

He'd told me about working out with Dominick Masters, how they'd started talking more because they were the only two showing up so early every day. As far as I knew, Joey hadn't taken a single day off since he'd returned to Vegas, four days after we separated.

His brows puckered. I didn't blame him. Every time he asked what I was doing, I changed the subject back to him.

He adjusted, draped his arm over him, settling his palm at the back of his neck. The view gave me a great view of those biceps and if he noticed where my gaze trailed on the screen, his muscles flexed.

"Nice guns." I laughed.

"They're waiting for you. Missing you too much."

"I miss you too. All of you." Every time we talked, I'd trail my fingertip over his jaw on my screen, like I could actually feel him. "Every day, I swear."

"This is killing me. Being so far away from you." He blew out a breath, opened and closed his mouth and then muttered, "Fuck it. Look, Gabby. I gotta know what's going on. You're not telling me anything and it's... it's driving me crazy."

"I know. I'm just... working on things. With my mom. And my—our—future."

"How can it be ours when I'm not a part of it, though?"

It was a damn good question. Shit, maybe I was messing this up. But I knew him. If I told him my plans, he'd swoop in, help me handle it. And yeah, in relationships people worked together, they supported each other. I no longer knew if I was being stubborn, but I needed to prove to myself I could do this.

"I know. I know it's hard and I know you're frustrated with me, but it's all *good* things, Joey, I swear. I just, need it to be *mine* for a moment."

His lips pressed into a line so thin and my heart squeezed. He sat up, and I could tell from the movement, the way the phone jiggled he was resting his elbows on his knees, giving me a delicious look at all those abs my fingers itched to touch and the body that was always the last thing I envisioned before I fell to sleep at night, softly crying out his name while I found self-pleasure in the memory of him alone.

"Don't look at me like that when I'm hours away from you." His tone had thickened, sending sparks of desire through me.

"I could... I could show you... what I'm thinking of when I see you like that."

His dark eyes flashed. "No."

"No?"

I slumped back in my bed. Maybe I really had gone too far with all of this.

"No. The next time I see you—all of you—it's going to be when *my* hands and mouth and body can take care of it. You tease me now and I'm breaking my fucking promise to you, hauling my ass to Seattle and kidnapping you back here."

Shit. My hand not holding the phone curled into a fist. Was it wrong of me to be turned on by the thought of him throwing me over his shoulder and kidnapping me?

"You can't say things like that to me."

His grin turned wicked, that devilish dimple dug into his cheek. "Then get your shit sorted and fast so I don't have to get arrested."

I barked out a laugh. "I'm working on it. And things are... moving quickly. Faster than I expected."

"Yeah?"

He wanted to ask. I could see the questions he had on the tip of his tongue. Instead, he drove a hand through his hair and asked, "How are things with your mom? Any better?"

She was looking over my shoulder constantly, questioning, helping me plan. I didn't think we'd ever get to the easy *Gabby can do no wrong* relationship she had with Garrett, but it was better.

"We got in a fight this morning. About Dad."

His shoulders tensed for a moment, that same look he got every time something didn't go right for me. I adored his protectiveness. "Wanna talk about it?"

"I yelled at her that I knew the reason she got so mad at me was because when she looked at me, she saw Dad."

"Damn..."

"I know. It was mean, but it was also true. I look just like him. She told me that once, when I was little and then she went and cried for three days. It keeps hitting me. *You're just like your dad. You look just like your dad*, but whenever she says it, it's never this happy thing. It's always—*how can you remind me of the man I love and can't have*. Like she hates me for it."

My chin shook as I forced it out.

"She doesn't hate you, Gabby."

"No, but it explains a lot. Why she pushes me differently than Garrett. They're so much alike, and I'm... not them." I pushed forward before I cried over it. Again. "Anyway, we talked about it. A lot. More today before she left for work. She wants me to be like her and Garrett, I think so I don't remind her of him, but I told her today she has to love me for me, accept me like I am, because that's what she did for Dad."

His brows arched. "That's... harsh. Wise, though."

"I think I made my point. At least, she gave me a nod like she got it. So who knows."

He rubbed his chin and gave me a look that had my toes curling. "If I was there with you, I'd be hugging you while you told me all this. God, I want to touch you."

"Me too."

"Mostly, I want to be there for you, in everything you need."

That uncertainty flared again and it killed me. A spike to the chest. "You are. I promise you are. Who's coming over tonight?"

He'd texted me earlier, telling me guys were coming over to watch the baseball games, have some drinks. I already knew Alix was coming and he'd said he was surprised Dom hadn't immediately turned down the offer and said he'd think about it.

"Most of the team, I think. Whoever's in town. Garrett said he doesn't want to leave Lizzie for long right now but might stop by. Did you know he's not drinking?"

"As soon as third trimester hit, he stopped. Said he wanted to make sure he was always ready to take her to the hospital if needed."

"How are the baby preparations going then?"

We moved to neutral territory, talking about Garrett and Lizzie and me becoming an aunt. She had a baby shower in two weeks and I'd thought about going down, using it as an excuse to see Joey but if I did, I'd never leave.

I didn't need everything settled and ready to open as far as the salon went before I saw him again—I just needed to know it was going to happen.

His doorbell rang and he glanced in that direction. "Guys are here."

"I'll let you go then. I love you."

"I love you too—hurry home and soon. Please?"

A thick knot grew in my throat. "I'm working on it."

"Good. See you soon?"

"Definitely."

His screen went black and I sunk back into the pillows behind me.

God, I hope I wasn't screwing this up.

30

GABBY

She wasn't thirty-seven weeks. Lizzie wasn't yet thirty-seven weeks.

The babies didn't care because they were coming.

I'd gotten Garrett's frantic call this morning, right after my mom went to work. Unfortunately, she was currently investigating an overnight stream of murders, so she couldn't take off.

I, however, could, so I absolutely did.

"I'm on my way," I'd told Garrett. "Be there soon."

While rushing to the airport, I'd texted Joey. **Getting first flight down to Las Vegas. Lizzie's in labor. Can you pick me up at the airport?**

I could rent a car, but it would take longer. And who knew if I'd be rested or calm enough to drive.

Already heard and yes. Absolutely. Time?

At first, I'd been surprised by his reaction. Given the circumstances, understandable.

Only, another text came in right after that still had me grinning ear to ear.

I can't wait to see you. Warning: I might not let you leave.

I love you too. I'd texted back.

Fortunately for him, for us, I wasn't sure I would leave. Things were moving along and quickly with the salon. Construction on the inside of the building was well under-way. I had my Nevada test to take already scheduled, planned around the time of Lizzie's induction date when I was already going to be there.

Now, though, I was only thinking of Joey as I rushed off the plane and through the Vegas Airport. I dodged other flyers who looked like they partied *way* too hard and were regretting their life choices as they stumbled, clearly hungover to their gates, until I saw the sign for passenger pickup.

I wasn't even down the escalator before a tingle spread through my body.

I glanced up and found him immediately.

It didn't matter he had a worn, well-loved green and gold Vipers ball cap pulled down low over his brow. It didn't matter he was only wearing a pair of athletic shorts and a short-sleeve plain top. It didn't matter one single bit he was wearing Adidas black slides on his feet.

He was here.

He must have sensed me too because as I gawked at the man I hadn't been able to touch and still hadn't told the full truth to for six weeks, his head rose, and those dark eyes of his I loved and missed so much found me.

His lips parted, and screw this. I shoved—politely—past the couple in front of me who didn't separate their glued together bodies or mouths as I pushed past them.

I must have blinked, or magic took me to him because in the next second I was in his arms, wrapped in them, his head burrowed against my throat and my face shoved into his chest.

"You're here."

His body shook.

Maybe it was mine.

Perhaps an earthquake.

As I tried to pull back so I could see him, touch him, kiss him, he held me tighter.

"I'm here." I squeezed him back until Joey released his hold and my hands *were* trembling as I cupped his jaw. "I missed you."

Dimples appeared, my knees wobbled. I playfully poked one with my fingertip and earned a wider grin.

"I can't believe you're here."

He blurred in my tear-filled eyes. Stupid happy tears. "I'm finally here."

My grin turned stupid and I rolled to my toes. I kissed him then, meant it as a quick peck but Joey shoved his mouth to mine until we were the ones glued together and mouths fused, right there, the stream of departing passengers shoving their way around us as they stepped off the escalator.

"We should go," he murmured against my mouth. "Get to the hospital, but you have to know there are a million things I'm going to do with you later and one of them might be not ever letting you leave my sight again."

The real reason I was here wiped away my smile.

But it was time for truth.

"You might not have to."

His eyes closed slowly. "Best fucking news I'd heard in a long time."

"Come on. Has Garrett updated anyone yet? How's Lizzie?"

"Doing well. They're trying to slow the labor but it's not working. Apparently, these Dubiak boys might be stubborn."

"Can't be helped. It's in their DNA make-up."

"No shit," Joey joked and flung his arm over my shoulders.

I laughed, but it was brittle. I'd spent the flight and all day a mixture of excitement and worry and fear.

They weren't thirty-seven weeks yet. This was too early. Things could go wrong. Sensing my impending panic, Joey kissed my temple. "Everyone and everything will be fine. Just like last time she was at the hospital."

"Right." Because then, we'd thought she was miscarrying and instead received great news. "Just like last time."

"Archer and Gavin." I hugged Lizzie carefully. "They're perfect."

"So tiny," she said and hugged me back. She was so tired.

We'd been at the hospital overnight. I'd refused to leave until the babies came in case there was an emergency but other than being born two weeks earlier than expected, they were perfect.

I hadn't showered, both Joey and I were still in the clothes from yesterday but this morning, at five-thirty-three and five-forty-two, Archer and Gavin made their entrance into the world.

And they were, like I told Lizzie, absolutely perfect.

"They'll grow," I assured her and swiped away tears from my eyes and pulled back. "Their dad is monster-sized. They'll grow."

"You're a pint-sized pain in the ass," said my monster-sized brother. "And where's my damn hug? They wouldn't be here if it weren't for me."

"Oh?" I arched my brow and went to him. "Did you bring them into the world? Did you do all the hard work?"

"No. I did all the fun work."

All four of us laughed. My mom was on her way, would be here in a few hours. I peered down at the tiny bundle wrapped in blue in my brother's arm.

"Hey, Archer." I gently trailed a fingertip over his cheek. "I'm going to be your favorite aunt in the whole world."

Garrett cleared his throat.

"Shut up," I mumbled without looking at him. "Just because I'll be his only aunt doesn't mean I won't be his favorite."

"We should go," Joey said, quietly resetting Gavin in Lizzie's arms.

The sight of him when he first took Gavin into his arms almost made my uterus explode.

"You don't have to," Lizzie said, but she had to be exhausted, and we'd already been in the room for long enough for us both to cuddle the babies, hear how they were doing.

So far, they'd each breastfed once perfectly. At thirty-five weeks they were just over five pounds. Nurses were keeping an eye on them, but APGAR—whatever those were—had come back perfect and since they were doing fine eating, there was no worry yet about them needing to stay longer than necessary.

"We do," I assured her. "I think Joey and I both need a shower. And a nap."

But first, I had a surprise to reveal to him. I didn't even care it was barely seven.

"You'll need your rest before everyone else comes to say hi, anyway."

"Okay." She yawned behind her hand and I chuckled.

"See you later?" I asked Garrett.

"You better. Thanks for getting here so quick yesterday."

I rolled to my toes and kissed his cheek. "Always. I'm always here for you."

"Me too, sis."

He and Joey shook hands and on the way down the hallway, I pulled out my phone. "I know you're exhausted, but can we go somewhere first?"

The building was only fifteen minutes away from the hospital. Thirty minutes from Joey's home.

"Breakfast?" he asked and I laughed.

"No. I have a surprise for you."

"A good surprise?"

"Absolutely."

"Then I'll take you anywhere you want to go."

He took my hand, his fingers playing with my wedding ring. I hadn't taken it off. Neither had he. He didn't say anything as the elevator descended and we headed to his car.

I gave him the address and he gave me a curious look as he punched in the coordinates.

"Those babies are so damn cute," I murmured. Now that adrenaline and excitement was wearing off, exhaustion was setting in.

"They'll be a lot of work. I can't imagine twins."

"I want a house full of them," I admitted, eyes drooping. I forced myself to stay awake.

"A house full of twins? Not sure that can happen."

"No." I slapped his chest and he grabbed my hand, settled both of them interlocked on his thigh. He hadn't stopped touching me since I arrived. Even while we slept, slumped over uncomfortable waiting room chairs, he'd always had a hand on me.

Like he was afraid I'd disappear, hop on a plane if he wasn't holding on to me.

He didn't have to worry. Soon, he'd see.

"I meant babies. Lots of them."

He cleared his throat. "Good." He flashed me a grin. "Me too."

Babies then. Lots of them. We agreed.

The drive was faster than expected, probably due to lack of traffic headed in the direction we were going, but soon, Joey pulled up to a building, a five-story condominium building on top of a row of businesses.

My business.

I bounced in my seat. "Park there. We'll walk over."

"Walk where?"

I could barely contain my excitement. Not only had I not seen everything yet in person, but I was also getting multiple texts a day from Kelsey. We'd started construction two weeks ago and I was already shocked at how fast everything was happening.

Joey pulled his car into the parking lot and I was out of my door, almost stumbling in my rush to see everything, and he met me at the front.

Brows furrowed, eyes squinting from the sun, he took the hand I offered, and I practically pulled him across the street.

"What are you doing?" Wariness drifted through his tone.

I flashed him a smile and kept tugging on him. "You'll see."

31

JOEY

"You'll see..."

I saw a building with apartments in an area of Vegas that looked full of fresh out of college rich preppy workers, and a boulder grew in my stomach.

Was she... *moving*? Here?

And yet she was so excited. Was this what she meant by taking care of herself? Actually living alone?

I followed her, my hand so tightly gripped in hers I couldn't pull away if she tried but she didn't take me toward the main entrance to the modern and chic building where a sign for the name of the building was plastered.

Instead, she dug into her purse with her free hand and pulled out a set of keys.

It was then I saw the other sign where she was dragging me.

And the words COMING SOON painted on the glass.

Elite Beauty Salon and Spa.

My heart raced and my palms grew clammy. She...

"You first," she said as she shoved the key into the lock and pulled open the door.

"What is this?"

"You'll see." Her smile shook and she rolled her lips together. With her foot, she gently tapped me in the back of my legs.

Holy shit. This was what she hadn't told me. This was the secret I'd been growing so concerned about.

I'd been worried.

For absolutely nothing.

I stepped into a space filled with silence, the roar of my heart causing enough noise for everyone in a two-block radius.

She slid in front of me, and pressed her back to my chest. Her voice shook as she said, "I haven't actually seen this in person yet."

"It's yours?" I needed the confirmation. Shock rushed through me as I wrapped my arms around her stomach and held her against me all while trying not to throw her onto the floor and ravage her.

"It's mine," she said quietly, practically a whisper in my ear. "My very own salon."

It was still in the construction phase but with the separated styling stations and sinks and then the small row of chairs with attached dryers, it was obvious what it was.

Holy fucking shit. She'd *done* it.

I slipped my arms from around her and stepped to the side. I needed some distance for my own sanity. My jaw tightened and I couldn't think of a rational thing to say. All the blood in my brain had raced south. "Your salon."

"Yeah, I mean." She scanned the space, excitement growing along with nerves as she bounced on her feet. "Not the building. But I was able to lease it and get a business plan and I have someone who's been helping me—Kelsey, you know, Dan's daughter—she did the walk-throughs. I called her to talk one day for advice. We'd hit it off at Lizzie's wedding when she did her hair and then, everything snowballed so she's been my eyes here while I worked on the financial stuff back home. And... you're not saying anything."

I covered my mouth and sniffed. Holy fucking shit. I couldn't...

Tears grew in my eyes and Gabby blurred in front of me.

"Oh. I didn't think you'd cry. Are you... are you okay with this?"

Okay with this? Had she gone absolutely batshit crazy?

"I want to fuck you. Right now. Everywhere. The floor. The chairs. The windows. I don't give a fuck but I'm afraid if I touch you I'm going to break you."

"So..." Her bottom lip found its way between her teeth. "You're happy?"

The thread holding me back snapped and I placed my hands on her cheeks. "You're moving here... not into this building but in with me, right?"

"That was the idea."

"Thank fuck." I slammed my mouth to hers and she yelped, which quickly turned to a moan and screw people walking by. Screw anything except the desperate need I had to be with my *wife*.

Who had done all of this. Figured out what she wanted and made her own damn dreams come true.

"Fuck, I love you," I gasped as I wrenched my mouth off hers. My need was too hot. Too heavy. Too needy and too... everything.

My hands went to her ass and she jumped as I lifted, locking ankles behind me. "I would take you home, be gentle, make love to you. We should shower and get the hospital stench off us, but I just... I need you."

"There's a massage table in the back. It's—"

She sounded as desperate as me.

I slammed my mouth to hers again. I'd find it. The place wasn't that big. I kicked open doors into rooms that weren't yet done, found chairs so huge I couldn't imagine their purpose, a bathroom, a small office area, and then the table.

Smaller than what I imagined. It'd do. I turned, settled her on her feet and then flipped her around, pushing my hand to her back so she was folded over the bed.

"When we get home, I will take you slow, make it good for you and do you in every position you want, your choice, but if I'm not inside of you in two seconds..."

She was already kicking off sandals and tearing down her shorts. No underwear. Jesus. I could have fingered her in the waiting room or something. Taken this edge off. Not that the thought hadn't crossed my mind while we were waiting for Lizzie to give birth. Sneaking off to a bathroom because she'd been away from me for so long and then next to me in a place where we couldn't touch. It was *all* I'd thought about.

But now she was here. Pulling off her shirt and bra and revealing herself to me and I did the same, grabbed a condom from my pocket, and tore it with my teeth.

"Bend over and pray I don't fucking break this table," I groaned, rolling on the condom. I was hard. Pulsing. So goddamn desperate to be with my wife.

She laughed but listened, curled her hands around the other side and laid her cheek on the table. "Hurry." She arched onto her toes, which made it easier to reach her.

I bent my legs, settled my cock at her entrance. She was already soaked and I slid like silk over her clit. She moaned, bit her lip. "Please. Joey..."

I shoved inside of her, and goddamn my wife was so

damn sexy, so damn warm and she gripped my dick like a vise as soon as I started to move.

I couldn't hold back, didn't want to. But I did need to make it good for her. I bent over her, kissed her neck, her shoulder blades, everywhere my lips could touch I kissed and found her clit with my fingers, the swollen bud. She writhed against me. The table screeched in tandem with my thrusts.

It was over fast, right as Gabby's legs started to tremble, I flicked her clit, hard, with my thumb and she exploded, went off like a rocket and I followed her into oblivion as the heat I'd barely contained unleashed into an orgasm that had me roaring her name into her spine.

Once we settled our breathing, stood, I planted a gentle kiss on her and handed Gabby her clothes. "Let's go home and you can tell me how this happened."

"Home," she whispered and gave me a kiss. "That sounds perfect."

Yeah. It'd never sounded better to me before, either.

"What the fuck is happening?"

That came from Joey, face pale, hands on his hips. I couldn't blame him. It was Christmas Eve. We were surrounded by the entire Taylor clan, along with Garrett and Lizzie, Archer and Gavin, and my mom. It was the rare time during the year when Carolina played Las Vegas, so his entire family came out to spend the holidays with us.

It was perfect. Between Sonya and my mom, I'd surrendered the kitchen over to them. We'd spent the last few days taking care of a gaggle of kids, swimming, drinking, and eating. Oh dear Lord, had we eaten.

It was setting up to be the best Christmas ever. I had Joey. His family. Mine. We were *married*—happily now, and my official name change to Gabrielle Taylor had happened in October.

I'd needed to pinch myself to ensure this wasn't all a dream up until fifteen seconds ago.

Joey and Garrett's phones had started going psychotic

with alerts and Garrett had barked out, "Turn on the news. Now."

"Shit." I flinched and kissed the top of Archer's head. "Sorry, buddy."

"This is... this can't be right. Dom's an asshole, but he'd never..."

Assault a woman. At least, that's what the reporter was claiming someone said happened. He'd been at a bar. Got in a fight with a guy, witnesses described as *beaten to a bloody pulp* and *shredded to pieces* and someone had caught him tossing what looked like a passed-out woman into the back seat of his Maserati.

"He wouldn't." In the four months since I'd lived in Vegas permanently, I'd gotten to know Dom. Not well. We weren't buddies. But he came around more than he ever had before. He was quiet. Didn't talk much about himself. But I got the sense he wasn't just a good guy, but one of the best. Yeah, he had issues. But this?

"This is going to fuck with the team," Joey said, shaking his head.

We've been able to confirm that Dominick Masters last year's Defensive Player of the Year for the Las Vegas Vipers has been arrested. Charges are pending during the investigation, but it appears...

The screen turned blank and we all spun.

"You don't need to see this. It's all speculation." Leave it to my mom to take control. With the remote in her hand, her brows puckered. "The team will handle this. Call their lawyers. Get in touch with them. But tonight is Christmas. It's about family. So we focus on that and figure out how to be there for your teammate tomorrow."

Damn.

Joey smirked at me and quietly said, "Now I know where you get your bossiness from."

I rolled my eyes. "You're the bossy one."

Hands there. Knees spread. Take it. Open your mouth. Suck my—

"You're right," John Sr., Joey's dad, said with a quick nod. He whipped me out of the memories of last night, in the shower, where I'd come with Joey's powerful thrusts at my back, his hand covering my mouth so I didn't scream the house down.

"Tonight is for us. We're all together and we're blessed for it. So let's keep Dominick in our thoughts. Think the best of him until we know more. But tonight, we take the moment to cherish everyone being here."

"He's right," Garrett said with a nod. He had Gavin in his arms, and I was learning my brother was rarely without one of his sons in his arms. At four months old, almost to the day, the babies were growing. Now they had fat rolls at their thighs and wiggled so much it was difficult to diaper them.

Archer was the fussy one. While Gavin would kick his legs and squirm to have his own space, Archer always needed to be held. Fortunately for him, his aunt Gabby *loved* to hold him. I was rocking and swaying him, the way he liked, brushing my fingertip over his cheek, I barely realized the room had grown silent until Lizzie stepped up next to me. "I'm going to take him before you drop him," she whispered, a twist of her lips I didn't understand.

Until she stepped out of my view.

And there was Joey.

"Oh."

My gaze flashed to the now blank television screen. "But..."

"Dad and Garrett are right. Tonight's about us."

As he said it, he lowered himself to one knee. Without Archer in my arms, I had no idea what to do with my hands. They went to my mouth. My hips. Across my stomach. To my sides. "What are you doing?"

He smirked. That damn dimple scrambled my brain, it took me a second to see the box in his hands.

"One year ago," he started, while every nerve in my body lit up. "I was miserable."

"He really was—" Jason cut in.

A laugh bubbled and I quickly swallowed down. My hands shook.

"Shut up." He oomphed and I imagined the slap Tessa gave him on his stomach, but I couldn't pull away from the intensity in Joey's dark eyes, in the tenseness in his shoulders as he glared at his brother before returning that gaze to me.

It immediately melted. "You have made me happier than I ever could have imagined being. Every day with you is an adventure and I can't wait to travel the world with you."

Tears streamed down my face and I was unable to wipe them away. I was unable to do anything but breathe, lock my knees so I didn't collapse from the trembles rolling through me and the words he was speaking.

We were already *married* and yet he was on his knees like he was proposing, unwavering in his intensity despite the muted sounds of the women around us, gushing over him.

"I know we're already married," Joey continued, undeterred. "But because of the way we did things, there are things you missed out on like a proper proposal, with me letting our families know how important you are to me, how I will break my back every day to ensure you're always taken care of, secure in my love for you, and how much I love you and desire to protect you forever."

"Joey—" His name was a rasp, falling from my dry throat as tears dripped off my chin. I swiped them away and went to him on shaking legs with my heart about to burst.

"So, Gabrielle Taylor." He smirked, loving to say my full name, especially when I was driving him crazy in the way it meant I was ten seconds from being tossed over his shoulder or bent over the nearest surface. "In front of our friends, our families, will you do me the honor of continuing to be my wife for the rest of forever?"

"You're a fool." I laughed. We'd already decided not to renew our vows or get remarried so family could be there. We might not yet remember every part of our original wedding but what we'd built on our honeymoon and in the weeks separating us after cemented our commitment to each other. I didn't need the production and ceremony when we already had each other.

"I'm your fool."

"Always," I said, and held out my left hand. It trembled as he took it in his, his hand so warm, so firm and confident. "I will always be your wife."

"And my travel buddy."

"Yes." I laughed again.

"And someday... the mother to my children."

"When we're ready."

There were things I wanted to do. Places I wanted to see. But soon. We'd get to all of it soon.

He removed the ring from its box, a thick band covered with so many diamonds I almost passed out and as that ring was slid onto my finger, he stood to his feet, brought his palms to my jaw, and tilted my chin.

"I love you, Gabrielle Taylor. Today, tomorrow, and forever."

He sealed his promise with a kiss and our families cheered.

"Best night of my life," I whispered against his lips. "Outside from our wedding."

"Every night with you is the best of mine."

We were hugged. Champagne was popped. Beneath the happiness and celebration was the lingering worry about Dominick, but tomorrow. We could wait until tomorrow. Tonight was ours.

No... the rest of forever was ours. And we could chase the remainder of our dreams together.

NEED MORE VIPERS? Dominick's story, Rule Breaker, is coming soon! Pre-Order today: http://mybook.to/vipers2

OR, join my mailing list and never miss a new release or sales announcement. https://bit.ly/3nC4exd

THANK YOU

HUGE thank you to Nina and all the incredible women at Valentine PR for throwing your full enthusiasm and support behind me and these books. I've loved working with you and can't wait to see what the future brings us.

Ellie and Virginia, as always, thanks for putting up with my mess and spit-shining each manuscript until it sparkles. Thank you especially during this crazy time in our world for your flexibility and your extra hard work.

Shannon, you're the best. Always. Forever. Your talent is astounding and I'm thankful I can call you a friend.

To my Sweeties! I love you ladies and your excitement for my books!

To all the bloggers who devote their time and passion into reading books, book tours, release events, leaving reviews, promoting and pimping – you are all rockstars! Thank you for all the love over the years.

My family— I love you all to the moon and back. I don't know what I would do without you in my corner, cheering me on every step of the way. Your support is everything to me and I love you all with all of my heart.

And last but definitely not least – to you the reader. I'm blown away with every release how much you adore my books. You have made my dream a reality and I hope I can cheer you on with yours.

ABOUT THE AUTHOR

Stacey Lynn likes her coffee with a dash of sugar, her heroes with a side of bossy, and her wine a deep shade of red.

The author of over thirty romance novels, many of which have been best-selling titles, she loves being able to turn her vivid imagination into a career that brings entertainment and joy to her readers. Focused on sports romance and emotional, small-town romance, she also loves stretching herself in different genres.

Born in Texas and raised in the Midwest, she now makes her home in North Carolina and loves all things Southern. Together with her ultimate tall, dark, and handsome hero, she has four children. Her life is a chaotic mess that fights with her Type-A, list-making, neurotically organized preferences and she wouldn't have it any other way.

Subscribe to her newsletter so you can stay up to date on all her new releases. www.staceylynnbooks.com

OTHER BOOKS BY STACEY LYNN

Las Vegas Vipers ~hockey romance

Game Changer

Dream Maker

Rule Breaker – May 2022

Shot Taker – June 2022

Ice Kings Series ~hockey romance

Playing With Fire (free on all retailers)

Playing To Win

Scoring Off The Ice

Hooked One Her

Hard Checked

Fighting Dirty

The Rough Riders Series ~football romance

Dirty Player

Filthy Player

Wicked Player

Cocky Player

Love and Lies Duet ~angsty slow burn, romance

All the Ugly Things

All the Beautiful Things

Love and Honor Duet ~angsty, romantic suspense

<u>Twisted Hearts</u>

<u>Unraveled Love</u>

Love In The Heartland ~small town romance

Captivated By You

This Time Around

Long Road Home

Before We Fell

Crazy Love Series ~West Coast romance

Fake Wife

Knocked Up

28 Dates

Weekend Fling

The Fireside Series ~small town romance

His to Love

His to Protect

His to Cherish

His to Seduce

Tangled Love Series ~erotic romance

Entice

Embrace

Enflame

The Luminous Series ~BDSM romance

Dominate Me

Crave Me

Long For Me

Just One Series ~rockstar romance

Just One Song

Just One Week

Just One Regret

Just One Moment

The Nordic Lords Series ~MC romance

Point of Return

Point of Redemption

Point of Freedom

Point of Surrender

Standalones

Remembering Us

Don't Lie To Me – billionaire romance

Try Me – A Don't Lie To Me Novella